"In my youth I read everything Isaac Asimov wrote," the head of the secret society said. "In his 'Foundation Trilogy' he postulated a science he called 'psychohistory,' not realizing that the statistical methods he postulated were very similar to what insurance companies of the time called underwriting. Asimov made no real attempt to explore them. But then, perhaps only an insurance man could see how that science could be put to use."

"An insurance man like you Mr. Douglas," his newest co-conspirator asked.

"Exactly like me. I've made Asimov's science fiction into science fact. Nobody before me realized how rigorous the statistical probability of human behavior can be made, provided you understand fundamental social principles... and provided you don't abandon the project when it starts to deliver bad news."

"What do you mean, bad news?"

"Our civilization is on the edge of collapse. We face a seventy-five percent probability of world civil war already. And it will be ninety percent by this time next year."

"You talk so calmly," the woman said. "But if everything goes smash, won't you go smash too, with everybody else?"

"No, my dear, I have a plan."

But Mr. Douglas had forgotten one thing: he too was only a psychohistorical statistic.

THE PROMETHEUS MAN

a nrobook
by

RAY FARRADAY NELSON

Illustrated by George Barr   Edited by Hank Stine

Donning
Norfolk/Virginia Beach

To Kirsten, for twenty-five years my mistress, guru, mother of my son, fellow outlaw, libertarian comrade, tormentor, business partner, co-conspirator, victim, and sexual obsession—but never ever wife to me or any man.

Copyright© 1982 by Ray Faraday Nelson

All rights reserved, including the right to reproduce this book in any form whatsoever without permission in writing from the publisher, except for brief passages in connection with a review. For information, write:
The Donning Company/Publishers
5659 Virginia Beach Boulevard
Norfolk, Virginia 23502.

Library of Congress Cataloging in Publication Data

Nelson, Ray Faraday, 1931-
   The Prometheus man.

    I. Title.
PS3564.E4745P7   813'.54   82-5025
ISBN 0-89865-192-1   AACR2

Printed in United States of America

THE PROMETHEUS MAN

INTRODUCTION
Robert Silverberg

Unless my memory is playing extraordinary tricks on me, I first encountered Radell Faraday Nelson a quarter of a century ago, at a science-fiction convention in London. I was then a very young and very new professional writer, and I remember Ray—who is a few years my senior—as a lean, cool-eyed, somewhat sinister-looking type, ominously bohemian in manner, who in those far-off and innocent days gave an immediate impression of having dabbled in opium, hashish, cheap red wine, and other forbidden pleasures while preparing himself in the traditional literary way for the life of an avant-garde artist of some sort.

Maybe I made the whole thing up. Decades later, the vicissitudes of time have brought Ray and me to the same corner of California, he from Detroit and a lot of other places, I from New York, and I am more or less the same in appearance and general world-view as I was at that long-ago London convention, bearded now, perhaps three pounds heavier, somewhat less shaggy around the forehead—but Ray, that primordial beatnik, how Ray has been transformed! The lean and (to me) sinister person of the late 1950s is now portly, amiable, sedate of bearing. He is married; he is a father; he is a partner in a bookstore; one might almost call him a *bourgeois*.

Almost.

Because behind that ample facade and under the yellow T-shirt that proudly proclaims, I WROTE BLAKE'S PROGRESS,

1

there still beats, I think, the heart of that fiery-eyed young subversive/radical/bohemian. Certainly the mind of that placid book seller of El Cerrito, California, is still the diabolical mind of the youthful Ray Nelson, who at the age of seventeen or eighteen had already taken a long cold look at the world's foibles and had begun his lifelong job of exposing and deflating them. The evidence is there in the man's writing. Decades of ingesting his wife's bountiful Norwegian cuisine have left their mark on the man's body, but his soul is still that of an anarchist. It shows in his fiction.

I imagine that Ray Nelson's fictional works include a ton of Kerouac-like stories of "How It Really Was in the Fifties," mostly unpublished; but for me his career as a writer begins with a long story called "Turn Off the Sky," which appeared in the August, 1963 issues of *Fantasy and Science Fiction*. A handsome Emsh cover illustrated the story, and just three names are displayed on that cover: Robert A. Heinlein, Issac Asimov, and Ray Nelson: A good start to a career, one would say.

And the first lines of the story are precisely what I would have expected from the Ray Nelson I had earlier met:

"As usual, Abelard Rosenburg came to the party stark naked except for a briefcase full of left-wing propaganda and two coats of paint below. The paint was a beautiful ice blue, forming a striking contrast to his black skin and still blacker beard. He stood in the doorway of the little bookstore a moment, silhouetted against the blazing artificial aurora borealis in the sky; then when a few people had dutifully greeted him, he entered and opened his briefcase.

"Share my burden?" he asked a young ballet dancer, handing her a thick fistful of printed and mimeographed sheets."

And there we have the Late Sixties—five years ahead of the actual event.

It's a fine, harsh, intelligent story, and why it has never been reprinted puzzles me. Why *I* never reprinted it in the days when I was editing anthologies puzzles me in particular. Nelson went on to write other fine, harsh, intelligent stories, some of which did get reprinted; he collaborated on a novel, *The Ganymede Takeover*, with no less than Philip K. Dick; and on his own he wrote a number of novels, some of them science-fiction, some of them not. One of the science-fiction items is a very good space-opera, *The Ecolog;* one is a crisp and funny political fantasy, *Then Beggars Could Ride;* and one, fabled in song and story and yellow T-shirts, is a magnificently whacky and profound thing called *Blake's Progress*, which should have been a cult classic and probably would have been had not it, like the other two, been published as part of an ephemeral series of pulp action-adventure paperbacks. Some shrewd publisher, perhaps even the one of the present novel, would do well to restore those books to print—and it might be a good idea to let Nelson expand them to their proper lengths, too, for they give every appearance of having been held down by main force to a predetermined 192-page format.*

Certainly no such compression has been imposed on *The Prometheus Man*. It is a big, sprawling, very Nelsonesque novel in the grand utopian tradition of Wells, Huxley, Zamyatin, and (to a certain degree) Orwell: a book by a man who has spent a great deal of time thinking about the future, which to be done right involves thinking about the past and present as well. If it is not as weirdly lyrical as *Blake's Progress* or as fast-and-furious as *Then Beggars Could Ride*, so be it; it has other virtues, considerable ones, which you are about to discover.

For me there was one special pleasure: the vision of all of Berkeley turned into a giant urban monad inhabited by hundreds of thousands of unemployables. That's more or less what Berkeley is right now, of course, but the current layout isn't a single structure a hundred stories high, and I found the image stunningly apt. So is a good deal more in this meaty and thoughtful novel by—do I dare say it?—this meaty and thoughtful novelist. I hope its publication marks the beginning of a period of close attention to his work.

---

* We're already ahead of you again, Bob. A much expanded version of *Blake's Progress* and the original novel-length *Turn Off The Sky* (from which the controversial Hugo nominee novelette was taken) are both already under contract—H.S.

If we could share this world below,
If we could learn to love...
If we could share this world below,
We'd need no world above.

> The Nrobook of Baboo

Chapter 1

In the hush of the Holy Hour before dawn, under a cloudless, gradually-brightening sky in which the stars and the waning moon were still visible, a magnetically suspended and propelled monorail, like some huge chrome and glass serpent, curved with a hissing rush down through the snow-flecked foothills of the Sierra Nevadas toward the broad, flat central valley of California.

A slender blonde in her early twenties, naked except for her fingerwatch, swiveled her leather-upholstered chair toward the floor-to-ceiling window and gazed for several minutes at the passing panorama: a wilderness of grey cliffs, boulders and pines. When at last she spoke, it was in a whisper, as if she had entered some vast, ancient cathedral.

"Eden."

"What's that you say?"

Behind her in the little room a guant, pajamaclad man of about the same age sat on the edge of a double bunk and regarded her with vague, sleepy puzzlement. His stubble-darkened face was almost expressionless, as if he had not yet had enough experience to decide what attitude to take toward life.

She gestured toward the window. "It's a new Eden, but this time God didn't make it. We did."

He frowned. "Only God can make a tree."

She picked up a gaudy brochure from the thick pile carpet.

"This travel folder says otherwise." She found the relevant paragraph. "God's trees were all logged out of this area in the late twentieth and early twenty-first centuries. Every pine you see out there is a clone of one superpine developed in a genetic engineering lab."

He yawned and scratched himself but did not reply.

She closed her eyes and tilted back her chair. "We take too much for granted. We don't realize that from the standpoint of our ancestors we live in an earthly paradise, a utopia. No racism, sexism, no ageism, no war, no starvation, almost no disease. We have an average life-expectancy of over a hundred and fifty vigorous years, machines to do all our dirty work, a world state in which all human beings are citizens, a government that guarantees us food, clothing and shelter whether we work or not, and up there...." Her skyward glance seemed to include the whole universe. "Out there among the stars we have our frontier, for those who crave adventure."

"Of late," he muttered, "most of the bold space adventurers have been robots."

She sighed. "You have no poetry in your soul, my dear. If your exams tested the ability to dream grand dreams, you'd flunk for sure."

"I may flunk anyway."

"Don't talk like that. You absolutely must pass your finals. Otherwise you won't even qualify for a job *interview*. And you know how hard it is just to get one of those, these days. It's either that or become an Un. Sometimes, Newton, I think you're practicing to become an Un. After all, how hard could the tests be? I passed mine."

"You're the passing type."

"There's no such thing as a passing type. Anyone who studies hard can pass those tests. Anyone with normal intelligence. You do have normal intelligence, don't you?"

"So I'm told, yet sometimes when I'm with you I feel I'm still back in my early teens when all the girls were smart and all the boys were stupid."

After a pensive pause she said reproachfully, "You could have taken your finals the same day I took mine. Then we wouldn't be dangling in this awful suspense."

"I wasn't ready."

"Are you ready now?"

"I think so."

"For God's sake, the exam is tomorrow. You mustn't think, you must know! Can I coach you on anything? Drill you a little where you're weak?"

"That wouldn't help."

She swiveled to face him, fists clenched. "You're just saying all this to tease me. You know how I hate situations where there's nothing I can do."

"That would be exactly like me, wouldn't it?" he answered tonelessly, without emotion.

She relaxed a little, an uncertain little smile playing about her lips. "Sadist! I wouldn't have married you if I'd known you were a sadist."

"We all make mistakes." He did not smile.

He thought, *A perfect society, But what if I'm not a perfect person?*

The sky grew brighter. Greys turned into greens and browns in the forest outside. Her orange lipstick began to glow as if with a light of its own. Wordlessly they began to get dressed in rented his-and-hers orange shifts and kneelength boots. She always insisted on wearing rented clothing on trips to avoid having to take luggage.

The recorded voice of Mary Danville, the video star, announced in a husky, insinuating tone, "San Francisco, fifteen minutes."

Holly and Newton McClintok prepared to disembark.

*

The monorail glided to a stop above the heads of throngs of unheeding tourists in the immense, cavernous lobby of the San Francisco Hilton. The doors slid open with a muted hiss and the passengers began to emerge onto the mezzanine, craning their necks to search for waiting family and friends. Occasional glad cries rose above the general murmur of voices and the endless soft featureless music. Here and there in the tiers of balconies above, clumps of one, two and three children peered down, admiring the monorail, wide-eyed, open-mouthed, while parents crossly tried to keep them moving.

As Holly stepped out through the doorway, she said, "Do you see the folks?"

"No, but I'm sure they'll be here," said Newton.

"There they are!" she exclaimed, and waved her hand excitedly.

Sure enough, the whole McClintok clan had turned out for the occasion, all of them, women as well as men, wearing the tartan kilt of their clan—the current height of fashion among Scots.

Adam McClintok the patriarch, led the pack, tall, thin, bony, looking a lot like Newton except he was bald—a grinning father figure, who deliberately aped the words, image and attitudes of the latter half of the last century, as part of the current craze for the past. Miriam, Newton's biological mother and the eldest of Adam's three wives, was still attractive and young-looking at sixty, thanks to a near-miracle of cosmetic surgery. Bringing up the rear were Newton's two other mothers and each of their sons; Newton had always wondered why his father had never elected to have the fourth child to which, as the law allowed one child to every adult, their family was entitled.

Newton endured a veritable orgy of embracing and handshaking as the clan closed in on him. He had never liked public displays of affection. Intimate emotion seemed something that ought to be reserved for video-dramas and the wall-screen. Finally he managed to disengage himself.

"Well, how was the vacation, Newton?" boomed the old man, getting in a last slap on the back.

"Wonderful!" cried Holly, before Newton could speak.

"Cold enough for you up there in Michigan?" persisted Mr. McClintok.

"I wouldn't know," said Newton distantly. "Detroit *is* under a dome. You could say we weren't outdoors once the whole time."

"Didn't you ski or anything?" asked Mr. McClintok.

"No," said Newton.

"You were there to relax..." Newton's mother gave him a look of vexation.

"I relaxed," said Newton. "I feel much better."

The old man broke in, "Don't nag the boy the first minute he comes home, Miriam. I wouldn't blame him if he got back on the train and headed for Detroit again."

Newton had actually been thinking vaguely of doing that very thing, but now the train doors slid shut and the monorail moved swiftly and silently out of the lobby.

The old man continued expansively, "You're like me, Newton. Not much for the great outdoors. I tell you the truth, I haven't seen a horizon for twenty years. Now come along and tell us all your troubles—because I know wherever you go, boy, trouble will follow." He led the McClintoks toward a nearby exit.

They crossed Market Street on a third floor pedestrian bridge, high above the divided bikeway where pedicabs, threewheelers and bicycles streamed by in the early morning rush. Newton had never been able to visualize what Market must have looked like in the Nineties when motorized vehicles had choked and polluted it.

"Did you get a chance to study at all?" Newton's mother asked anxiously.

"I doubt if he opened a book or switched on a processor the whole time," said Holly bitterly.

"Your loyalty overwhelms me, dear," said Newton in a flat voice. "Tell all! Tell all!"

"Here, here, my boy, relax," said the old man with alarm. "Don't take offense. Your poor wife was only having a little joke. You're so tight-lipped, so rigid. Maybe you'll share a drink with your old dad."

At this Newton's mother became even more axious. "You know, Adam, there's no such thing as one drink with Newton."

"Are you implying, woman, that Adam McClintok's son is an alcoholic?" demanded the patriarch.

"I don't have to imply anything," she said, drawing herself up indignantly. "We all know..."

The other wives broke in, both talking at once, a chorus of shrill, tense voices arguing, arguing, arguing. Newton's brothers looked at him with expressions that said more clearly than words, "Same old Newton, causing trouble wherever he goes."

They took the elevator to the ground floor and emerged on Powell Street where the cablecar had just been turned around on its turntable. Its appearance hadn't changed for a couple of hundred years, but the cable was now a dummy, there was no motorman, you punched your destination into a computer keyboard as you got on, and the merry rattle and clang was only a recording. Untouched by human hands, it rolled into position like a ghost car. Newton was the first to climb aboard, his family close behind. Only a few others joined them; these days the cablecar was more to be seen than to be ridden on.

Clang, clang, said the recording, and they were under way.

Newton found himself seated between his father and his wife. He shifted uncomfortably as the car lurched along.

Adam leaned toward Newton to make himself heard over the din of the soundtrack. "You ready for the tests, my boy?"

"Ready as I'll ever be."

"We'll all be rooting for you, lad." He patted his son on the back. "The whole McClintok clan! We'll all be right outside the testing rooms."

"All except Holly," said Newton.

Old Adam reared back with surprise. "What's that you say? I don't believe it!"

"Holly will be in Los Angeles," Newton explained.

9

"That can't be!" cried Adam, as the others chimed in with exclamations of dismay.

Holly said defensively, "I got a notice from an employment agency while I was in Detroit. I have to go to Los Angeles to try out for placement. I have to think about my own career, you know. Two can't live as cheaply as one, anymore—as the saying goes. There is only point seven eight jobs per each member of the graduating class."

Newton grimaced.

"As it is I was damn lucky to get an interview so soon. The average wait is three months after graduation, and some people wait as much as a year or more—if their scholastic standing is sufficiently low." She looked pointedly at Newton.

"Can't they wait just one day?" demanded Newton's mother.

"You know they can't," said Holly. "It wouldn't be fair to the other applicants. I'll only be gone about forty-eight hours."

"But this particular forty-eight hours?" said Adam. "You'll have other chances."

"Maybe so," said Holly, "but what good would I do here? I can't go into the testing room with Newton and hold his hand. If you ask me, you all are doing him more harm than good by babying him along like this. He is an adult, you know."

"In some ways, maybe...." said Newton's mother.

"All your fussing and hand-wringing just make him nervous!" said Holly angrily. "He knows his subjects well enough, but you people make him so tense he forgets everything. I ask you, will the world stop rotating if he flunks?"

Adam was aghast. "A McClintok? Flunk?"

"He could take the test over," said Holly.

"That's not easily arranged." Adam was pale. "It might take months before they'd let him try again."

Miriam McClintok was paler. "And in the meantime what would he do? What would we all do? He's such a difficult child when he has nothing to occupy him, when he lies around the apartment all day...."

"Getting drunk," added one of the other mothers under her breath.

"Don't worry," said Newton. "It's now or never!"

"That's the spirit!" crowed his father, ignoring the undertone of irony in Newton's voice. After that they talked to each other, not to Newton, and he was glad. He didn't want to answer any more questions today. There would be questions enough tomorrow morning. Instead he stared fixedly at the bicyclist who clung to the side of the cablecar, getting a tow up the steep hill.

When at last the poor man became aware of being stared at and let go. Newton smiled faintly, as if he had won a small and secret victory.

*

The door of Newton's room recognized the timbre of his voice and greeted him with a synthetic but unctuous, "Good afternoon, sir," then slid open to admit him. Holly followed close behind. The door closed with a sound very like a human sigh.

"I haven't got much time," said Holly, walking briskly toward their little private bathroom, pulling off her orange shift over her head as she went. Newton sat down listlessly on the edge of the bed and listened as she turned on the shower.

"They don't understand us, do they?" she called out to him over the hiss of the water.

"You mean my folks?"

"Right! Sometimes they seem like a throwback to the guilt-ridden Twentieth Century when that United States President, John Kennedy, said 'Ask not what your country can do for you, but what you can do for your country.' Sounds grand, but of course there's a logical flaw at the center of it. If I sacrifice for you, and you sacrifice for your father, and your father sacrifices for your various mothers, and you all sacrifice for the government, where does it all end? Who finally benefits from this endless chain of misery?"

"I'm sure I don't know."

"The eternal truths of morality! Twentieth Century moralists thought they would never change, that right would always be right and wrong would always be wrong, but actually society has always defined and redefined morality as circumstances demanded. A world that had too few people banned birth control: A world that has too many people demands it! A monoculture necessitates only monogamous marriage: a global multiculture necessitates all sorts of marriage arrangements. Every human situation creates its own special potentials and limitations. If you're going to win whatever game is currently being played, you must learn how to exploit the potentials and evade or adjust to the limitations."

"What you're saying in your roundabout way, Holly," Newton observed, "is that you think it's okay for you to go to Los Angeles on the day I take my finals."

After a pause she answered, "You always have to drag in personalities, don't you? No use trying to have a philosophical discussion with you."

"I really wish you'd stay."

"Now you sound exactly like the rest of your family, trying to manipulate me by making me feel guilty. That's the way they control you, Newton. They pull the guilt strings and you dance like a puppet. I'm disappointed in you, dear. I'd thought you'd grown beyond that, but now I see they still have you dancing for their amusement. Sometimes I wonder why I ever married into your family. When I get back we'll talk about this, have to make plans. By that time we'll have some idea about our future careers."

"One day, Holly. I'm not asking much."

She emerged from the shower, toweling herself vigorously, her body as appealing as ever. "Don't be such a baby, Newton. You're disgusting when you whine. You know if I don't show up, it'll be entered in my record for future employers to see."

"I might flunk."

"Flunk or pass, at least the suspense will be over. At least we'll know where we stand." Her tone had become increasingly brittle.

"If I fail, you'll leave me? Is that it?"

"For God's sake, Newton, don't ask me things like that. Do you think I have a crystal ball? How do I know what I might do in some hypothetical situation in some imaginary future? I told you every situation has its own potentials and limitations. We'll deal with them when we come to them." Now she was flustered and embarrassed, and he knew his suspicion had been right. Newton gazed at her with bruised resignation, fearing her selfishness and admiring it at the same time.

"Can we make love?" he asked in a low voice.

"Now? I haven't time." She glanced nervously at her fingerwatch.

"We may never get another chance."

"Newton! When I get back we can spend a week in bed if you like." She ripped open the sterile plastic package that contained a fresh rental dress, exactly like the one she had so recently discarded. "Promise me you'll see that these shifts get back to the rental agency. Intercontinental Rentals. Don't forget."

"I won't forget."

She slipped into the orange shift, then sat down on the bed to pull on her boots. Newton reached out a bony hand to gently touch her on the cheek. She glanced at him and saw, to her amazement, that he was silently weeping. "Jesus, Newton! Stop that! You want to drive me crazy?" She stood up. "Now come give mama a kiss goodby."

He sat motionless, head bowed.

"All right, don't give me a kiss," she snapped. "'The hell with it!"

The door opened at her command with a dignified, "Yes madam" and she was gone.

He got up, not bothering to wipe away the tears that trickled down his cheeks and dripped off his jaw, and walked over to his computer terminal where he sat down and activated the "on" stud. On the video screen appeared a menu of programs, including drills in the subjects he would be tested on in the morning. He hesitated, then punched up a game of Advanced Wizards and Mazes.

*

After hours of tossing and turning, Newton lay still and stared up into the darkness. Knowing that Holly was right didn't make things any easier. He had never been religious, and might even now have remained silent if he had not known the walls of his room were soundproof, but suddenly, as the tension reached an unbearable pitch, he screamed out at the top of his voice, "God! Please make me just a little smarter!"

Then, feeling better, he managed to sleep.

Chapter 2

The setting sun on the Pacific horizon threw the man's face half into shadow, half into a ruddy glow, emphasizing his resemblance to the Neo-Baptists notions of Satan, with his little beard and mustaches and a hairline that receeded at the edges of his forehead but not in the middle. His polished manners only added to the satanic impression; everyone knows the devil is urbane. His name, he claimed, was Hal Waterman.

"You are monogamously married?" he said, with self-mocking bathos. "My bleeding heart is garnished by the onions of sadness."

Holly giggled in spite of herself.

She had left her compartment and come to the lounge car for amusement, for diversion, and no one could deny that Mr. Waterman was diverting. She lifted the speared olive from the vodka martini on the table before her and popped it into her mouth, testing the taste to see if it had soaked long enough. It had.

"I hope I didn't disappoint you," she said.

"Ah my dear," he answered wistfully, "my penis, like the sun, sinks slowly in the west. At the least sign of maidenly reluctance, I invariably retreat. Invariably! I shall not force myself upon you. I'm much too lazy for that, and as everyone knows, lethargy is the mother of virtue." He sipped his whiskey sour with eyes closed.

She had been sitting alone, watching the surf exploding against the swiftly passing rocks beyond her floor-to-ceiling window, listening to the low murmur of voices, the clink of glasses, and the unobtrusive music, when this huge, grinning man in a grey business burnoose had startled her with his unexpected request. "May I share your table?"

"Of course," she had replied automatically.

And he had, as soon as he was seated across from her, begun to ask her all sorts of questions in his sophisticated way, flattering her, titilating her with an occasional suggestive remark. Even now, when he knew she was monogamous, he continued to turn on the charm. As she went on answering his questions, she realized he already knew a great deal about her, while she knew almost nothing about him.

"Who do you work for, Mr. Waterman?"

"Call me Hal."

"Who do you work for, Hal?"

He leaned back with a sigh and gazed out the window as if admiring the riot of colors in the sky. "I'm in insurance," he said.

"What company?"

"Ah, let me not bore you with shoptalk about my disgustingly mundane profession. When one is with a lovely lady, does one talk of percentages and policies? Certainly not! One talks of beauty, of love, of the higher things. This is a dull, drab world, wouldn't you say, Mrs. McClintok?"

"Why no. Not at all."

"Have you ever longed to take this little sphere of clay we live on and mold it into a shape nearer your heart's desire?"

He began shaping an imaginary ball of clay with his big, powerful fingers. She watched him with considerable uneasiness.

"What if you could, with a single stroke, wipe out all this, destroy it!" He slowly crushed the imaginary ball. "Would you do it?"

"No. Certainly not."

"Then you are content, Mrs. McClintok, with things as they are?"

"By and large, yes."

"But there may be some details you'd like to, let us say, adjust?" He studied her face intently.

"As a matter of fact, I do think we put too much emphasis on tests. A few wrong answers on a test can ruin a man's whole life."

"True indeed, but nature demands the elimination of the unfit. Our tests are far less demanding, I assure you, than those of the jungle."

"We don't live in a jungle, Mr. Waterman."

"Don't we? If the great cats keep their claws sheathed for the moment, that does not mean they don't still have them. We have lived at peace for a long time, but that does not mean we will live at peace forever. At certain points in history the future suddenly and without warning bursts forth like a longslumbering volcano to destroy the past. At such points you and I must chose either to die with the past or live with the future. Which would you prefer?"

"I'd rather live, of course."

"At any cost?"

"Whatever are you talking about, Mr. Waterman?" she demanded uneasily.

"Oh, pardon me, my dear. I see I've upset you. Please excuse an awkward old fool. I was only trying to get your reactions to certain ideas. I'm an amateur student of psychology, you see."

"And I'm one of your guinea pigs?"

"I wouldn't put it so indelicately, Mrs. McClintok. But you must pardon me a second time for leaving you so abruptly. I have certain matters to attend to." He stood up and, to her surprise bent and kissed her hand. No one had ever kissed her hand before. It was unheard of.

"What a strange bird," she mused under her breath as she watched his wide, massive back threading its way through the crowd to disappear at last through the forward exit.

She dismissed him from her mind and retired early, sleeping deeply and without dreams she could remember.

*

The employment agency was on the hundred and tenth floor of the San Pedro Arcology. In a hush broken only by the murmur of soft recorded music, Holly crossed the thick carpet of the reception room, gave her name to the sleek high-fashion robot and sat down in a dark vinyl-upholstered chair, taking her place among the dozens of other young women waiting there.

The walls were painted a pale creamy off-white, almost the color of human skin, and on the wall opposite her hung a square viewscreen displaying an everchanging three-dimensional panorama of the surface of Mars, including the all-but-abandoned spaceport and occasional glimpses of the weathered entrances to Troglodopolis, the vast underground colony where a skeleton crew of repair personnel, employees of Triplanetary Mining, Inc., still lingered on after everyone else had gone home. These scenes, which one might encounter almost anywhere, were supposed to soothe the unconscious according to current psychological theory, but Holly, perhaps influenced by her husband's gloomy viewpoint, found them vaguely depressing, like a long sad farewell to the dreams of youth.

She turned to the young, slender, oriental woman seated next to her and, to make conversation, asked in a low voice, "Have you been waiting long?"

The woman blinked as if awakened from a trance and glanced at her fingerwatch before replying, "Seven hours."

Seven hours, Holly thought with dismay. *And she's ahead of me.* "But you did have an appointment, didn't you?"

The woman smiled. "Oh yes. This must be your first job interview."

"Why yes, it is. How did you know?"

"Because you seem to think seven hours is too long to wait for a chance at a job. I have waited a week or more in other places. May I suggest that you regard job-hunting itself as your profession until you get another one, and cultivate the virtue or patience." The woman spoke with the air of some ancient Zen monk, smiling all the while as if imparting eternal wisdom to a confused follower.

Holly was indeed confused. "I was summoned here all the way from Detroit!"

Imperturbably the little woman answered, "I was summoned here from Tokyo."

A blonde, seated nearby, chimed in, "I was summoned here from Oslo, and I've been waiting since yesterday." Her tone was resigned, fatalistic. The other women in the room, all speaking at once, called out the names of various cities and various time periods, and it seemed to Holly that they took a perverse pride in the distance they'd come and the length of time they'd been waiting. One, in fact, with a short, military haircut, claimed to have come all the way from the Moon colony.

With a sinking feeling Holly realized that her promise to Newton to be back in San Francisco in forty-eight hours might prove impossible to keep. If all these women were ahead of her, and waited days on end without thinking twice about it, when would she ever get home again? During her school years, they had drilled her in how few jobs there were in this automated world, and how competetive it was just to get an interview—but she had never imagined anything like this.

The woman from Tokyo said, "Don't worry. They have a bunk room across the hall where you can sleep."

Holly thought dazedly, *Is she some kind of Mother Superior*

17

of the Holy Order of Jobseekers, and I a green novice? Will I be trapped forever in the limbo between the employed and the unemployable, spending my life in an endless pilgrimage from one hushed and sacred waiting room to another in search of a mere job? And what other choice was there? To be an Un? The daughter of a Tech, Holly shuddered at the thought.

She glanced wildly around at her "sisters," reading in their faces varying degrees of pity and condescension. The woman from Oslo said gently, "You'll get used to it."

Abruptly the receptionist called out in a faintly bored tone, "Holly McClintok? You may go in now." A languid, graceful mannequin hand gestured toward a door.

As Holly stood up and started across the room, she felt the eyes of the other jobseekers glaring at her, excommunicating her, damning her. Only the woman from Tokyo continued to smile, as if she had somehow known this would happen, as if this had happened to her a thousand times before.

In front of the receptionist's desk Holly blurted out, "There must be some mistake. It's not my turn."

"You may go in now," the robot repeated with its plastic lips.

The door slid open. Holly entered, not daring to look back.

The office was illuminated with dim, indirect lighting, so she did not at first recognize the hulking man in the long burnoose who gazed at her from behind an immense reddish brown mahogany desk. Then he spoke, his voice deep, ironic, faintly mocking.

"We meet again, Mrs. McClintok."

"Hal Waterman!"

"At your service, my dear."

"Are you the one who will interview me?"

"No, my dear. I am the one who already did interview you, on the train." He heaved himself to his feet and advanced, hand extended. "Congratulations, Holly. You're hired."

She was so stunned, he had finished shaking her hand before she realized he had started. Hired! When she had expected it would take a year or more to find a job. The idea made her dizzy. But—

He snapped on the intercom on his desk and said, "Receptionist, you can send the others away." He grinned at Holly impishly, enjoying her surprise.

Holly gathered her wits enough to ask, "I'm hired...for what?"

For the first time the big man showed signs of unease. "We can discuss that later," he said briskly, glancing around as if afraid of being overheard, though there was nobody else in the room, then he brightened. "I'm sure you'd rather not go out through the waiting room. Some of the other applicants might still be lingering about." He pressed down firmly on an ornament—some sort of ancient coin—on his pen and pencil set. A bookcase in the rear of the room slid to one side to reveal a hidden doorway. "Let's go somewhere where we can talk, Holly," he said, favoring her with a broad and disturbingly satanic wink.

"Yes, Mr. Waterman. I mean, yes sir."

"Didn't I tell you to call me Hal?" he demanded, taking her hand to draw her after him into the dark passageway. The bookcase slid into place behind them.

She did not speak, but her mind cried out, *Newton! Help!*

*

I'm afraid you flunked out, Newton," said the haughty-looking professor. He made no attempt to break it gently and obviously wanted only to have the whole business over with as soon as possible, so he could get on to a successful student, one who was worth his time and effort.

The shadowless indirect lighting in the room where the two men stood made Newton's looks even paler and gaunter than usual.

Newton stood swaying, silent, expressionless.

"I'm sorry," the professor added, but the gesture was transparent.

Newton was not surprised. As he had answered the questions he had felt a sick and helpless sense of his own ignorance, his own stupidity. Under pressure, a dark fog drifted in over his brain, and he was forced to guess and bluff. Sometimes he felt his subconscious was rejecting the entire bullshit of the social fabric, which seemed an absurd and senseless farce to him. For now that the test was over, Newton knew the right responses to many of the questions that then had seemed to read like the riddles of the sphinx. Yet, unreasonably, Newton had clung to a desperate hope that somehow....

"I can't believe it," Newton whispered.

With a shrug the professor punched up Newton's score on a display screen. Newton stared at his grade a long time. Only two points below passing! But it might as well have been one hundred.

The professor removed his horn-rimmed glasses and cleaned them impatiently. Newton had noticed that the glasses had no correction factor. They were merely a prop, one more example of the obsessive modern preoccupation with escaping to the past.

Newton felt an urge to snatch those phony glasses from the professor's fingers and stamp them to fragments. The professor put them back on.

"You aren't thinking of doing anything to yourself, are you?" the man demanded sternly.

A skeletal smile twitched around Newton's lips. "No sir. Suicide...is for the living."

After Newton had left the room, the professor discovered Newton's printout on the floor. He shook his head sadly, and then wiped the scene from the screen; he did not push the "save" key. He knew Newton would not be back.

*

Old Adam McClintok glanced up from the program chart he was working on as the computer terminal in the corner of his bedroom chimed softly. With a grunt he dropped himself in the contour chair by the console and pressed the infeed stud. On the display screen Holly's face faded into view.

"Well, hello girl, Did you get the job?"

Yes, Dad. Isn't that great!"

"Wonderful! I can't believe you lucked out so soon. And where are you now?"

"I'm still in Los Angeles. I'm afraid I'll have to stay here for awhile, maybe a week or more."

Adam frowned. "That's not so good. Newton...."

"That's what I called about," she said anxiously. "Did Newton pass or flunk?"

"Maybe you'd better ask him yourself. He's in his room."

"He is? I've been chiming the room for the last hour and nobody answers."

"He's in there all right, but I guess he doesn't feel like talking."

"So he did flunk?"

"You guessed it," Adam sighed.

"Oh my God," Holly whispered. "What will we do now?"

"I'm open to suggestions, daughter. Any suggestions at all."

"Can you go down the hall and pound on his door? Can you tell him to answer his terminal?"

The old man stood up. "I can give it a try."

The door opened at his command and he stumped off along the apartment corridor. The soft amber lights in the ceiling turned on as he approached and switched off after he had passed. A moment later he planted himself before Newton's door and knocked vigorously.

"Open up there, Newton! I want to talk to you."

Newton's muffled voice drifted out from behind the door. "Go away. Leave me alone."

"If you won't talk to me, at least talk to Holly."

"Is Holly out there with you?"

"No, but she's trying to reach you on the terminal. Next time it chimes, you can have the good manners to answer it, boy."

"So she didn't come home like she promised?"

"She's still in Los Angeles. Unavoidable delays."

"Delays are always unavoidable, aren't they? Did she get the job?"

"Yes, she did. That's why she's delayed. She's lucky, and you know it."

"How nice for her." His voice was toneless, without emotion.

"You don't sound well to me, Newton. Are you sick?"

"I'm all right. Give me a little time to pull myself together."

Adam shifted from foot to foot uncertainly. "What will I tell Holly? She's on my terminal right now."

"Give her my congratulations." Again the flat, cold indifferent voice.

Adam returned to his terminal.

"What did he say?" Holly demanded.

"Congratulations and leave me alone. I doubt if he'll answer if you chime him. Listen, can't you come home for just a few hours? We can't even get in to see if he's all right."

"I can't leave. I'm on call twenty-four hours a day. Jobs don't grow in algae tanks. There are plenty of people waiting in line who'd consider this little inconvenience a priviledge. But you can't get into our rooms. I realize that. The door is keyed to my voice and Newton's, nobody else's. What a mess!"

Adam hesitated, then said, "Actually it will open for the rest of us, too, but I don't dare let Newton know that. You know how touchy he is about his privacy. I had it reprogrammed while you two were in Detroit."

"You old fox." Holly appeared more amused than angry.

Adam explained apologetically, "We thought you two would be getting your own place after Newton's graduation."

"Of course. I understand."

"Don't tell Newton. Not while he's in this mood."

"I don't see how I can tell Newton anything at all. I'm here and he's there and never the twain shall meet. He can be so unreasonable at times!"

Adam sighed. "Nobody knows that better than Miriam and I, my dear."

"I've got to run, Dad. I'll chime you later."

Her face faded from the screen as Adam realized he'd been too concerned about Newton to ask Holly her terminal number or message bank or even what kind of a job she'd gotten, and also... There'd been something in her voice when she'd mentioned being on twenty-four hour call, something Adam, as he thought back, might almost have called fear.

*

The nose was fleshy and pink and taller than a man. Blue veins and large pit-like pores showed in its surface. The hairs in the nostrils hung black and thick, like a nest of cables. In ominous silence it slowly turned from full-face front to profile.

Newton turned a dial and the nose moved back. The rest of the face came into view, smiling, filling the giant screen that was one entire wall of Newton's room. Without a clue from the audio, which he had turned off, Newton recognized the face as that of the famous Reverend Roger, and knew what the media evangelist was saying.

"We'll be right back, brothers and sisters, but first a word from our sponsors."

Reverend Roger had been dead for fifty years, but death had not brought about so much as a pause in his ministry, for he had gained a special kind of immortality through the vast library of video recordings he had made in his youth. Perhaps the first clergyman to realize that the repetitive nature of religious ritual made it an ideal subject for automation, Reverend Roger had made a study of all the elements in a religious broadcast which were unchanging...the openings, the closings, the Bible readings, the sermons keyed to certain holidays...and had carefully and expertly recorded them, dressed in the dark timelessness of his priestly robes.

His regular daily programs mixed these recordings with new live portions to give exactly the right balance between the familiar and the novel. No television show of any kind had enjoyed such enduring popularity.

But now, in silence, the commercials continued, for Bibles, prayerbooks, pictures of Yehshuh, as the orthodox Christians called him, crucifixes, and even a walking, talking, preaching Reverend Roger doll that said, "Forgive them, Lord, for they know not what they do."

A profit is not without honor.

The only illumination in the little room came from the flickering, glowing screen, but that sufficed to bring into visibility the rumpled, unmade bed, the scattered clothing, the overflowing waste receptacles, the broken toy spaceships, and the piece of crystal from the moon that glittered atop the bookcase. The light from the screen blinked rose a moment, then bluegreen, glinting on an empty whiskey bottle; two, three, four of them. Still others lay almost invisible in the shadow of the room's only chair. To the right of this chair—an antique of sorts, from the last decades of the Twentieth Century—stood another whiskey bottle, three-quarters full.

There between the partly-filled bottle and the chair dangled Newton's hand, lean and bony, hardly moving. After several minutes of stillness, the long fingers moved slightly, first rubbing together aimlessly, then groping around, searching. At last they touched the partly-filled bottle, almost overturning it. They clutched the neck of the bottle as if to strangle it, then raised the bottle off the floor. The bottle moved slowly upward and sideways on a halting, zigzag course that brought it finally into contact with his stubble-covered chin. The scratch of glass against whiskers broke the long silence, seeming to Newton unnaturally loud. Through trial and error he at last brought the mouth of the bottle to rest against his tense, thin lips.

The bottle tilted and liquid flowed with a subdued gurgle, some of it overflowing and spilling down his chin onto his filthy tunic.

Whiskey bloomed like a soft sick rose in Newton's mouth. He drank deep, watery eyes momentarily straying from the TV screen where Reverend Roger had returned to mouth his closing benediction. Newton once again thought to himself how much more reliable the world of television was than the real world. Reverend Roger would smile exactly the same comforting smile ten thousand years in the future. Like God, Reverend Roger was eternal.

Newton set the bottle on the floor again with exaggerated care and wiped his mouth with the back of his hand. He hated the taste of alcohol. He hated its smell. He even hated its hesitantly oily texture, but like Reverend Roger, alcohol was predictable.

In all the rest of the universe, as he'd seen on the newscasts, lurked surprises; usually ugly, painful surprises. How much safer to content oneself with the role of spectator rather than participant, to watch other people as if they were actors on television with the sound turned off.

Newton took another drink and went back to watching the screen, half-awake and half-dreaming. The choir sang in silence, their mouths opening and closing as if they were fish on land, dying. They were in fact probably all long dead.

Newton spoke aloud to himself with boozy contempt. "You're a failure, Newton McClintok."

"Maybe so," he replied, "but even if I am a failure now, this is the last time I ever will be one."

"Oh yeah? How do you figure that, Newton?"

"If you never try, you can never fail. Right, McClintok?"

"Right, but if you care about anything, you will try. Right, Newton? They'll made you try."

"Right! So just make damn sure you don't care. Whatever you do, don't let them make you care. Right?"

"*Right!*"

Newton heard one of his mothers setting a tray down outside his door, probably the youngest one, Wilma. Wilma had been doing that ever since he flunked out.

Wilma didn't pass judgment on people, just did her best to give them what they needed, or at least what they said they needed, or so Newton supposed. For some reason he had never gotten to know her too well. But then maybe he'd never gotten to know anyone, including Holly, very well. There'd been so much vital stuff to watch on the screen.

He shuffled into his private bathroom, washed his hands, then stumbled to the door and gruffly commanded it to open. It obeyed. It too was predictable.

On the hall rug sat a tray containing a chow-mein dinner and a pint of whiskey. He took the tray inside. It had been exactly one month and nine days since he had last been outside the room.

*

After talking to Adam over the computer net, Holly had left the booth and returned to the decaying motel in the neighborhood of the ancient movie colony which Hal Waterman had rented for her. She had expected him to make some sort of sexual advances, but he had acted like some impossible screen ideal of a Victorian gentleman, never going further than to kiss her hand with elaborate ceremony. Moreover, a short walk around the court had revealed to her that she was the motel's only guest.

That shouldn't have been too surprising. After all, what good was a motel in an age when the private motorcar was almost extinct?

Now she sat on her bed watching the sunset through an open window where tattered curtains swayed in a hot, sluggish breeze.

There was no air-conditioning.

For that matter, there was no electricity, and when she had turned a faucet, she had discovered there was no running water either, and the antique telephone on the bedtable, vintage 1980 or thereabouts, was not connected. When Hal had left her here, he'd told her to use the restrooms in a nearby restaurant, but only now did she know why.

Her cabin was one of about fifty identical cubic stucco buildings that enclosed a wide expanse of lawn. The whole complex, she guessed, could easily have been built in the Art Deco craze of the Nineteen twenties or thirties, and if that was true, one could only marvel at how well it had been preserved. The Hollywood district harbored many little enclaves like this, she knew, sentimental "historical monuments" to the days when this was the entertainment capital of the world.

Darkness came on quickly now. On the horizon she could see the skyscrapers, and arcologies lighting up their nightly display, and above them the stars, clear and bright. She had read about the dreadful smog that had blanketed this area in bygone days, and felt a kind of abstract gratitude that smog had followed the internal-combustion engine into oblivion. Here in this cabin, exposed to the open air, she would have had no protection against it.

But what could she do here, all alone in the dark without so much as a flashlight? She would sleep. She pulled off her boots and climbed into bed, laughing aloud when the bedsprings squeaked, for she had never slept on bedsprings before. But she soon found they were less comfortable than an airbed. She did not undress however, keeping on her rented orange shift and her underwear. In spite of the heat, she pulled the covers up to her chin.

It was then she heard the heavy footsteps approaching across the grassy courtyard. She lay still, hoping the footsteps would pass by. Instead they came up to the door of her cabin and stopped. The vague fears that had been building up in her since her first encounter with Hal Waterman suddenly came into sharp focus. What did she know about this demonic looking man? Nothing. What did she know about his company? Nothing. Did she even know for sure he had a company? No.

What could be more clever, if one happened to be a rapist or homocidal maniac, than to contact the victims through an employment agency? In this job-starved era nobody asked questions about a potential position. Everyone was too desperate. For that matter, the employment agency itself might be a phony. Then the maniac would take his victim to a lonely, out-of-the-way abandoned motel where there was no computer terminal, not even a functioning telephone, and where nobody would hear her screams.

There came a gentle knock on her door.

She thought of remaining silent, hoping he would go away, but what good was that? He know she was here. He had come right to her unlocked door without hestitation.

"Are you asleep, Holly?"

"No, Hal. Come on in." She tried to remember a self-defense course she had taken many years ago.

The screen door squeaked open and banged shut.

He advanced into the room, feeling his way in the dark, at last finding a chair and sitting down gingerly, as if afraid it might collapse under him. Holly could not see his face, only the black looming bulk of his body.

Mind if I smoke a little tobacco?" he asked mildly.

"Tobacco? That's forbidden."

"Nothing is forbidden to those who can pay."

His face was briefly illuminated by the flare of an antique petroleum lighter such as Holly had never seen outside a museum, then he sat back with a creak and blew a stream of smoke toward the ceiling. "The vices of the present are so quickly exhausted. One is forced to reach back through time for the vices of the past. Haven't you noticed, our whole world is doing it?"

Holly sat up in bed, hugging her knees. "Why did you bring me here?" she demanded, her voice shaking in spite of all she could do to prevent it.

He chuckled. "To this God-forsaken place, you might say? Ah, have no fear for your virtue, my monogamous lady friend. I have no designs on you. The company owns this place, maintaining it ostensibly as part of our Cultural Heritage, a tidbit of folksy americana, but actually as a hideaway where our employees can enjoy a good night's sleep away from the watchful eye of the hotel patrol."

"But you have no terminal here, not even running water or electricity."

"Such things would certainly attract the attention of the authorities. No, my dear, in our time the great luxuries are not computer hookups or electrical gadgets, but anonymity, blessed anonymity." The tip of his cigarette glowed, a tiny red dot in the blackness.

"And this company of yours...you haven't even told me what it's called or what it does."

"Haven't I? An oversight, a simple oversight, I assure you. I thought I said I was in insurance."

"But what kind of insurance? What kind of a company?"

"Our name may not be familiar to you. We're called the Promethean Underwriters. We don't lend money to the general public. You, as a private individual, can't buy one of our policies, and we couldn't dream of advertising, but we do rather well for ourselves anyway. You have no doubt heard of the International Debt. Have you ever wondered to whom this debt was owed?"

"To the citizens of the world state, I thought."

Hal laughed outright. "I see our company's practice of keeping a low profile has been only too successful. But if you think the affairs of a world state can be financed by your pitiful little bonds and stamps, you must be so lacking in intelligence as to be unfit for the job you have so recently accepted. If you think your friendly corner insurance broker can insure the risks taken by government agencies, you must be ready to retire to an Unemployables' camp."

"So you sell insurance and lend money to the world state?" Holly had a sense of suddenly rising out of the depths of a dark sea of ignorance and bursting forth into the air of another, higher level of reality. It was a level she had always half-suspected was there but had never before had the time or means to investigate, one that held all the temptations people dreamed of.

"To the world state, and to the national governments. One does not hear much about national governments anymore, but even in their present semi-atrophied condition they manage to devour billions every year with their endless impact reports, feasibility studies, investigations and general bureaucratic thrashing about. Not that I or my company would dream of discouraging the busy little devils."

"I still don't understand. Why all this mystery? Why these secret passages? These abandoned motel hideouts? These interviews disguised as casual traveler's chitchat?"

Hal chuckled again. "I could tell you all sorts of rational reasons for it, but let's go straight to the bottom line. *It's fun!* Don't you think it's fun?"

"Fun?" Holly was dumbfounded at the concept. That was never the way she had seen power before.

"Of course. And if you think what you've been through so far is strange, wait until tomorrow."

"Tomorrow? What's going to happen tomorrow?"

"Have you ever been up in a balloon?"

"No, but...."

"Tomorrow you will decide whether or not you're willing to spend the rest of your life in one."

With that the big man lurched to his feet, snubbed out his

cigarette, and exited laughing.

*

No wind disturbed the eon-ancient snow that stretched almost unbroken to the horizon. The snow glittered faintly in the starlight...white, grey and bluewhite...reflecting particularly the light of one star that was brighter than the rest. The stars did not twinkle, but shone steadily with a hard, unblinking glare.

There was no air in the sky. The air had been frozen long before the first life stirred on Earth. Frozen air formed the white blanket that stretched, sparkling, to the horizon, broken only by an occasional jagged black crag of rock. The star that was brighter than the rest was the Sun.

On all this vast cold sphere of Pluto dwelt not one living creature.

Yet something moved.

There, in the distance.

First a single, faraway peak, then a strange beetle crawling awkwardly through the wastes, then a grim, long-necked charging dinosaur, starlight glinting on its reptilian scales, it advanced and grew. Now it was almost here, a vast behemoth, obscuring the sky with its bulk, towering over Newton like a living mountain.

But it was not alive!

It was a machine, a mining machine, and though it moved purposefully, there was nobody at the controls.

The scene shifted.

Newton saw an aisle in a vast plutonian factory. The only illumination in the immense building came from occasional flashes of electrical fire and here and there a phosphorescent glow. Without a single human being to tend them, the machines on both sides of the aisle toiled in the gloom, moving steadily and rapidly in silence. Now and then a little driverless robot truck scuttled past like a frightened crayfish and vanished in the shadows.

Newton liked to watch the telecasts from other planets, though most people found them painfully dull. As a boy Newton had dreamed of becoming a space pilot. Now Earth had colonies on every solid planet, moon and asteroid in the Solar System— sometimes huge industrial parks covering a hundred square kilometers or more—but less than a hundred space pilots. There were few men and fewer women in space any more, only machines.

The scene shifted again and Newton found himself looking

into the very heart of one of those machines, watching the green flywheel spin and the pistons pump, but he smelled no grease or ozone, only stale bedsheets, garbage, spilled whiskey and himself. He had not had a bath in weeks. He reached down and clutched the cold smooth glass of a whiskey bottle. He lifted it, but found it too light. He shook it hopefully, but heard no friendly, familiar slosh. He sighed and set it down, licking his dry, cracked lips. Some of his dinner came up for a moment, but he quickly swallowed it.

Behind him a feminine voice called out, and he heard his door slide open.

Damn them, he thought, twisting in his chair. *They've reprogrammed the door.*

A woman stood in the doorway.

"Holly!"

"Hello, Newton."

With a shaking hand he switched off the television. He stood up, swaying and shuffled toward the door. "Hello, l'il wifey." He tried to ape the tone of humor that he used in the days when the term had been a joke between them.

She wore a spotless orange dress and stood perfectly still, silhouetted against the light from the hallway beautiful as ever in her streamlined way. A pain in his chest told Newton he still loved her.

"May I come in?" she asked softly.

"Of course! This is as much your place as mine!" he stumbled about, switching on lights, pushing things off the bed so she could sit there.

She entered hesitantly. The panel shut behind her. As she passed him, Newton let her smooth bare arm brush his fingertips.

"Where were you?" he demanded. "I haven't seen you for months. Not since the day I flunked out."

She sat down gingerly on the bed. "I chimed you every day for the first couple of weeks." She glanced at the computer terminal. "You never answered."

"I couldn't talk over that thing. I had to see you in person, to explain...."

"I wrote to you." She glanced toward his desk where her letters lay in a pile, most of them unopened.

"I'm not much of a letter writer." He felt hot and embarrassed. He forced a smile. "Anyway, the main thing is you're back. But tell me, really, where were you? I won't be mad. You had things to do, right? I understand that, But where were you?"

"I was up in a balloon." Her voice shook, ever so little.

"Up in a balloon? All this time?"

"All this time," she said softly, not looking at him. "I'm sorry Newton."

Feeling dizzy at the implications in her tone, Newton leaned against the wall. "I don't believe this. I just don't believe this. I'm lying here, damn near dying, and you're up in a balloon somewhere. Wait. I get it. You're joking! Right?" He tried to laugh.

"I'm not joking."

"But you're back now, that's the important thing. Back to stay."

"No, Newton."

"What do you mean? Are you going back up in the balloon again?"

"That's right."

"To stay?"

"Yes."

"Oh my God, I don't believe this. Up in a balloon. To stay." He began pacing the room. "Don't tell me things like that, l'il wifey."

"I'm not your l'il wifey any more, Newton. I never was. That was just a joke. This isn't the twentieth century. I divorced you yesterday. Didn't you read any of the notices the court sent you?"

"Junk mail! I thought it was junk mail! Who reads junk mail?" He collapsed in his chair, his back to her. "I really don't believe this, you know. Come off it, okay? Enough is enough."

"There was no way you could fit in...on the balloon," she said. "Try and understand. I asked them. They saw your test results. They couldn't make an exception. And it's a good job, Newton. I could never get a better one. If I turned it down, that would be on my records. We can't just think of you. I might never get another job. I have a career, too."

"You have a career? Well, I don't. I'm an Unemployable. That's not a career. That's a black hole you disappear into." Again he tried to laugh. Again he failed. "I don't believe this. Listen, Holly, don't hand me any crap about balloons. Maybe you did divorce me. How can I blame you? When the ship is sinking, who blames the rats for leaving? Go on, then. Opportunity knocks and you answer. I can understand that."

"Thank you, Newton," she whispered sarcastically.

"But no more bullshit about balloons. Okay?"

"Okay, darling." Her voice was barely audible.

Newton knew when she began crying, even though his back was to her. He always knew how she felt, even when he was in the next room. He always knew when she was crying. This time, however, he made no move to put his arm around her and comfort her.

Don't let her make you care, he told himself sternly.

He knew she still felt something for him, he knew by her voice. Maybe she wouldn't leave if he got down on his knees and begged. Maybe.

Don't hope, Newton, he silently cautioned himself. *Don't care about anything, remember? That's they way they get you. Don't try. Don't fail. Hope is the hook.*

But in spite of himself he turned in his chair to face her. She had been watching him, but now looked away quickly. Tears left slimy snailtrails down her cheeks.

He said, "What's wrong, Holly? Can't you even stand the sight of me?"

She looked at him for a long moment, then haltingly she answered, "It's only that I hardly recognize you, sweetie-baby. Couldn't you maybe clean up a little?"

She's going to stay, he thought suddenly.

With frantic haste he stumbled into the bathroom, shaved, and took a frenzied shower. He put on a clean robe, a white robe with blue floral trim, and combed his hair. "I need a haircut," he muttered.

He re-entered the bedroom.

Holly was gone.

The door to the hall stood open.

Newton commanded it to close, then thought, *She maybe left a note.* He searched feverishly but found nothing, only the faint lingering aroma of orange perfume.

"I don't believe this," he murmured.

Gradually, as the days passed, he learned to believe it.

Chapter 3

Under a cloudless night sky shimmering with aurora borealis Holly crossed the Bering Straits on the Alaska-Siberia monorail. Midmorning found her disembarking in the Russian industrial town of Solzhenitsyn, hiring an electric propellor-powered snowmobile on thumbprint credit, and skimming out beyond the cyclopean city walls into the white silence while a worried Monoglian cabbie tried, in broken English, to persuade her to turn back.

From under her parka she studied the passing terrain through greenish polaroid goggles, a terrain flat and featureless as a tabletop except for an occasional boulder or stunted, leafless tree. In the breast pocket of her bulky, insulated coveralls a small radio bleeped from time to time in code, and it was to this she listened, not to the driver's increasingly voluble warnings. Now and then she glanced up into the bright, empty sky and frowned.

At last she said, "Here, driver. Let me off here."

He cut the motor and let the snowmobile coast to a stop, but continued to scold her. "*Nyet, Madam, nyet!*"

"Yes," she insisted. "Here. That's a good boy." She pushed open the door and clambered out, her boots sinking deep into the snow.

"But Madam! Nothing here! Nothing!"

"I know. You may go now."

"I not leave you here alone!"

"Go on, scat!" She shooed him away with a mittened hand, her breath drifting in little white clouds.

Muttering a passionate Russian curse, he slammed the door, slewed the snowmobile around in a ragged half-circle, then sped away toward Solzhenitsyn.

Holly stood quietly, scanning the heavens, as the insect whine of the snowcab faded in the distance.

Though there was no wind, the cold began immediately to seep into her garments. She stamped her feet and slapped herself. Her radio beeped comfortingly, but contributed nothing to her warmth. "Hurry up, damn you," she whispered through chattering teeth.

Then she saw it, a tiny dot near the zenith, circling slowly like a buzzard. *About time,* she thought with relief. A moment later she could make out its gull-like wings, its slender, graceful fuselage, its V-shaped tail where rudder and elevators combined in a single set of control surfaces. Then she made out its four-bladed propellers, feathered and stationary at the midpoint of the trailing edge of each wing. "Bleep, bleep" sounded the radio. The aircraft banked sharply.

Its shadow passed directly over her, it banked again, and, flaps extended, drifted in for an almost soundless landing nearby.

Holly ran over to the plane where it lay, leaning slightly to the left, bright blue against the painfully white background. She pulled open the door with clumsey mittened hands and climbed into the first of three tandum seats, then strapped down, plugged in, and slipped on her flight helmet and oxygen mask, sucking the relatively warm air thankfully into her lungs, not minding the faint smell of rubber. In her headphones a low masculine voice said, "Welcome home, Holly."

"Thank you, Hal," she answered, still in the process of strapping on her throat microphone.

There was no one else in the plane.

She dogged shut the door and leaned forward to press the button labeled "Program Start."

The propellers on the wings leaped to life, blending into a silver blur. Behind her, she knew, the cryonic-loop batteries were feeding current to the plane's compact but powerful electric motors, current that had been collected by the coating of solar cells that lined the upper surface of the wings.

In hardly more than a few paces the craft was airborne and climbing. As it banked she caught a glimpse of the snowcab, the driver staring up at her open-mouthed.

33

Aircraft, she reflected, had become a rare sight since the worldwide network of magnetic trains had rendered obsolete that gas-guzzling, pollution-vomiting, ozonosphere-destroying plague of jet planes that had once swarmed the skies. Almost all of the airplanes that remained outside of museums were the fleet of space shuttles that serviced the needs of the Solar Colonies (these shuttles being powered by hydrogen-oxygen rockets that produced no pollution, only the purest of pure water), and a few solarvolatic-assisted gliders such as the one she now occupied, mainly playthings of the rich.

The snowmobile dwindled away below her, and even the dark ugly huddle of buildings that was Solzhenitsyn shrank to some toy city one might find under a Christmas tree.

She turned her attention to the sky ahead, and soon located the slow-moving dot she sought.

"Valhalla!" she breathed.

Her aircraft, particularly when climbing steeply, was not fast, but she closed in rapidly on her objective and minutes later could distinquish its main features.

Valhalla was an immense transparent geodesic sphere, its surface webbed with triangular leaded glass panes that gleamed and flashed in the sunlight, its lowest quarter walled in except for a few small windows and one large protruding transparent half-bubble at what one might call its south pole. Egg-shaped white pods clung to opposite sides of the equator, their fatter ends terminating in a transparent, downward-pointing canopy, while along its "Antarctic" belly ran a maze of struts and wires supporting dish antennas of various sizes, bits of irregularly shaped equipment like dead flies in a spiderweb, and two straight tracks where dangled four other power-assisted gliders similar to the one she rode in.

Below at the end of a long, thick cable, a spherical lump of ballast swung slowly, like the pendulum of a grandfather's clock.

She smiled, remembering the solemn guided tour Hal had given her on her first visit to Valhalla, how he had led her up to the roof of the occupied lower fourth of the great globe and shown her the gardens growing there and the big suspended-barrel composters where every bit of waste, including human excrement, was recycled into fertilizer. She had felt ill that day, and half-repelled, unable to understand Valhalla's preoccupation with garbage, dirt and excretions, unable to adjust to the rich earthy aroma of the roofgardens, unable to accept the ceaseless pitch and roll of the deck, so she only half understood Hal's explanation of how the sun coming in through the panes of glass in the upper sphere heated the black floor of the garden, and caused the air within the sphere to expand; how it was released through valves into the colder, outer air during the day, then not allowed to return during the night so that Valhalla gained altitude like a hot-air balloon but, unlike a hot-air balloon, did not come down again. One could walk in the garden, protected from ultraviolet by the leaded glass, protected from the thin air outside the sphere and the still thinner air in its upper portion by the thick roof of the gardens, but not protected by anything against airsickness. Yes, she had been ill that day, disgustingly ill.

Now nothing on Valhalla was unfamiliar enough to her to make her ill, though the craft still held more than one mystery that intrigued her, not the least of which was the reason why anyone would want to build a hot-air balloon that was an independent, self-contained ecosystem, a balloon that would perhaps never descend to Earth.

Her aircraft leveled off and, guided by a radio beam, droned steadily toward the gently rocking sphere . She checked her air mask. Up here she would have quickly lost consciousness without it.

She heard the skyhook rise and snap into place, then the propellors stopped spinning and their blades feathered. With one last long graceful glide her little plane swooped in and hooked itself on one of the inverted carts hanging under Valhalla. The sudden stop would have smashed her head against the windshild if she hadn't been strapped in. This was one thing she was not quite used to.

As the plane dangled from its track, bobbing and rocking, falling in with the long slow swing Valhalla always had, she unstrapped, unplugged, removed her flight helmet, and with a deft and newly-learned motion transferred her airmask to a small portable oxygen bottle.

A shadow fell over her and she glanced up. Hal had come down to meet her. Big, gentle, clever Hal Waterman. She wondered how she could have ever thought him demonic.

He took her mittened hand in his gloved one and helped her up on the catwalk. She couldn't see his face behind his airmask, but somehow she was sure he was smiling. Arm in arm they ascended a short flight of steps and passed through an airlock into Valhalla's pressurized interior.

He pulled off his mask an instant before she pulled off hers.
"Did you get the divorce, Holly?" he asked softly.
She nodded.

"You won't regret it," he told her.

She had her mask off now. "I've already regretted it many times," she said. Coming in so abruptly from the bright sunlight into this dim, narrow locker room, she could not see Hal clearly, but she did hear him sigh.

"I know how you feel," he said.

"I doubt that, Hal."

"I had to say a few goodbyes before I came here. We all did." His self-mocking, bantering tone had vanished for the moment. "But sometimes there's no room in the lifeboat for any more survivors. Then you have to cut off a few fingers."

She angrily pushed him away. "There you go again with one of your mysterious remarks. What in hell are you talking about?"

"Today you'll understand everything," he reassured her. "No doubt you've already guessed Promethian Underwriters is more than a mere insurance and loan company.

"I've had a feeling something was going on here," she admitted.

"Today all will be explained, after you have sworn your oath."

"My oath?" She stared at him blankly.

He lapsed again into his usual teasing tone. "Of course. Isn't it traditional to swear an oath when you join a secret society?"

*

The face was unforgettable; it was the marks of suffering that made it so; the dull grey eyes that might have stared into the face of Medusa, the downturned lips that now began to move silently, as if pleading for mercy; but suffering was not the only emotion Newton saw there. The man had intelligence too, and a tattered remnant of arrogant pride. He could have been Casanova...in Hell.

Suddenly the forehead began to sweat and the pupils of the eyes dilated. According to a digital clock in the upper right hand corner of the picture, it was almost time. Three seconds, two seconds, one. Now! The face contorted in agony, tears streaming down its paperwhite cheeks. Then the pain passed and on the face appeared an expression of infinite relief. The video camera backed away a little to reveal a nameplate in front of the man's Adam's apple.

"Jesus Sanchez, presidential assassin."

The camera pulled back still further so Newton could see the outlines of the sealed glass hemisphere in which the man rested. As Newton knew, Jesus Sanchez was already one hundred

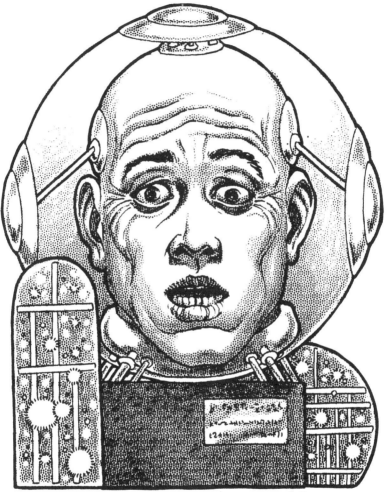

twenty-seven years old and theoretically immortal. Newton could also see the place in Jesus' head where a small portion of the scalp and skull had been removed and replaced by a cluster of wires. These wires led directly to the pain centers of Sanchez's brain. Every fifteen minutes a timing device sent a feeble electric current through these wires, causing Sanchez to experience the greatest pain known. The man had no real existence, only a lifesupport machine that regulated the chemical composition of his artificial bloodstream to prevent fainting, sleep, shock, insanity or death. He would remain in this state until his combined term of two hundred and twelve years was served out; then he would be allowed to die.

Thanks to humanitarian reformers, the death penalty had been abolished, but only to be replaced by a near eternal torment, a punishment that in previous centuries only God had been powerful enough and monstrous enough to administer.

As the camera receded, more heads came into view, each under its own glass bell, a multitude of faces all bearing the same expression of dreadful anticipation.

"The Hall of Heads," whispered Newton. "You're famous, you'r immortal, and you're in the Hall of Heads, Sanchez, but you're still a loser."

The Hall of Heads was a popular and authentic program. Soon the dramatic portrayal of Sanchez's life would begin. Newton opened a fresh bottle of whiskey and tasted it experimentally. His eyes strayed to his rumpled bed and rested a moment on the two pillows there. His and hers. He still always slept on his own side of the bed, pretending Holly was only a little late coming home, not really gone.

She's getting at you, Newton, he told himself bitterly, silently, *and she's not even here.*

He stood up, went over to the dresser, opened the top drawer, and began once again pawing over his treasures...the stupid, sentimental souvenirs, the wedding pictures, the honeymoon snapshoots. He took out his wedding ring and slipped it onto his finger. He had always refused to wear it when Holly was with him, claiming it made his finger itch. Why put it on now, when it had lost all meaning? He took it off and for a moment felt like hurling it across the room. Instead he dropped it into the drawer. He often felt violent these days, but never actually did anything violent.

He muttered, "I'm alone too much."

Being alone all the time in a windowless room with the silent video people did strange things to his mind. He had lost track of time and had no idea of the date or month. In spite of his placid exterior, his emotions had climbed onto a manic-depressive roller coaster. At the top of the cycle he felt an almost supernatural ecstasy, and at the bottom felt a depression so oppressive he would have killed himself except that it was too much trouble.

He closed the top drawer and opened the next one down. There lay one of Holly's old nightgowns, pale orange, rumpled, with a rip in the skirt. Gently he took it out, as he had often done before, and felt its flimsy softness in his fingers, rubbed it against his cheek, and buried his face in it, breathing the faint scent of orange perfume that still lingered in the fabric.

A fury welled up inside him, but he surpressed it. He walked slowly into the bathroom and hung the gown over the nozzlehead in the shower.

He thought, *The tile is fireproof.*

He returned to the dresser to seek out the ancient antique cigarette lighter he'd found in childhood. He tried it, and it still lit, though he had not used it since the years of his adolescent experiments with forbidden pleasures. Once again in the bathroom he applied its tiny flame to the hem of the gown, ready to jump back when the nylon tricot burst into flames. The fabric merely turned black where the fire touched it and gave off a black, oily smoke while sticky little drops fell to the floor of the shower. Patiently Newton continued to ply the lighter. He had no appointments, nothing better to do. The smoke stank and he started coughing. His eyes smarted. Still he watched, with tear-blurred vision, the interesting way the delicate gossamer retreated before the oncoming flame; melting, writhing for a moment as if alive, then falling—drip, drip, drip.

"What the hell are you doing?" came a startled voice from behind him. Newton turned and saw his older brother, Einstein McClintok, standing in the doorway and staring at him through the smoke.

"A little housecleaning," mumbled Newton, snapping shut his lighter. He felt ashamed and guilty, but also suspicious. "How did you get in here, anyway? Is the door programmed for your voice?"

"Stop acting like a lunatic and come out here," Einstein commanded. "I want to talk to you."

Meekly Newton obeyed.

Einstein took the one chair and Newton sat on the bed. Behind Einstein's crew-cut head the silent TV show continued unwatched.

"What were you trying to do in there? Burn the building

down?" Newton wondered why his brother was shouting. Was it because Einstein was so short compared to Newton, even though older? Did the little fellow feel threatened? Or did he not want to admit how he'd gotten into the room? "Every light on the monitor in the kitchen lit up. We almost called the fire department."

"I'm sorry."

"Newton, I'm worried about you. We're all worried about you. Dad, Grandad, your mothers...."

"Really?"

"You think we don't care about you? You think I don't care about you?"

"That's right."

"Why do you think I spent all that time coaching you for your finals? You could have passed those finals, you know, if you had only tried."

"I did my best."

"You did not! Sure, you went through the motions, but you didn't give your whole self to it. You've never in your life given your whole self to anything, except that damned screen. Why is that, Newton? Can you tell me why that is?"

Newton thought, *Because there's nothing in this world worth giving my whole self to.* He said, "Did you say you wanted to talk to me? What about?"

"What about? Well, we would all just like to know what your plans are, Newton."

"I have no plans," said Newton softly.

Hours later, when Einstein had gone, Newton carried to completion the only plans he had. After smashing the smoke detectors in his room, he finished burning the nightgown.

*

Seated in a kind of electric chair, with electrodes taped to her forehead, chest and palms of her hands, Holly raised her right hand and repeated the simple pledge Hal had just taught her. Hal stood nearby, studying a bank of cathode-ray tubes where green wavy lines glowed against a black background.

"I pledge allegiance to Promethean Underwriters," she recited. "And to the great project for which it stands, one policy indivisible, with benefits and coverage for all." It was not her idea of humor.

"Good readout," Hall commented, turning away from the display screen.

"Is that all there is to it?" Holly demanded, as he came over to begin removing the electrodes.

"You still have to meet the President of Promethean Underwriters and learn what this company is really doing. Our agents have checked on your divorce, by the way, and everything seems to be in order. The President is always impressed by divorces. Divorces show real company loyalty."

She had caught glimpses of President Bradbury Douglas during her first stay in Valhalla, but had never spoken to him. He had seemed like a kindly old man with long white disheveled hair, unusually dressed in a plain, grey, conservative business kilt. She wondered when these agents had checked on her divorce. In the time since she'd come aboard? Or before? If before, why had she had to tell Hall about it?

In answer to her unspoken questions, Hal added, "We always confirm these things with both our agents and the subject. You know how insurance people are always trying to reduce risk."

"When will I meet President Douglas?" she asked.

Hal glanced at his fingerwatch. "About an hour and a half from now. The appointment is all set up."

"Thank God I'll have time to change." She left Hal and hurried out into the general office area where about twenty unusually good-looking young men and women carried on the business of the company in a low but lively murmur. All wore blue knee-length tunics—the Company Blues, they were called—and walked about from desk to desk briskly but without undue haste, ignoring the steady pitch and roll of the floor like seasoned sailors. Holly exchanged absent-minded greetings with some of them in passing, then darted up the central spiral staircase to the next deck, which was devoted mainly to individual staterooms.

In Valhalla the doors were never locked and were opened manually. Theft was unknown aboardship, perhaps because of the careful screening of the personnel, perhaps because of the difficulty of making a getaway. She stepped into her room, a narrow, windowless cubicle carefully designed to take up as little space as possible, and slammed her door behind her. The ceiling light too required manual operation, but she was used to it by now, and had actually been startled at first when she returned to the Earth, where lights usually turned on by themselves when they sensed your presence.

She opened her closet and checked over her wardrobe. She considered wearing an orange shift, but decided against it. Nobody had laid down any rules to her about dress, but she had noticed that the only one aboard who regularly wore anything but the Company Blues was the President. Company Blues it would be, then! And the warm, ankle-length blue slippers everyone seemed to wear here, that looked like elves' slippers.

She inspected her reflection in the oval mirror on the door, deciding she'd have to wipe off that orange lipstick. Nobody wore orange lipstick in Valhalla, or any other lipstick for that matter. But her blonde hair was exactly right...shoulder length and straight, like everyone elses' here.

When Hal knocked on her door she was ready, both physically and psychologically. "Let's go," she said, with such enthusiasm Hal laughed.

President Douglas' office was located at the bottommost part of the sphere, occupying nearly all the lowest floor. Holly had never been inside it before, but some of her new friends among the office staff had described it to her. Now she could scarcely contain her impatience as Hal led her down the central spiral staircase, along a narrow featureless passageway, to a door made of some dark wood and carved in low relief with the image of Prometheus descending Mt. Olympus, huge fireball in hand, that was the company trademark.

Hal knocked.

"Come in," said a gruff, good-natured voice. Hal and Holly entered. Holly understood immediately why it was call "The Round Room." Not only was the room itself disk-shaped, but the walls curved upward, making no attempt to conceal the fact that they were the inside surface of a sphere. The only source of illumination appeared to be a large circular window in the center of the floor that was ringed with curved couches to form a kind of "conversation pit." President Douglas advanced with hand extended, crying, "Welcome to the inner circle, Miss McClintok. Or would you like to return to your maiden name?"

"McClintok will be fine, sir," she answered as he vigorously shook her hand.

"Drink?" Douglas asked.

"No thank you, sir," she answered, surprised that the highest official of the company was waiting on her like a bartender.

"I'll have the usual, Brad," said Hal.

Douglas crossed to a curving bar and began cheerfully mixing a whiskey sour. All the glasses and bottles had clamps that held them to the wall so they would not spill or fall in rough air. He handed Hal a glass and began mixing something for himself.

"First, young lady, I want you to stop calling me 'sir.' I consider anyone with an IQ of one hundred and fifty-six or more to be my equal, for all practical purposes, and I understand you check out at one hundred and eighty."

"That's right," she said.
"Call me Brad, then."
"All right, Brad."
Brad led them to the conversation pit, saying, " And if you don't mind I'll call you Holly. Please be seated. I'm sure you have a lot of questions."
As she settled into the overstuffed leather upholstery she had a twinge of acrophobia from staring down through the window at a sheer drop of at least 14 kilometres. Slowly, majestically, the white landscape moved to her right, paused, and moved to her left. The President noticed her discomfort and chuckled. "Fear not, young lady. That glass is thick, and beyond it is a bubble canopy, to be on the safe side."
"Of course." She forced a smile and avoided looking down.
The old man drained his glass with evident pleasure, then glanced at her kneely. "Holly, have you ever read Isaac Asimov?"
"No, but I've heard of him. He was a twentieth-century science-fiction novelist, wasn't he?"
"Very good, young lady. Yes, that's right. I read almost everything he wrote when I was a boy. He's had a great influence on me, though now, as an adult, I am aware of his shortcomings. In his 'Foundation Triolgy' he postulated a science he called 'psychohistory,' not realizing that the statistical methods he indicated had already been invented by the insurance companies of his day under the name 'underwriting.' He also postulated something he called 'The Foundation,' a hidden storehouse of knowledge that would survive the collapse of human civilization, a storehouse he called *The Encyclopedia Galactica.* Interesting ideas. I was impressed at the time. But he did nothing with them, made no attempt to really explore their implications, only flew off in all directions with a lot of routine adventure nonsense. Perhaps like so many brilliant men, an inferiority complex prevented him from properly evaluating the products of his own mind. But we shouldn't be too hard on him. He was very young when he wrote the thing, and perhaps only an insurance man would be able to see the vast potential of these ideas. Right, Hal?"
"Wouldn't be surprised," Waterman agreed, staring into his drink.
Douglas leaned forward. "Only an insurance man would be able to develop underwriting into a real science of psychohistory, a solid, quantified, mathematical discipline like physics, something you can program into a computer. And only an insurance man would see how that science could be put to use."
Holly couldn't help saying, "An insurance man like you,

Brad?"

Douglas grinned boyishly. "Exactly like me, Holly. I flatter myself that I've made Asimov's science-fiction into my own science-fact. Nobody before me realized how rigorous the statistical probability of human behavior can be, when you have a large sample. Nobody realized how the same equations that worked with gases and quarks also work with masses of people, provided you understand fundamental social principles, and provided you don't abandon the project when it starts to deliver bad news."

Brad's tone now was one she'd learned to recognize here in Valhalla, the tone that said something awful was happening that nobody was willing to talk about. "What do you mean bad news?" asked Holly.

"Our civilization is on the verge of collapse," said the old man, no longer smiling.

"That's absurd!" Holly's reaction was as instantaneous as if it had been instinctive.

"I could show you the math, but you wouldn't understand it yet," said Douglas. "Let me put is simply. Evolution, in Darwin's sense, ended when the unfit learned to gang up on the fit. Now anyone, no matter how defective, can survive if protected by the slavering, drooling horde, and nobody, no matter how strong and clever, can survive without the horde's permission. In a society there's a point very much like critical mass, a point where something like a psycho-historical chain reaction begins, where the ratio of winners to losers tips too far, where the losers suddenly revolt and, with a temporary sense of blessed freedom, exterminate their betters."

"Losers? Betters?" Holly was surprised, but quick to follow the man's line of reasoning. She had often had similar thoughts, but had brushed them away.

"By losers I mean, in particular, the Unemployables. Please believe me when I say that we face a seventy-five percent probability of world civil war already, and the figure is rising. We expect a ninety percent chance by this time next year. We know what we're talking about. We've gotten very good at this sort of fortune telling."

"A world civil war? What will that mean?"

"The Unemployables will exterminate the Techs, and that will only be the beginning. When the Techs are gone, the Uns will find themselves in a world full of machines they do not understand, cannot repair, and can hardly even operate; a world that will immediately begin to break down as they look on helplessly, a world that will grind to a halt, leaving the Uns without even the rule-of-thumb technology of preliterate savages, without even the instinctive knowledge of a wild animal. They'll be free at last! Free to die."

Holly broke in, "You can warn the authorities."

"No, no, no," the President said briskly. "They have their own theories, their own computers. They wouldn't believe us. Besides, you must understand the nature of the relationship between us and them. Our own survival, the survival of any insurance company, depends on outguessing the client. Let's say I am the underwriter and you are the client. We're talking life insurance. Right? To make my percentage I must at all times have a better idea what might happen to you than you have. I must insure you for what you wrongly think will happen to you and avoid insuring you for what really will happen to you. I can put it still more simply. I bet you that you'll live. You bet me you won't. The only way you can win the bet is to die."

Holly objected, "But if the government falls, won't you have to pay off on their policies?"

"Pay who? The government will no longer exist."

"You talk about this so calmly," said Holly. "But if everything goes smash, you go smash too, along with everybody else."

Brad straightened triumphantly. "No, my dear girl. Don't forget, I'm up here in Valhalla."

*

Einstein McClintok stood gazing out the living room window, shoulders hunched, hands in pockets. Here, at the apartment's large but only window, he could stand close and peer down into the park one hundred and ten stories below, crane his neck and catch a glimpse of the afternoon sky, or stare across at the mirrorlike glass facade of the neighboring building. Behind him, in the center of the room, Old Man Adam McClintok lounged on a low couch, smoking marijuana in an antique Arabian waterpipe, his number one wife Miriam reclining beside him in a clinging translucent tunic. The old man was the only member of the family who always kept up the fashion and wore the ancestral kilt.

Einstein broke the silence. "Dad, what are we going to do about him?"

His father smiled dreamily. "Nothing."

"Nothing? But Dad, everyone on this floor is talking about him. It's a public scandal! By doing nothing about it, we make it appear we condone his outlandish behavior. People will start wondering about us next. The authorities will investigate. That marijuana you're smoking isn't exactly legal, you know."

The old man shrugged. "Who cares? It isn't as if I was smoking tobacco, you know."

"We've got to do something."

"What would you suggest?"

"Send him to the Unemployables' Camps." Einstein began to pace the floor. "That's where he legally belongs."

Old McClintok sighed, "He's still my son. I haven't the heart to kick him out."

Mrs. McClintok added wistfully, "He has lived in that room all his life. All his possessions are there. I'm told an Un doesn't have a toothbrush to call his own."

"He's still my son," the old man said again, apparently unaware he was repeating himself. The waterpipe gurgled softly and the intoxicating aroma of Marin Gold permeated the atmosphere.

"Are you sure?" Einstein loomed over his father. "He's not like us."

"He looks like me." said Adam reasonably.

"He doesn't act like you. Think, Dad! I'm a computer man, your father is a computer man. Your wives are all computer people. Your children are all computer people except Newton. He can't be a real McClintok!"

"I'm afraid he is," said Adam sadly, "and there's nothing we can do about it."

Einstein played his trump card. "If there's a scandal, we could all lose our jobs. Then when he went to the camps we'd all have to go with him."

Old McClintok slowly shook his head. "As long as he stays in his room nobody will pay any attention to him. Why don't you take a drag on my waterpipe to settle your nerves?" He offered him the mouthpiece.

Einstein stamped out of the room in disgust.

The old man turned to his frowning wife and said, "Einstein is so wholesome, like Holly was. Wholesome people don't know how to enjoy life. It's vice that makes a man human!"

"He's right, though," she mused sadly, "Sooner or later Newton's got to go."

*

I wonder (thought Newton) whatever happened to the Reds.

When I was a kid playing guns, the Reds were still the bad guys. The Commies. The Russians. The Russians were fighting us Americans for control of the Solar System. I can still remember the newscasts about them, and us nuking each other on Mars. I can still remember how excited I used to get, how I used to hate the Russians with a blind, murderous hate. Nobody won. The war just sort of petered out, stopped being important. There's still a lot of bitterness over the American Civil War and even the Black Liberation War, but nobody calls anybody a dirty Red anymore. There aren't any Reds. There aren't any Capitalists. There isn't any real Russia and there isn't any real United States. There's just the Techs and the Uns all over the world. The Great Cause I was eager to die for when I was a kid somehow faded away without my noticing, so now it's less real to me than the stupidest comedy on television, and I'm still a young man. That was only a few years ago.

What happened to the Reds?

Can't I even depend on my enemies?

*

"The gods were angry at Prometheus for stealing fire from heaven and giving it to mankind. Would they have been quite so angry if Prometheus had kept that fire for himself?"

Hal chuckled dutifully at President Brad's question, but Holly could only answer. "What do you mean?"

Bradbury Douglas, elbows on knees, peered down through the circular window in the floor at the white wastes of Siberia so far below. "We all know what this so-called Promethean fire symbolizes, don't we, young lady? The folklore of every nation abounds in such stories. Adam and Eve. Pandora and her box. The Japanesse Izanami and Izanagi. The fire is knowledge, forbidden knowledge, but the gods, it seems to me, only feel threatened when the forbidden knowledge is distributed wholesale to all comers. The democracy of the thing offends the naturally aristocratic deities. In all times and all places our best and wisest leaders have cautioned against casting pearls before swine, and I, unlike so many would-be reformers, have heeded the warning. Your IQ is one hundred and eighty is it not, Holly?"

"That's right, but...."

Brad leaned back and templed his fingers. "Bear with me. You'll soon see my point. No one in Valhalla has an IQ of less than one hundred and sixty, nor is anyone here sickly, mentally unbalanced or descended from ancestors who were stupid, sickly or crazy. There are no swine up here. Valhalla's inhabitants have been selected, to mix a metaphor, like thoroughbred horses. No matter what happens down on Earth, up here we have preserved a gene pool for a new and, one would hope, a better human race. My motives, you see, are not totally selfish. I have the best interests of our species at heart."

"And you're willing to exterminate the species to prove it!" Holly felt a sudden flash of anger at finding, here at the heart of the beautiful dream she had sworn to support, the same old Nazi fallacy of the Superior Race.

Brad raised his hand and said mildly, "Please, Holly. I exterminate nobody. I merely wait."

"While they exterminate themselves?"

"I could not stop them if I tried."

"You could warn them."

"They wouldn't listen. We would only draw their attention to ourselves, and I think we would be better off if they utterly forgot that we exist, which they will in their eagerness to leap at each other's throats. Far better to let them slide merrily down the shoot into a new dark age, at which time we will be able to reveal ourselves and play out the story science-fiction writers have always loved so well. We will be the airmen of H. G. Wells' 'Shape of Things to Come.' We will be the 'Connecticut Yankie at King Arthur's Court,' the 'Foundation' of Asimov's trilogy, the heroes who triumph over barbarians by means of superior technology."

"They'll shoot you out of the sky with ground-to-air missiles," said Holly.

"I think not, my dear. Remember how long the world has been at peace. Remember how long the skies have been virtually clear of aircraft. According to our best information, the whole planet possesses not one functioning ground-to-air weapon, nor one soldier trained to fire it. In the unlikely event we've been misinformed...in the very unlikely event that's not true, the ground war and the technological collapse that follows will make it true."

Holly did not at once reply, but sat staring down at Siberia, letting the full implications sink in. The ballast ball, at the end of its long, slightly curved cable, moved slowly to the left, paused, and moved slowly to the right, carrying the Valhalla with it. "So you think you can actually conquer the world?" she said in wonderment.

"By default. Issac Asimov showed me how."

"But what do you have that corresponds to Asimov's *Encyclopedia Galactica?*"

"I have, in subatomic storage, all the knowledge of mankind

down through the ages, a kind of vastly expanded Alexandrian library locked in a single memory bank, a crystal the size of a baseball. And no one will get a chance to 'burn' it."

Holly had read about subatomic storage computers, but only as a theory, a prediction of the future. For Promethean Underwriters, it seemed, the future had already arrived. There was nothing impossible about the idea. The quantum jump made by an electron changing orbits could be used for binary coding as easily as any other electronic phenomenon. "Here on board?" she asked, looking directly at him for the first time since the interview began.

He smiled and chuckled, "The location of the crystal must remain my secret. I should trust you with everything I know, but paranoia counsels prudence. You may, however, consider yourself an initiate into the highest order of our little masonic lodge, short of Grand Mastery, which I reserve for myself." He stood up and extended his hand. "Welcome to the Promethean Order, Holly." She rose to meet him.

They shook hands, he warmly, she numbly, and as they stood on the window in the floor she did not dare look down, but looked her President right in the eye. She saw in that eye a certain calculating glint she knew only too well.

My God, she thought, *he's got the hots for me!*

Chapter 4

One year had passed since Newton had last been out of his room.

He celebrated the first anniversary of his exile by watching television. The news broadcast concluded, as usual, with a majestic shot of the tall, silvery World Government Pylon at Oiltown, Antarctica. Oiltown, captial of the whole planet and indeed of the whole Solar System, lay two kilometers below the surface, safe from the nuclear missiles which, even at the height of the Russo-American War, had never come. Here, in shadowy, echoing caverns, reigned SERCON, the master computer, the socio-economic extrapolator. World Presidents came and went, but SERCON never left office, never ceased to make itself more and more indispensable and autonomous, to make more and more of the really important decisions. No human could think fast enough to even check these decisions, let alone control them.

The Pylon was an impressive symbol, rising imperturbably above the violently swirling snow flurries around its base. *A symbol*, Newton wondered, *of what?* The Conquest of Nature? Unity? Liberty? Fraternity? Equality? Peace? Freedom? The male sex organ? Who could say?

Next came a comedy, a variation on the old-time minstrel shows, except that burnt-cork "darkies" had been replaced by a row of men and women with shaved heads and the yellow monkish robes of Uns, the inmates of an Unemployables' Camp.

In the place of Mister Interlocutor, the fat white slave owner, now sat Cap, a pompous busybody in the uniform of a captain in the Security Police. The Uns sat around him in a semicircle, like a row of grinning yellow teeth and, at a gesture from him, leaped up and began dancing in a parody of the Can-Can, lifting their robes as if they were skirts and kicking high. Some wore bloomers, some long red flannel underwear, some nothing at all under their robes.

Newton muttered sarcastically, "How very funny." He raised a sloshing bottle to his lips. He had had a stomach ache for more than a week. A few shots of whiskey had usually killed the pain, but today it seemed the more he drank the more it hurt. In an effort to distract himself, he broke his own longstanding rule and turned up the sound. The dancing Uns were singing:

"*Oh, we've got nothing to do all day,*
But dance and sing and laugh and play,
We're always happy and always gay,
In Barracks Twenty-Four."

"Bullshit," Newton muttered, switching off the sound again. He took another drink, but the pain remained.

Unfortunately he had, with no conscious effort, begun to pick up the knack of lipreading and now, in spite of himself, began reading fragmented phrases off the dancers' lips.

"Never a care," they mouthed, then, "Love to spare" and finally, "My little Un baby and me."

With a curse Newton changed the station, shaking his head in wonder at the stupidity of people who actually believed this was how the Uns lived. *I guess they want to believe it,* he decided. *People will always pay more for a soothing lie than a bitter truth.*

He found himself watching some ancient pornographic films, coy, simpering and touchingly naive. Newton smiled, then laughed out loud at the way the pubic hair was shaved off in conformance with the tribal taboos of the period.

Still grinning, he took another drink.

His stomach felt as if it had exploded. He screamed with agony and surprise as, lurching to his feet, he tasted vomit coming up. He ran for the bathroom.

There he knelt before the toilet bowl and let himself go, then stared down at the result.

Blood!

He gazed at the redness with stunned disbelief, then heaved again.

More blood.

"I'm dying," he said softly, with wistful bathos, trying the idea on for size. "I'm actually dying." He felt no trace of fear, only a kind of weary relief, yet like an actor who has learned his part too well, he began to go through the motions of survival, dragging himself to his front door, commanding it to open, and sprawling in the corridor where he listened like a drama critic to his own screams. "Help! Help! I'm dying!"

As his vision blurred he heard running footsteps approaching, then the voice of Wilma, his youngest mother, saying, "Yech! What a pig!"

But she did help him to bed and chimed the doctor on his terminal.

*

A stomach ulcer.

The doctor told him firmly from the large screen, to which Wilma had switched the image, "Booze did this to you, young man. My prescription is simple. No more booze. No smoking, not even marijuana. No spices. No rich foods. For a while you get nothing but milk with a raw egg in it and vitamin pills. Understand?"

Newton, in bed, nodded weakly.

"Good," said the greybearded medical man. "Shall I debit your account?"

"Debit mine," said Wilma, pressing her thumb against the thumbprint reader of Newton's terminal.

"Very good, Mrs. McClintok. Take care of this boy. I leave him in your capable hands, and I know they're capable because of the fine job you did on his physical examination."

"I just followed your instructions," she said, pleased.

"Like a registered nurse!" the doctor boomed. "I'll have the pills sent up. All right?"

"All right, doctor," she said.

His image faded from the screen.

As Wilma unplugged the medical telemetry appliances from the terminal, Newton's family began to tiptoe in through the door which Wilma had neglected to close.

Old Adam read aloud the motto Newton had scrawled on the mirror of the medicine cabinet in the bathroom. "A fool's paradise is better than none." With effort Newton remembered writing it there months ago with a tube of orange lipstick Holly had left behind.

"What does that mean?" Einstein demanded, with more than a shade of hostility, glowering at Newton from the foot of the bed.

"I don't remember," whispered Newton truthfully.

"I think it's rather clever," said Wilma, returning the examination appliances to their place in a drawer under Newton's terminal.

"Don't encourage him to any more acts of vandalism," scolded Miriam, the number one wife.

They all continued wandering around Newton's room clucking their tongues, shaking their heads, touching things, staring at things, even picking up things and sniffing them distatsefully.

"I need sleep," Newton called out weakly. "Could you all leave me alone for a while?"

"We're taking the liquor with us," said Miriam firmly.

"Yes, yes, of course," Newton croaked, "Just go. That's all I ask." He hated himself for the whining tone that had somehow crept into his voice.

"We're going." Wilma leaned over and kissed Newton's cheek, much to his surprise. "Pleasant dreams."

When the last one had reluctantly departed, Newton raised up on his elbows and barked out the closing command, then listened with relief to the satisfying swish and thump of the door shutting.

Then he noticed that someone had borrowed his favorite book, *Ancient Japanese Poems,* without asking permission. Gazing fixedly at the gap in the line of familiar books on his shelf, he said softly, "Newton, Newton, Newton, don't let it get to you. Don't let them make you care."

He fell back on his pillow and drifted off into a troubled sleep.

When he awoke he at last knew for sure they had programmed the door to respond to their voices, because someone had come in and cleaned up the mess. Holding his still-aching stomach, he made a slow, shuffling inspection tour of the whole apartment, finding most of his clothes gone, the motto washed off the mirror, and the tube of orange lipstick confiscated to prevent him from scrawling it up again.

The tour completed, he collapsed into his chair and reactivated his television set. As the image flickered into life, he thanked whatever gods there be that his loving family hadn't disconnected the TV. He wouldn't have been surprised if they had.

*

Wait a minute. Wait. Wait. *Now!*
Orgasm.
Relaxation.

Miriam McClintok gave a long satisfied sigh as Jim Moran rolled off her and lay, breathing heavily, by her side on the bed.

She thought, *God, that was good!*

As the dim morning sunlight filtered through the curtained window, she gazed fondly at his muscular, handsome, sweaty body, at his wonderful youthfulness. She had almost forgotten what a young man was like.

She thought, The Old Man has young wives. Why can't I have a young husband?

She whispered, "Do you love me, Jimmy?"

"Huh?"

"Do you love me?"

"Sure I do, baby. You know I do."

"Do you want to marry me?" She knew he prided himself on always doing the right thing, the respectable thing.

After a long pause he answered hesitantly, "Sure, baby." then more assertively, "Of course I do."

Smiling, she touched his soft rumpled blond hair. She thought, *What a perfectly luscious blue-eyed everlovin' hunk of beefsteak!*

Later, around noon, as they walked hand in hand in the park, he thought, So what if she is a little old. Her co-wives ain't—That Wilma is really something—and I'll be able to get away from my parents at last and have a room of my own.

It was Newton's room he had in mind.

*

Miriam McClintok marched into the living room and confronted Old Adam, her fists on her hips and her feet planted firmly apart.

"I have something to tell you," she announced.

He leaned back in his chair, set down the flow chart he'd been working on, and swiveled to give her his undivided attention, smiling politely. The smile faded as she launched into her proclamation, ending with "...Jim is a servomotor maintenance man and he wants to marry me and come here to live with us."

The old man had turned quite pale, but only for a moment, then he brightened and said, "I'd be the first to welcome him if you invited him, but of course it's quite impossible. We have no room in the apartment."

"What about Newton's room?" she demanded.

"Newton's in it!"

"Then kick him out. He has no legal right to be there."

"What kind of a mother are you, Miriam? I'm not going to have it on my conscience that I shipped off my own son to the Un camps. No, I'll have no part of it. If you want the boy out, you'll

54

have to evict him yourself." His expression said more plainly than words that he knew she was too soft-hearted to really do it.

And he was right. It was Jim Moran who said, later that day, "I'll have a little man-to-man talk with this here Newton guy!"

Newton's stomach had healed somewhat, so that he could eat mush, fruit and in fact almost anything not too spicy, rich or indigestible. He could, according to the doctor, have ice cream every day, but Wilma cautioned him against gaining weight. Since discovering his family could enter his room at will, he had resigned himself to visitors and had actually begun looking forward to Wilma's intrusions. She came daily to oversee his diet and even play him an occasional game of chess, always losing with good grace. No woman had ever beaten Newton at chess, not even Holly with her famous IQ.

Thus when he heard a knock at the door, it was hardly surprising that he called out expectantly, "Wilma?"

"No, it's me, Jim Moran."

"I don't know any Jim Moran." Something in that hail-fellows-well-met voice put Newton instantly on guard.

"I'm going to be your new co-father."

Newton, with resignation, commanded the door to open.

Jim entered, face fixed in a rigid, masklike smile. Newton noted the profusion of zippered pockets in the man's blue denim tunic and classified him as a maintenance Tech. Among the programmers such workers were regarded with amused contempt as being perfectly suited for their jobs but otherwise as stupid as cows.

Jim, on the other hand, classified Newton as a bum, with his long tangled hair and beard and his thin wasted body, like the body of a Hindu holy man. Jim thought, *This guy is going to be a pushover.*

He asked Newton, "Do you know how it feels to be in love?"

"I have some dim recollection of it."

"Well, I'm in love."

"So?"

"And I need your help."

"I have no help to give."

"I need your friendship. Whaddya say, Newton?" He extended his hand.

Newton regarded the hand coldly. Jim's smile faded slightly, then returned. "I envy you, Newt."

"For what?"

"You're free of the rat race, once and for all. No more worries, no more pressure. How did you do it?"

"Easy. One false step and bingo, you're there."

"I can't get out of the old rut, Newt. Maybe someday...."

"My name is Newton. A newt is a salamander."

"No offense intended, Newton. No offense intended. Maybe someday I'll join you there at the Un camp, dancing, singing, playing ball."

"The Un camp?" Newton sat up in bed abruptly.

"Sure. I mean, this is your opportunity, like an early retirement. While I'm slaving away my life in the shop, you'll be off there whooping it up twenty-four hours a day, like in the pop songs." He stopped, nonplussed by Newton's stare.

"So you want my room," said Newton softly. "That's what this is all about, isn't it?"

Red-faced, Jim said, "I have a right to it. I'm employed. I'm going to marry one of your mothers. I'm going to be your father."

"And you're even in love, aren't you, Moran? And that means there's no trick too dirty for you to pull. Love triumphs over everything, even conscience. Right?"

Jim decided to have hurt feelings. "Don't take it like that, Newt. Here I come, wanting to have a friendly little talk, and you get abusive. Listen, buddy, if you want to get tough, two can play that game."

"Get out," said Newton in a low voice.

"You can't tell me...."

"Get out!" Newton screamed, and Jim took a step backward. Newton stood up in his bed, swaying, like some reanimated corpse rising from the grave. "Get out!" he screamed again.

Jim fled.

Newton waited until the show he had been watching was over, then turned off the television, changed into fresh clothes, and commanded the door to open.

Barbara, Newton's second mother, was fixing supper in the kitchen when Newton appeared in the hallway.

"Oh!" she cried out, her hand touching her throat. "You startled me, Newton."

He stood in the doorway, tall, gaunt and hairy. "Where's Wilma?"

"Out shopping."

He considered this a moment, then said, "Can you give her a message?"

"Of course."

"Tell her I said 'thanks.' "

"All right."

He pushed rudely past her and she heard him command the

front door to open, then a moment later heard the elevator. Beyond being a little surprised at seeing Newton out of his room, she thought no more about it, for just then the computer signaled that the roast was done, and she had to return to preparing supper.

On the ground floor Newton came out through the broad main air-door and stood squinting, unaccustomed to even the dim afternoon sunlight that filtered down among the skyscrapers. The smell of superpines was good. He sucked it deep into his lungs. His vision cleared and he saw, among the trees in the park across the bikeway, his mother Miriam and Jim Moran holding hands engaged in heated conversation. He smiled, glad to see that Miriam was the one who had brought in this intruder, not Wilma.

He crossed the bikeway on a pedestrian bridge but did not turn toward Miriam and Jim. They did not notice him, did not see him walking quickly away down a winding path into the park. Soon he reached a children's playground and paused.

Here, he realized, he had played endlessly while waiting to become a man, to begin to really live. He had been a man, but oh so briefly. Three years? Four? He had spent his childhood looking forward. Now he could spend the rest of his life looking back. He stood a long time, as if photographing with his mind every detail of the scene before him, the flocks of fluttering pigeons, the old people on their benches, the glittering monorail trains high above that flashed from building to building like startled goldfish. Especially he stored the images of the children, the laughing, unsuspecting children, who knew so little of what awaited them. The children saw Newton, too, and pointed, whispering to each other. Newton, the wolf man. Newton, the boogie man.

He shuffled briskly away, hoping they would not follow him and jeer at him as he might have done at their age, but they hung back, fearful.

He trudged along the bank of a little stream, not looking up at the buildings, pretending he was in some wild, unspoiled forest far from civilization, and only glanced up when a crashing in the underbrush told him he had startled one of the many tame deer who lived here.

At last he emerged on the broad sidewalks of the oval fishpond at the park's center, a gathering place for old retired Techs, secure in their pensions and their prejudices, and for soapbox orators who shouted the virtues of every conceivable political or religious panacea for the ills of humanity. Orphists! Antisexualists! Starshippers! Christians! Neo-Baptists! Computerites! Scientologists! Chanters! Drummers! Jews! Techno-

logical Anarchists! Communists! Capitalists! Astrologers! Witches! Warlocks! Zen Buddhists! Zen Methodists! Immortalists! Reincarnationists!

Scowling apelike Security Police stood in twos, alert for any sign of mob violence, armed with deadly needle guns and hypnotic gas grenades. Wherever they walked, crowds parted to make way for them.

The largest crowd seemed to be gathered around a little white-haired old prune of a man who stood on a stone bench, shouting and gesturing violently like a second Hitler. Newton stopped on the outskirts of his audience to listen.

"Those who don't work, don't eat!" the man proclaimed, drawing scattered applause. "Our forefathers lived by that rule. America lived by that rule when it was great, before it surrendered its greatness to the tyranny of the World State, before it was rotted away by the poisons of foreign ideologies."

The crowd murmured agreement.

Encouraged, the orator lifted his voice. "Why should we slave our lives away to support the lazy, the useless and the incompetent? Why should we, the Techs, carry those no good Uns around our necks like an albatross? Darwin laid down the Law of the Survival of the Fittest, yet the unfit are supported by us in indolence, luxurious idleness. What do they really deserve? Death! Death to the Uns!"

"Death to the Uns!" echoed the crowd, like spectators at some sports event.

Newton turned his back on the cheering throng and marched onward, smiling faintly, bitterly.

The sky faded from blue to red to black. The fog came in, the cold San Francisco fog that tourists love. The children and retired Techs had all gone home. The park lamps, their poles invisible in the gloom, glowed like fuzzy moons, feeble and yellow. Newton alone remained in the park, wandering aimlessly, shivering, rubbing himself, delaying as long as possible his arrival at his inevitable destination.

Midnight found him slowly along a long broad cement walkway toward an elegant floodlighted imitation of the Greek Parthenon that rested on a low artificial hill, a building Newton had often seen but never entered.

"It will be warm in there," he whispered to himself to convince himself not to turn back.

He ascended the white marble staircase and entered the offices of the Security Police.

The uniformed man at the desk glanced up, bored, and

demanded, "What can I do for you?"

With a dignity that could only be absurd under the circumstances, Newton replied, "I'm an Un. Take me where I belong."

Chapter 5

The Aleutian Islands, Holly knew, lay somewhere beneath that bright white expanse of clouds that stretched on all sides to the horizon. She stood at the railing that circled the indoor farm area, holding tight and gazing down across steeply tilted banks of photovolatic cells, trying to make out some trace of land. She longed to see some sign of the familiar world she had so recently left; an island, the wake of a ship, anything. She wanted to reassure herself that Valhalla was not the universe, that Valhalla's inhabitants were not the entire human race. Yet if President Douglas was right, the society in which she had been born and raised, the society that lay hidden beneath that overcast, would soon be only history, like Victorian England, like medieval Europe, like ancient Rome and Greece and Egypt.

A new, strange society would be born and grow, and Valhalla would be its seed.

Behind her she could hear the cheerful voices of her co-workers, hear the clunks and creaks of coffinlike terrariums as their plastic lids were opened and closed. Overhead she could hear the muted groan of the huge evacuated sphere above the garden's transparent roof, a gentle, periodic sound synchronized with the pitch and roll of the deck.

Without warning an arm draped itself around her shoulders and, startled, she glanced up into the ironic dark eyes of Hal Waterman.

"Airsick?" he asked with concern.

"No. Why do you ask?"

"You're gripping that railing so hard your knuckles have turned white."

She saw that he was right, and, with a conscious effort, relaxed. "Better?" she said.

"Perhaps you miss the old world down there. Each of us has something of the old society we wish we could have brought along. I, for example, daydream about hamburgers."

She laughed. "Hamburgers?"

"With everything, on a toasted sesame seed bun, with a side order of exceptionally greasy french fries." He licked his chops with grotesque exaggeration. "If the Good Lord DNA had wanted me to be a vegetarian, he would have given me rabbit teeth, but how could the evolutionary process have predicted I would find myself marooned on an ark with no animals? That I would go to the great soybean diet in the sky, never taste meat unless someone died?"

She pulled away from him. "Someone died? Do you mean we're cannibals up here?"

"Of course!" He twisted his mustache like a silent-movie villian. "I'm surprised you're surprised. You should have deduced it from our policy of recycling absolutely everything. But it's not hamburger you miss, is it?"

She shook her head slowly. "No, not hamburgers."

"Your husband?"

"Newton? Yes, in a way."

"If you need a man, I would be delighted to loan myself out to you as a stud." He made a low, sweeping bow.

She laughed again. "Women never have needed men in that way, the way men need women. No, what I miss about Newton is his way of thinking."

"Thinking? Holly, my dear, you can't be serious. I've seen his IQ rating, his grade average, and frankly I've wondered what you ever found to talk about with someone so far inferior to you mentally."

She turned away from Hal and looked pensively upward, toward where the blue sky shaded into the black of outer space. "He wasn't quick like I am. I know that. He wasn't clever like everyone is up here. But he digested ideas slowly and thoroughly, and in the end understood things in a deeper, sadder way than I did. Maybe I can explain it in terms of the old dichotomy between cleverness and wisdom. If Newton tried to join in our bull sessions here in Valhalla, I'm sure we'd cut him to pieces verbally, make him look like a dropout from a school for retarded children, but after a while we'd start going to him for advice."

"Not me!"

"You, too," she said seriously. "Beyond IQ, beyond cleverness, there's something else; a vast, sad sense of life, of how things really are. You can't test it like you can IQ. You can't measure it. You can't even prove it exists, but it's there, and you can recognize it when you encounter it, sense it intuitively. In the greatest Japanese poets—men like Basho and Issa—you find it in its purest form, shorn of every vestige of mere cleverness."

"We are rational people up here," said Hal. "We're not Zen monks and nuns running giggling through the mountains. When you talk like this I wonder if you really belong here."

"I wonder that, too, Hal. In some ways I love Valhalla. In some ways I feel really at home for the first time in my life. I can hardly believe the way I can make a joke and not have to explain it, or if I do explain something, how I can leave out steps and have my audience fill them in for me instantly, effortlessly. What luxury to be able to drop a single word, a hint, and have everyone else immediately and correctly reconstruct my whole thought, as a paleontologist reconstructs a dinosaur, given one small bone! But then, just when I feel the most at home, the most accepted and understood, I blurt out something and see, by peoples' faces, that I've stepped outside the bounds, that I'm really among strangers as much as I've ever been."

Hal said uneasily, "Of course no two people are exactly alike. You can't expect...."

She cut him off. "At such times I have an intuitive feeling that you made a big mistake bringing me here, perhaps a fatal mistake. At such times I see myself as a serpent in your Garden of Eden, a threat to everything Valhalla stands for."

"Good grief, my dear!"

"You don't understand what I'm like, Hal. I'm not a happy little ant in the nest like you and everyone else here. Let me tell you how it was with Newton and me."

"Go ahead, Holly. Get it out of your system."

"We played chess."

"And of course you always beat him."

"No."

"You let him win. How kind of you."

"No, he always won, and won fairly."

"What does that prove?"

"Let me finish, Hal. He taught me the game when we first met. We played almost every day, and not once did I beat him, yet I went on playing. Hundreds of times he beat me! I studied chess books. I played chess against a computer. I asked other players for tips. I practiced alone in my room. Still he beat me."

"Are you telling me you're a masochist?" He raised an eyebrow.

"I'm telling you that toward the end I began to almost fight him to a draw. I'm telling you that if we hadn't split up I would have beat him in a year or two, first only once in a while, then more and more often, until at last I'd be winning all the time. I'd whip his ass, Hal. I'd whip it good, because I'd study and practice and he wouldn't. That's the kind of person I am. And he wouldn't care. That's the kind of person he was."

Hal patted her gently on the back. "Holly, Holly, Holly, don't be so intense. You like to win? So do I. So does everyone in Valhalla. Just being here is winning."

"Not for me. I want to be number one." She met his gaze, and it was he who looked away.

"Brad is number one in Valhalla," he said, glancing around as if looking for evesdroppers.

"For the moment," she said softly.

"Well well, my dear," he said. "You really *are* ambitious, aren't you.?"

And she looked into his devil face and saw that he was a little bit afraid of her. She had figured him right.

*

The Unemployables' Camp was not a camp, but a huge barracks occupying the entire area of what had once been Berkeley, California. It loomed over the San Franciso Bay a hundred stories high, and extended deep underground in a series of basements and sub-basements that finally ended in a grid of buttresses and what one can only call pontoons; exending, as it did, well below the water table of the area, it was quite literally afloat, though on dry land. The most violent earthquake spent its energy in the water table and did not so much as rattle the knives and forks in its many mess halls.

Newton, having been assigned to a section called "Telegraph Avenue," entered one of these mess halls, a vast room about two blocks wide and five blocks long. The tables were thronged with men, women and young people—a surprising number of young people—all dressed exactly alike, with yellow monk-like robes, plastic sandals, and freshly shaved heads that glistened in the blueish fluorescent ceiling lights like so many polished eggs. On each righthand wrist was clamped an identification bracelet containing, in magnetic code, almost anything anyone might want to know about the wearer. The identification bracelet could not be removed. Newton had tried.

Newton, of course, looked exactly like everyone else.

A similarly garbed man with an armband saying "Trustee" handed him a tray and muttered mechanically, "Please remain seated after you finish your meal."

That this task was done by a human being instead of a machine impressed Newton, showed him that he had come to a place where human labor was cheap, almost worthless, an impression confirmed by the presense of human countermen behind the cafeteria-style counters.

He got in line and waited.

In the early morning hours Newton had been transferred by a squad of security police in a monorail from San Francisco to the Berkeley Camp, and there had been issued his yellow robe, plastic footgear, and steel bracelet. Together with a multitude of other Uns, he had then been shepherded through a series of brightly-lit, bare rooms.

In the first room a barber had, with a few deft strokes, removed Newton's beard and long hair.

In the second room Newton had endured an extensive series of medical examinations run on a production line basis. They had detected his ulcers and warned him about them, but he had said nothing.

The third room had been devoted to immunization shots, administered with high-pressure jets, and blood tests, taken by a trustee orderly who, from the looks of his dialated pupils, was probably high on drugs.

The fourth room had been filled with long lines of what had appeared to be telephone booths. Instead they had been psychological examination booths where Newton had been wired for electroencephalograph, polygraph, biofeedback monitor and E-meter and had been asked a long list of questions beginning with:

"Do you masturbate?"

When the robot voice had asked him, "Are you happy?"—he had answered yes, then wondered if the machine had called that a lie.

In the fifth room a kindly-looking old doctor had, with a laser knife, performed with only local anesthetic a "simple little sterilization operation," *a vasectomy.*

As Newton departed, the doctor had said, with surprising gentleness, "You may have a little swelling. Ask the trustee in your bunkroom for an icepack."

Now, in the mess hall, Newton felt a burning pain in his lower abdomen but tried to ignore it. He could tell by the expression of the other new men that he was no worse off than they.

The line began to move.

A freckledfaced boy ahead of him looked with misgivings at the bowl of green soup and slice of black bread that had been given him and demanded, "What's this?'

"It's good for you," answered the burly counterman, a trustee, to judge from his armband.

"It smells like algae," said the kid, sniffing the soup.

"That's because it is algae," said the counterman.

"I won't eat it!"

The counterman shrugged. "Maybe not now, but later."

"You mean this is all we'll get?"

"You're a smart lad for an Un. You catch on fast."

The boy angrily returned the tray and stomped away. The counterman gave the tray to Newton, who accepted it without protest, thinking, *A good boy eats what is set before him.*

Newton sat down at an unoccupied table and tasted his soup. It tasted moldy but he sipped it anyway. The bread tasted saltless, but he ate it.

A fat lady asked Newton, "Is your table vacant?"

"As you see," Newton replied.

She sat down next to him and began to shlurp. Newton ignored her.

She made a face. "Oof! It tastes awful, doesn't it?"

"I won't argue with you," said Newton distantly.

"What are we all waiting for here?" she asked him.

"I don't know."

"Something dreadful, I imagine." She bit her lip fretfully.

When Newton didn't answer, she leaned toward him and whispered, "You were sterilized, weren't you?"

"That's right."

"I wasn't. I wonder why they did only the men."

"If all the men are sterile, how can the women get pregnant?" he said.

She brightened, as if a great light had dawned for her. "Why, that's right, isn't it? How clever of you to figure it out!"

And how stupid of you not to, thought Newton contemptuously, but almost immediately he realized that this stupidity which so disgusted him was the very thing that made them both Uns, which bound them inseparably together. As a student Tech he had been taught always to strive for the best.

Now, as an Un, he would have to learn to hate the best and swear an unspoken pact of solidarity with the worst.

Others sat down at the table and the fat lady turned her attention to them, much to Newton's relief. More and more Uns filed into the mess hall until all the seats were taken and Newton had to stand to let someone else eat.

The waiting continued.

What were they waiting for?

Something dreadful, Newton thought, remembering the woman's words.

At last two Techmen entered and made their way through the crowd, which parted, murmuring, to let them pass. One of them inserted a key into the wall and a panel slid open to reveal a small stage furnished with a long table, four folding chairs, and a microphone. The hum of expectant conversation grew louder. One of the Techs jumped up onto the stage and walked over to the mike.

He blew into it a few times, then said, "Testing, one, two, three. Testing." Loudspeakers in the ceiling echoed his words. Both men existed, smiling, through a door in the back of the stage.

A moment later the same door reopened and four high-ranking Techs entered, talking with each other in low voices, their coveralls bearing the insignia of their rank and branch of service.

When the group was seated, the highest-ranking of the lot, an old but well-preserved man with a certain dignity about him, pulled the microphone close and began:

"Congratulations." The room fell silent. "Congratulations on passing your entrance examinations with flying colors. We can now be sure you are all loyal citizens of the World State, not criminals or members of the so-called 'Underground.' We know you are not psychopaths or any other type of dangerous lunatic. We know you carry no serious infectious deseases. We know you are sexually secure, safe from the burden of unwanted offspring. Therefore I feel free to say to you all, welcome to Utopia!"

This announcement produced no more than a scattering of bewildered applause, and Newton did not move a muscle.

The old man continued, "You may call me Mr. Emmanuel. I'm the director of the Telegraph Avenue section, of which all of you are now members. Regard me as a sort of father—a strict father, perhaps, but a fair one. You won't see much of me unless you, er, do something naughty. We have our rules, you know. You cannot leave this floor without special permission in writing, nor can you visit the other sections. You cannot leave the camp without an official release, and you cannot have visitors from outside the camp under any circumstances. We have no computer terminals here, and the video will receive a wide variety of programs but does not function in the sending mode, and the number of video screens is limited, one to a bunkroom. But if you don't see me, always remember I'm thinking of you and watching out for your best interest."

Newton, standing close to the stage, could see beads of sweat on Mr. Emmanuel's forehead, could see how Mr. Emmanuel's hands shook. *He's scared*, thought Newton, *but of what?*

Emmanuel continued, "Let me introduce to you some of the people you will be seeing: my staff. First, Captain Clark, Chief of Police on our floor." A worried-looking man stood up and smiled stiffly. His eyes were a pale blue and his grey hair was touched with white. He seemed more like a file clerk than a policeman

After taking the mike, he hesitated a moment before beginning, "I can't think of anything to say except, well, don't forget that the policeman is your friend. He's here to protect you. If you are threatened by anybody or forced to do anything illegal, the only sure way of protecting yourself is to report it to me." Seeing Old Man Emmanuel frowning at him, Clark cut short his speech and sat down. Newton thought wonderingly, *The Chief is scared, too.*

"Next," said Mr. Emmanuel, "I want you to meet our recreation director for this floor, Miss Normandy Taylor." Miss Taylor stood up. She had green eyes and her short-cropped hair, which could have been that on an Un who'd missed a few cuts, was bright red.

"Hi, kids," she said. "My job is to keep you busy and keep you from getting soft, and you'll find I do my job. We've got a full sports program here—team sports, swimming, boxing, track, the works. We got hobby clubs and special interest groups of all kinds. Something for everybody! If anyone wants to go a few rounds in the ring, I'll be glad to take them on personally. If you'd rather not get physical, I'd take great pleasure in beating any one of you at a little game of chess."

Chess? Newton smiled.

With fists on hips, Normandy Taylor glared out at the audience with good-natured belligerence. "Our motto is, 'Keep spirits up and costs down." Only a few people laughed at her attempt at humor. Her bravado visibly fading, she sat down.

"Last but certainly not least," said Mr. Emmanuel, "here's our Interfaith Chaplain. Most Gentlemen of the Cloth like to be called 'Father' or 'Reverend' or 'Rabbi,' but your Chaplain would rather you just called him 'Bill.' That right, Bill?"

"That's right," said Chaplain Bill, lurching to his feet. Bill was a round little man with a bald head and very thick glasses. He wore black coveralls with a turn-around clerical collar, and on his chest, in a neat row, he displayed the symbols of all the major respectable religions.

"I know this has been a trying experience for all of you," he said gently. "You may have difficulty adjusting to this new environment. I want you to know that, no matter how dark things seem, there is someone who cares. I care. I have worked with people like you for a long time, and I understand. If something troubles you, come and talk it over with me. Burdens grow lighter when shared."

He's scared, too, Newton thought, as the little fat man lowered himself into his chair.

"Well, that's all for now," said Mr. Emmanuel. "As you leave the mess hall, the trustees will give you each a room assignment and a bunk number. You have been computer-matched with people of similiar backgrounds and interests, so I'm sure you will have no trouble making friends. And remember, you have just one duty here. Be happy!"

Hardly anyone applauded.

As lines began forming at the exits, Newton again asked himself, *What are they afraid of?* Suddenly the answer dawned on him. He looked first at the immense but crowded mess hall, then at the four figures huddled together on the stage as if for mutual protection. A ghost of a smile tickled the corners of Newton's lips.

The Uns outnumbered the Techs by more than a hundred to one.

Chapter 6

At an early age, Holly had discovered that she was very different from other people—quick to learn where they were slow, far seeing where they were short-sighted, and (she faced it plainly because it was self-evidently true) competent where they were incompetent...When it came to organizations that had something to offer her, whether the high school Computer Club, or the Junior businesswoman's League, she saw inefficiencies no one else had seen (and the Valhalla proved no exception)—and to make them run more efficiently for everyone, she'd inevitably had to take them over. And when she had, everyone agreed, she ran them better than they had ever been run before.

With her brains, it hadn't taken her long to work out an infallible formula for taking over any kind of organization
    (1) Hobnob.
    (2) Volunteer.
    (3) Command.

In the first stage, the hobnobbing, she would enter a group for the first time, playing dumb, asking questions, flattering people by letting them explain things to her. She would memorize everyone's names. She would listen to everyone's troubles, everyone's life stories, and people would begin to like her because she was such a good listener. Then she would write down whatever useful information they had imparted to her in a notebook, alphabetized by last names and, in a separate section, by subjects. She would determine by observation who the real powers in the organization were, as opposed to the elected or appointed officials. She would investigate the organization's financial system, find out who paid who for what, find out what form the records took.

She would research the organization's history, study its constitution and bylaws. She would make note of discrepancies between principle and practice. (No organization ever remained faithful to its founding principles) She would make note of discrepancies between official history and fact. (No organization ever told the truth about its origins.) She would make note of where the decisions were actually made, as opposed to the official meetings. She would tactfully trace the flow of cash through the organization, and the flow of power, and would locate the places in the corporate structure where a small action might produce a large effect, what she called "Domino Points."

Most of all she would simply observe the organization in action, gradually picking up an intuitive feel for it, gradually learning its ingroup jargon, its style. She would learn to walk like a member and talk like a member, but in her mind she would never really become a member, always retaining her objectivity, her maneuverability, her freedom of choice, her personal power. Nobody who really understood an organization could swear unconditional allegiance to it, she would tell herself.

At the end of the hobnobbing stage she would be the perfect wolf in custom-tailored sheep's clothing.

Then came the second stage, the volunteering.

In every organization there were certain jobs nobody wanted to do but which must be done, and these jobs invariably were located at some of the organization's most vital domino points. Whoever did these "shitwork" jobs gained entree to the places where the decisions were actually made, that inner circle which never quite matched the roster of officials. Whoever did these jobs became part of the power structure.

Yet those who reluctantly did these jobs almost never saw the domino points within their grasp, almost never understood their own power, or even the power of the inner circle they now associated with, almost never did anything with their opportunities. Instead they concentrated on doing as little as possible and getting it over with. They were that sort of people; blind, unimaginative, uncreative drudges "doing their duty."

Holly, on the other hand, bided her time until the right job became available, then, suddenly and without warning, she would volunteer for it.

And she made damn sure to do that job brilliantly.
Someone was needed to collect the money? Holly would do it.
Someone was needed to edit the newsletter? Holly would do it.
Someone was needed to plan the program? Holly would do it. You name it. She would do it, and always brilliantly, brilliantly.

People often complained to Holly that they were helpless pawns of fate, that some vague abstraction called "Society" was responsible for all their frustrated ambitions, all their moral lapses, all the greyness of their lives. Holly felt like saying to them, "Society does not control you. I control you. I and a handful of others like me." Of course she remained silent, nodding and making, at most, a few sympathetic grunts.

For sooner or later the second stage gave way to the third, the stage of commanding.

To lead, you first must follow. Holly understood this, and followed with a will, feeling an almost sexual excitement as power flowed from her superiors through her to her inferiors, a great gleaming exaltation such as a hawk must feel as it plunges downward to catch a rabbit in its claws.

But she always knew the day would come when her superior would get lazy, or careless or simply get old. Then the power would fall into her hands like a ripe fruit, and she would be Number One. For they were white ants; and she was a red ant.

At least until another like her rose up to contest the throne.

Only Newton had been neither a red ant or a white one, but had seemed to stand mocking and indifferent outside the whole struggle. That was why she had been attracted to him.

But in Valhalla it was still hobnobbing time.

Holly listened. Holly observed. Alone in her tiny stateroom at night, Holly made entries in her alphabetized notebook, updated her dossiers. She did not warn anyone, "You have the right to remain silent. Anything you say now may be used against you later."

*

The gaunt scarecrow Newton pushed his way through the confused throngs of yellow-robed Uns.

"Thirty-one, thirty-one," he muttered, listlessly moving down the aisle between two rows of double-decker bunks. "Ah, here it is." With a sensation of mild relief, he climbed into the upper and lay there staring at the featureless glowing ceiling, oblivious to everyone else.

A disrespectful forefinger poked him in the ribs and a playful young feminine voice said, "Hi!"

He ignored her.

She giggled, then demanded, "What's the matter? Are you hypnotized or something?"

Newton rolled over, rested his weight on one elbow, and found himself gazing into the teasing brown eyes of a hunchbacked but rather cute young lady. He vaguely remembered having seen her in the mess hall.

"What are you doing here?" she asked him, grinning.

"This is my bunk."

"Well, whaddya know! I have the bunk right under you. If we're going to sleep together we ought to get acquainted. What's your name?"

"Newton McClintok."

"I'm Mickey."

"Mickey what?"

"Mickey McClintok, if you'll let me be your wife."

Even stonefaced Newton had to smile at that. "Sorry, Mickey, but...."

"Why not? We'll be together all the time anyway, and we must be compatible or the computer wouldn't have made us bunkmates." When he still looked unconvinced, she added wistfully, "Don't worry. Everybody know Uns don't really get married. They just sort of pair off—but we can pretend!"

Newton shrugged. "If you like.

She climbed up and perched on the edge of his bunk. "How did you get here, Newton?"

"Flunkout. Computer college."

"I'm a flunkout, too," she announced gaily. "High School. The top third of our class went on to college. The rest came here." She indicated the teenagers settling into the neighboring bunks with an indifferent wave of her hand. Some of them waved to her and called out greetings.

"You're taking it very well," Newton commented.

"Why shouldn't I? School's out—forever!"

She went on talking, but he stopped listening. Instead he studied her, thinking, *So what if she does have a few pimples? And she's not really very hunchbacked. What can you expect in a place like this?*

*

When the senator in charge of North America left the halls of the World Parliament he found, to his annoyance, the Director of the Bureau of Unemployables' Camps waiting for him in the elevator.

73

As they rose slowly from floor to floor, deep beneath the surface of Antarctica, the director began, "They voted no, eh?"

The senator nodded. "No additional funds for the Un camps."

"But why?" The director mopped his damp bald head with a large handkerchief.

"The Big Computer advised against it."

"I need those funds! We're talking simple survival. The Underground is growing. I need policemen. I need brain probes. I tell you, a full-scale revolution is brewing."

"How do you know?"

"Have you ever been in the camps, sir? I have. And you can feel revolution in the air!"

"SERCON doesn't go by feelings. It operates on cold, hard facts."

"Facts distorted by the Snafu Syndrome. You know how, whenever things start going wrong, every little department head starts covering up, concealing failures, magnifying or inventing successes. The worse things go, the more these little clock-punchers lie, until the head office announces victory just as everything collapses. All the data fed into SERCON shows everything's rosy, but everyone knows it's not. Even you must sense something."

"I abide by SERCON's decisions."

"Can't we bring in a second opinion? Another computer programmed to compensate for the Snafu Syndrome?"

"Does such a machine exist?"

"Promethean Underwriters has one."

The senator laughed harshly. "Old man Douglas keeps his computer to himself. You ought to know that."

"Please, sir, at least ask him...."

"I'll be damned if I'll go crawling to that intellectual snob! Ah, but this is my floor. Goodbye, director."

Alone in the elevator, the director thought about history and went on sweating.

*

Two hundred and fifty kilometers off the coast of British Columbia, at an altitude of thirty four thousand meters, the Valhalla drifted southeast at a groundspeed of a hundred and ten kilometers per hour, airspeed zero, moving into the January Polar-Front jet stream in the wake of a particularly stormy low-pressure area. Ahead towered a black wall of cumulonimbus, flickering with sporadic lightning, behind another dark wall followed, but the Valhalla sailed in weather so clear Holly could look down through the transparent surface of the Pacific below her and see the brown rugged mountainous ocean floor.

"What will happen if we're drawn into the storm?" Holly asked uneasily.

Her companion laughed. "We will not be drawn in. At this altitude storms push us away rather than draw us in. The wind moves toward a thunderhead at the bottom, but away from it at the top. In between we can find airflows going in almost any direction. That is how we steer."

"Steer? Can the Valhalla steer?"

"Oh yes, Holly. We can control our altitude by pumping air in and out of the sphere, though really we don't need to do that often. If you know what you're doing you can select an altitude hours in advance and reach it almost entirely through the natural heating and cooling effects of the sun. And we can travel pretty fast sometimes, if we can get into a jet stream. Over Japan we have more than once reached a speed of five hundred kilometers per hour."

Holly had strapped down as a precaution against that clear-air turbulence that always lurks in the neighborhood of jet streams, and now swiveled her leather-upholstered chair to face her companion, to study the woman, for Holly was far more interested in the emotional climate of her shipmates than in the merely physical weather outside.

Juanita Castro was a dark-haired, dark-skinned, dark-eyed hispanic, in her late thirties, neat, calm and businesslike in her "company blue" tunic and boots. Like everyone else in the crew, she was physically perfect and mentally so alert Holly had to handle her very carefully. Hal had assigned Juanita to train Holly in the more technical aspects of the Valhalla. Promethean Underwriters did not encourage specialization, but shifted employees regularly from job to job so that, if need be, anybody could do anything, and do it well.

Juanita, with the air of an old-fashioned schoolmarm, went on, "You will become quite a meteorologist here, far more wise to the ways of clouds and winds than any Mundane." Mundane! Holly had well learned by now the special meaning these sky-dwellers put on this word, pronouncing it as their grandparents might pronouce "kike," "nigger" or "honky." It was a dehumanizing word, a distancing word, that prepared them psychologically to sit quietly and watch while the Mundanes destroyed themselves.

The two women sat alone in a control room adjoining President Douglas' suit at the bottom of the sphere, surrounded by more or less mysterious electronic equipment and looking out through a curving window that began as a horizontal continuation of the floor, then swept up to meet the ceiling at a sharp angle. Outside the solar-powered airplanes hung from their hooks and swung gently.

Juanita continued, "No one really sees the Earth until they see it from above. I think we understand the Mundanes and their little civilization far better than they do themselves. We see how imaginary their boundaries are, how trivial their interests are, how narrow their mental horizons are. We see them as they really are, as self-important insects scurrying to and fro as if what they did really mattered. And if we want to study the poor things more closely, we have video-telescopes in this room that can read a newspaper headline down there, and some of us have learned to read lips. Then of course we monitor their television and radio broadcasts regularly," she gestured toward the downward-pointing dish antennas. "And as long as we are in line-of-sight communication with one of our branch offices all over the world, we can laser down messages and be patched through into the world communication net. Many people talk to Brad every day by two-way video and have no idea he's up here, not down there in New York or London or someplace like that. One clever vice-president had a secret mistress in his backyard. She always kept outside the picture area, but one day, while this guy was talking to Brad, Brad was watching him from up here. You should have seen the Mundane's face when Brad signed off with, 'Give my love to that lovely young lady sitting beside you.' " She chuckled. Holly chuckled too. They were the best of friends.

"But doesn't all this electronic stuff have some more practical purpose?" Holly asked.

"It certainly does. For example, we can predict earthquakes by photographing patterns of heat distribution, predict floods by measuring snowfall, predict the location of various natural resources. You'd be amazed how many things you can predict when you start shooting pictures from up here in infrared and ultraviolet, and prediction is the soul of insurance. You'd be amazed at how much we make, for example, by selling earthquake insurance to Mundanes we are certain won't have any earthquakes. When the pressure builds up along a tectonic plate, it always generates heat that shows up on our infrared photographs years in advance of any quake, but there's no way in the world they can separate that heat from the general ambient heat from down there."

"How long have you been aboard the Valhalla?" asked Holly.

Juanita sighed and stared off at the distant stormclouds. "I've been here since Valhalla was launched, since before that. I was here before Valhalla was built. I'll never forget that damned tropical island where they started putting this thing together, never forget the hot day—God, it was hot!—when they uncovered it to the sun and waited until it seemed like it would rip up the cables holding it down, then let it go, and we had to chase it in those little electric airplanes. There weren't many of us then. Just a handful, and now you are probably the last one he'll take aboard." She sighed again. "Brad and I were close then."

"How close?"

"You could say we were lovers."

"Really? Tell me, what's Brad like? I mean personally."

"Personally? I don't want to bore you."

"You won't bore me. I promise you!"

That night Holly wrote for a long time in Brad's dossier, lying in bed with her notebook propped against her knees.

*

When someone in the Un dorms died, what meager property that might remain was divided among those present. One day Newton, sharing in the bounty, obtained a dairy, completely blank, with a cheerful red leather cover.

That evening, just before 'lights out,' Newton began writing as follows:

Monday.
See the happy little moron.
He doesn't give a damn.
I wish I were a moron.
My God, perhaps I am!

With this bit of immortal verse, surpassing Shakespeare, Dante and Dostoyevsky in its profound insight into the life of my bunkmates and myself, I begin my record of daily life among the Uns. In sweet poetry I present what will undoubtedly form the underlying theme for the entire opus. Everything else will be variations on this theme, as I develop for you, dear reader, a vast symphony of stupidity, overwhelming in its magnitude and complexity. I plan to report each empty day in relentless detail, capturing every nuance of our boredom. You ask me why?

Because misery loves company.

All around me as I write I hear the night sounds beginning, the moans and snorts and grunts of the human beast in heat, stranger than the cries of any jungle bird. We, alone of all animals,

are always in heat, never satisfied. We alone must consumate the mating ritual all year round, and, here in the bunkroom, every night. Without any semblance of privacy, we get caught up in it almost against our will, stimulated by the sight and sound and smell of the others. One couple starts, and soon we're all doing it.
I sit in my bunk writing, putting off the inevitable, but I know that by lights-out I will have clambered down to Mickey in the lower, or she will have climbed up to me, not like gentle lovers, but like drug addicts, hating the drug but unable to resist it. I would never have dreamed that humanity could make so many different noises. Little cries. Sighs. Whimpers. Even screams. The boy on the bunk across the aisle makes a sound like a rattlesnake rattle at the moment of orgasm, the exact same sound every time. Otherwise there seems to be very little variety. No wonder pornography has always been so popular! Anything to give this mechanical performance the semblance of joy, or style, or rough hewn beauty.
As Mickey spreads her legs for me, I try to imagine Holly. I never call Mickey by Holly's name, of course. That wouldn't be polite. But sometimes Holly's face shifts and changes in my mind. Sometimes her eyes are the wrong color. Or her hair. Last night I lost her image completely and in a kind of terror began to cling to Mickey. Before I'd never touched Mickey's hump, thinking she might be embarrassed, thinking it might make it harder for me to imagine she was Holly.
But this time I found myself gripping it with both hands, as if to anchor myself with it, and I dug my knees into the mattress and seemed to plug into some vast, ancient source of sexual energy that drove me on remorselessly, possessing me like a demon, brushing my individuality to one side with a heedless, mighty paw. And Mickey threw her head from side to side, her face a fixed, almost metalic mask of pleasure, drool flying from her mouth. By some perverse logic it seemed to me the hump was an excuse to let go of myself, to surrender to my animal nature in a way I never could with Holly. And perhaps revenge helped fuel the fire! Revenge against Holly for leaving me, the bitch! And perhaps an ecstasy, a frantic wallowing in my own degradation fueled the fire too. The hump! The hump! How exactly right it was! Just what I deserved!
And after the orgasm, as I lay gently on top of her, not pulling out yet, she whispered, "I love you, Newton." She wanted me to say I loved her, but that I would not do. That I could not do. Even I have principles.
This diary contains three hundred and sixty five pages. If I

write small, that will keep me going a while, and later I'll find other books like it and continue my story. The trustees will give me blank books if I tell them literature is occupational therapy, if they see writing keeps me quiet and out of trouble.

My life's work!

A gigantic immense sprawling autobiographical novel, and all for your causal amusement, dear reader, to help you kill time, though of course it is really time that kills you.

So let us talk about Mickey, my little camel, my heroine, my dingdong Quasimodo. She tells me she has met a new friend and wants to introduce me to him. Victor Tarachenko in his name, and I hate him already because he has such a high class name.

I don't want to start the book with him.

Instead, in the opening scene (after a rousing fanfare), we see a fly walking across the page of this book. (Really). He has beautiful bluegreen iridescent wings and pauses now and then to rub his face with his front legs. The fly doesn't deserve his reputation for filthiness. Can't you see how he's constantly cleaning himself? But perhaps it is only the filthy who need....

He put the book up, and like everything else, never went back to it again.

*

"The worth of an idea is measured by the number of people who are willing to kill for it." Victor Tarachenko glared at Mickey across the mess hall table, as if daring her to refute him. She was thinking that Victor was handsomer than Newton, in a pretty Latin way, except for that one glass eye that didn't always look in the same direction as the real one, and his limp. One of Victor's legs was shorter than the other, which he explained as the result of standing at the bar too much, or walking around a mountain in the same direction too long, or of being a reincarnation of Lord Byron.

"You mean 'willing to die for it,' " Mickey corrected, momentarily resting her spoon in her algae soup.

"No, I mean kill! An Un could give his worthless life away, but killing takes conviction."

Mickey stared down into her soup. She could never meet Victor's eyes. She wondered if it was because of the intensity of his gaze or because she couldn't tell which of his eyes was false. He had told her at their first meeting that the false eye was the one that showed a glint of human kindness. He was full of jokes like that, cruel jokes directed against himself.

"Wouldn't you like to kill someone?" he demanded softly.

"What? No, of course not."

"Not even a Tech?"

"Why should I want to kill a Tech?"

"Wouldn't a rabbit like to kill a wolf? Wouldn't a mouse like to kill a cat? Be honest, Mickey. Wouldn't you like to kill a Tech?"

"Can't you talk about anything but killing?"

"I see you're not ready for my message yet. First you must become a little more bitter."

"If you want somebody who's bitter, you ought to talk to Newton. He's a regular pickle."

Victor leaned forward, interested. "Newton's your boy friend, isn't he? The one who can't manage to say the word love? I like that."

"I'll introduce you to him sometime," she said, but no sooner were the words spoken than she wished she could unsay them. Who knows what awful ideas Victor might put in Newton's head.

"When?" Victor asked sharply.

"Oh, sometime or other."

"The sooner the better."

Mickey couldn't help thinking Victor was kind of scarey, but exciting.

Chapter 7

"I want a drink," said Newton with sweet reasonableness as he lay on his bunk, eyes half-closed. He had had not so much as a thimbleful of alcohol since his arrival in the dorms, yet scarcely a day, scarcely an hour went by in which he did not think about it. He liked to think about it, to lie alone in the bunkroom while everyone else was off somewhere basketweaving, watching television, or doing pushups. He did not need a drink. That would have meant he was an alcoholic. He just wanted one. He just thought one would be very nice, thank you.

"Hello, Newton," said a quiet baritone voice near his ear.

Startled, Newton rolled over to face his visitor. "What do you want?"

"I'm Victor Tarachenko. Perhaps Mickey told you about me. She told me a great deal about you."

"I'll bet she did," Newton said resentfully.

"Don't you like her?" She likes you."

"I don't like anyone, least of all myself."

"Do you like Techs?"

Newton considered this question. Was Victor a Tech spy, come to test him? Newton couldn't care less. "Nobody likes a Tech around here, not even a Trustee, not even another Tech."

"Would you like to do something about it?"

"Like, for instance, what?"

"You could join the Underground."

"Underground!" Newton snorted contemptuously. "Forget it. You want a reservation in the Hall of Heads?"

"If we win, the Techs will be the ones going to the Hall of the Heads."

"And then what? Instead of having the boot of the best man on my neck, I'll have the boot of the second-best man."

"We don't do things that way, Newton. We share. We're equals. Have you heard the expression, 'From each according to his ability, to each according to his need?' "

"Of course. That's from Marx."

"Marx borrowed it from an earlier source. It was part of the rule of life adopted by the first Christians. The Christians tried it out and found it worked."

"They still had God's boot on their necks. You and I will always be on the bottom of the totem pole, and to us it doesn't much matter who's on top."

Victor grinned good-naturedly. "I'll win you over sooner or later, but I don't quite know how."

"You might try offering me a drink," Newton suggested, returning to his contemplation of the ceiling. When Newton glanced his way again, he found that Victor had departed as silently as he had arrived.

*

Holly knocked gently on the carved wooden door.

"Come in." Brad Douglas' voice drifted out to her from the other side of the door. "It's not locked."

Holly entered hesitantly. "Juanita said you wanted to speak to me." The room was dark except for a feeble reddish glow from the circular window in the center of the floor. Brad came toward her, a drink in each hand, in that slightly-crouching way everyone learned to walk on board the swaying Valhalla.

"Vodka martini is your drink, isn't it?" he asked. "Hal told me it was."

"Sometimes," she conceded, accepting the cold glass. "Are you keeping a dossier on my personal habits?"

"As a matter of fact, I am. Very early in my career I formed the habit of keeping files on everyone I dealt with. I recommend the practice to anyone wanting to become a success in the business world, or any other world for that matter."

For a moment Holly wondered if Brad were baiting her, letting her know he knew what she was up to. Then she rejected the idea. He was too friendly, too warm for that.

"Come over to the conversation pit," he suggested. "I want to show you something."

He led her to the curved couches and settled into the cushions with a satisfied sigh. She sat down beside him uneasily. The light from below threw his eyes into deep pools of shadow, turned his face into an enigmatic mask.

"Look down there," he commanded, pointing.

Looking down was exactly what she had been trying not to do. In the reasonable part of her mind she was certain this thick glass floor was perfectly safe, but some deeper, more instinctive mental level kept sending up frantic warnings of an impending fall. Far below she saw a glittering cluster of lights like sparks scattered on a dark hearth.

"Do you know what that is?" he asked softly.

"San Francisco."

"That's right, as few have ever seen her. Your home."

"My home is here, Mr. Douglas."

"Spoken like a loyal Promethean! But don't be hasty, my dear. You are not my prisoner. If you say the word, I can send you down in one of my planes. You could be saying hello to your father-in-law and to your mother-in-law by sunup tomorrow."

"I think I'll stay." She sipped her drink.

"Your ex-husband is down there, Holly. Would you like to know where?"

"Since you've gone to all the trouble of finding out."

"He's in the Un camps in Berkeley."

"I'm not surprised." She listened to herself approvingly, noting the absence of emotion in her voice, yet in her chest she felt a sudden tightness, a sudden pain. How good it would feel, she realized, to whisper all her plans to Newton, to share with him her delightful evilness, to take comfort in his amused contempt for all scheming, all ambition, to wallow in his quiet acceptance, the acceptance of a man who would never stoop to keeping dossiers on people, because to him it was only bullshit, anyway. What use to play a joke on the world if nobody is around to help laugh?

"Thank you," said Brad.

"For what?"

"For staying when you could have gone. I wasn't quite sure you would."

"What would it matter if I did? You could just have hired someone else."

He shook his head slowly. "No, I couldn't have replaced you that easily. You're not like the others. I sense something different in you. I did when I first saw you. You're never completely a part of anything, always a little outside. You're a game player, an island, a human computer. You're...like me."

"How flattering."

"Flattering? I don't know. People like us suffer a kind of damnation, a kind of loneliness ordinary people can't even understand. We can't be close, not even to others of our own kind. We don't trust each other, and with reason."

"You can trust me, Brad."

After a long silence Brad sighed and said gently, "Horseshit."

*

"Newton?"

"Yes, Mickey?"

Mickey bit her lip nervously as she lay in her bunk in the darkness. All around her she heard the rustle of her dorm-mates and an occasional snore. The smell of stale sweat, which had made her a little ill when she first arrived, now had become so familiar she might have missed it if it went away.

"Can I come up and visit you for a minute?" she whispered.

"Well...okay."

She bounded from her lower bunk and mounted into Newton's upper, where she crept under the rough blanket and huddled, shivering, skin to skin, against his warm body, her head resting on his shoulder.

"Comfortable?" Newton murmured.

"Um hmm."

"What's on your mind?"

"Oh, nothing much."

"Come on, tell me."

"Do you like me, Newton?"

"Why do you ask?"

"You don't think I'm ugly? I know I don't look my best with my head shaved and those silly old monk's robes."

"You're a very nice-looking girl. Really."

"Then why aren't you nicer to me? It could be so much easier here if you loved me."

"If I loved anybody, I suppose it would be you, but I've learned from experience that what you call love is only a futile dream."

She considered this a moment, then asked, "Don't you ever dream?"

"Every night, but the world of my dreams is exactly like the world of reality."

"You ought to dream when you're awake. Then you can control it. You can do as you please in a daydream."

"I assume you daydream quite a lot. What do you daydream about?"

She thrust her nose familiarly against Newton's sandpaper cheek. "I'm daydreaming right now, about a van trip."

"What's a van?"

"A van in an automobile big enough to hold a bed and a small kitchen. They used to have them back in the Twentieth Century," she explained.

"No wonder we call the Twentieth Century 'The Crazy Years.' I mean, what else can you say about people who ban something as harmless as pornography and embrace something as deadly as the automobile? This van you're talking about...If it's big enough to carry a bed and a kitchen, how much irreplaceable petroleum does it burn? How much poison gas does it spew into the atmosphere? How many small animals does it run over? How many children? If it rams into another of its kind, how many people are killed? How many permanently crippled? How many trees are cut down to make way for its roads and parking lots? How many acres of grass are paved over?"

"Hush, Newton, hush. My dream van doesn't hurt anyone. It runs on stardust and gentleness. Can't you stretch your imagination a little? Can't you let yourself think, just for a few minutes, like our grandparents and great-grandparents?"

"They were insane, vicious..."

"No, no, not really. They were sweet, innocent, much more innocent than we are. They didn't know they were doing anything wrong. Why should you defend the judgments of our time, a time that has rejected you and me as completely as it has rejected those poor ignorant people of the past? Can't you let go a little and join me in my dream? We won't hurt anybody."

"Well...all right. This van trip...Where are we going?"

"Anywhere we like. Right now we're on our way to the seashore, driving down a dirt road. You're wearing pants the way men used to do then. Blue jeans! Cowboy boots and a cowboy hat! It's the early Eighties, the era of the urban cowboy. I'm wearing a big blowy full-circle squaredance skirt with a bathing suit on under it. What's your favorite color?"

"Orange."

"Okay, the skirt is orange and I have an orange scarf over my western-style beehive hairdo, and I'm even wearing orange lipstick. My blouse though, that's white, and very full. The ocean wind blows it around. A warm wind, not a cold one. Can't you taste the salt in it?"

"Not really."

"We both have sunglasses on, because of the brightness. You have a wristwatch, not a fingerwatch, and it shows noon with an acutal minute hand and hour hand. Seagulls fly over, squawking. We laugh and talk as we roll along, bumping over stones and ruts and things, and we don't see anybody for kilometers, and we have such a good time we don't notice we have a good time. The sea says whoosh, whoosh, whoosh and sparkles so much we can hardly look at it even with our sunglasses. They're cheap sunglasses, you know."

"Cheap? Why?"

"We're not rich. In those days poor people could own a van, and maybe a car, too. Anyway, now our destination heaves into view, a point of land sticking out into the Pacific with an old lighthouse, tall and proud but kind of weatherbeaten. We park alongside and unload our picnic basket."

"Picnic basket?"

"People in the Eighties used to carry baskets full of food out into the country to eat."

"Algae soup and kelp bread?"

"No! No! You monster! Can't I have a harmless little daydream without you spoiling it? I won't tell you any more. You don't understand. You never will understand."

Newton laid a soothing hand on her arm. "Easy, now. You can have your picnic if you want. Go on and tell about it."

"Well, all right. We walk hand in hand through the dunes to the beach with our picnic basket, and there we spread out a blanket and unpack our food. You smoke a cigarette while I get things ready, without worrying about being arrested. And we can drink all the Coca Cola we want, and eat all the candy bars and cupcakes we please, and nobody stops us. Can't you just taste it?"

"Almost," said Newton, melting a little.

"After lunch we lie down in the sun side by side, in the same positions we're in now, and let the sun penetrate to our bones, not worrying about ultra-violet. The ozonosphere protects us. We lie there, half asleep, not afraid of anything. Nobody wants to make us do things for our own good. Nobody tells us to eat this and not eat that. Nobody tells us not to get too fat. Nobody walls us in or messes around with our minds or gives us tests that excommunicate us from the human race." Her voice had gradually taken on a desperate, almost hysterical tone. He touched her cheek to calm her, and found tears. "Newton?" she blurted.

"Yes, Mickey?"

"That's not a daydream. That's the real world. This world we're in can't be real. People wouldn't make a world like this on purpose. It's a nightmare! The Uns! The Techs! All a nightmare, and soon we'll wake up there on the beach where we dozed off in the sun and I'll cry and you'll say,"There, there, my love. I'm right here—and I'll smile and kiss you. That's where we really are, Newton, not here. Isn't that true?"

"If you say so," Newton said soothingly.

"We'll always be there, together, on that beach. Isn't that right, Newton?"

"Sure, Mickey, sure."

"Not here!" she screamed *"Not here!"*

"Be quiet! snarled a voice out of the darkness. "If you don't wanna sleep, the rest of us do."

"Yeah," came another voice. "Shutup, willya?"

A chorus of other complaining voices chimed in.

Mickey wept silently for about a quarter of an hour before climbing back down to her own bunk. Newton lay awake trying to visualize the beach again. While Mickey had been talking, he had almost seen it, but now he somehow couldn't manage to make it real.

And he wondered what Coca Cola had tasted like. In old bartenders' manuals he had seen how it could be mixed with rum, and on old buildings he had seen faded, flaking paintings of quaintly innocent girls drinking it and smiling, always smiling. Yes, he was sure it must have been wonderful. Otherwise it wouldn't have been banned.

Chapter 8

"Shut up, Victor," said Newton abruptly.
"Who are you telling to...."
"You hear that?"
Newton and Victor paused in the hallway on the way to the mess hall. An old woman stood, back to the wall, singing, ignored by the passersby. The tune had a haunting modal quality, like an ancient English folksong. The words also suggested a folksong:
"If we could share this world below,
If we could learn to love...
If we could share this world below,
We'd need no world above."
Victor said impatiently, "Come on, Newton. I'm hungry."
"Wait." Newton stepped up the the woman, noticing she was blind. "Where did you learn that song, m'am?"
"Baboo," she croaked.
"What?"
"Baboo, I am you," the woman said.
"I don't understand," said Newton.
"Baboo, I am you, I am you."
She extended a feeble hand. Newton realized she might need help finding her way to supper. Gently he grasped the thin dry fingers. She followed him trustingly, without resistance.
"Are you in a circle?" she asked him as they started down the hall. Victor was smiling scornfully.

"What kind of circle?" Newton asked in return.

Her only reply was to recommence her singing, her voice high, unearthly, without vibrato, yet curiously moving.

"Join hands, join hands, and form a ring.
Join hands, join hands, with me.
Join hands and dance and act and sing,
And love and share and be free."

Victor laughed outright at Newton's puzzlement.

Newton turned to him and demanded, "Do you know what this is all about?"

"It's a drug, a poison," Victor snapped. "It's a delusion! It's an anesthesia for the revolutionary spirit. She would as soon say 'I am you' to a Tech as to you or me. Can you imagine saying 'I am you' to a Tech?"

"I don't know. I haven't the foggiest notion what it means."

"More of that Universal Brotherhood shit."

"But Victor, you told me you were for Universal Brotherhood."

"Of course, but after the overthrow of the Techs! Baboo can't wait for that."

"Baboo, Baboo, I am you," babbled the woman. "Baboo, King of the Ring!"

"King Baboo is their leader," said Victor contemptuously. "Baboo, Lord of the Invisible Kingdom! A madman! The mad leader of the mad. The Pope of Fools! You've never heard of him?"

"No," Newton admitted.

"That surprises me, my friend. He's the most famous person in the Un dorms. His songs travel around the world, passing through doors and walls, leaping from camp to camp. Whenever an Un is transferred, the first thing his new bunkmates ask is, 'Do you know any new Baboo songs?' And inside the dorms you can hear his fans singing in the other sections, on the other floors. His songs have even joined the underground movement, through he hasn't. He laughs at the movement, can you imagine? Laughs!"

Newton answered with a bleak smile, "I have to respect anyone who can laugh at anything in a place like this."

"Do you want to meet him?"

"Why yes, I do."

"All right, Newton. He lives in this building, though not on this floor. I'll introduce you to him."

"But we can't leave this floor, Victor."

"That's what you think. I get around, sweetheart. You'll see."

The woman went on singing:

"Join hands, join hands and sing about the Buddha.

Join hands, join hands and sing about peace."

*

"Well, Holly," said President Bradbury Douglas, "this is the third time I've called you in to speak with me."
"That's right, Brad."
Brad and Holly sat on opposite sides of the circular window in the floor. Below them patches of brown and green farmland laid out in chessboard squares peeped up through the bright white overcast.
"And I have yet to make a pass at you," he added.
"Congratulations."
"Why is that? You're an attractive woman, recently divorced...."
"Perhaps I frighten you. Newton always found me a little frightening."
"Frightening? I wonder. Or are we exploring a different level of relationship, above the ritual mating protocol of our mammalian ancestors? Sometimes I feel you are a kind of answer to the questions that drove me to build the Valhalla, a solution to problems I had come to think had no solution. When I was a young man, before the Russo-American war, I joined an organization called Mensa, which was limited to people whose IQ was above a certain minimum. I hoped to find peers there, equals, people I could talk to." He shook his head. "No. go. So I joined another organization with still higher IQ requirements, a group called Sigma. Still no go. I realized then that my mind was different from other people's, not in amount of intelligence, but in kind."
"You have a big ego, Brad," said Holly, smiling.
"I've needed it to survive, to cling to my own way of thinking when I knew I was completely alone, when everyone else looked at me with dumb incomprehension. I cannot remember a time when everyone around me did not seem like mental pygmies, my parents, my classmates, my teachers, even the supposedly enlightened elite in Mensa and Sigma."
"What was wrong with them?"
"First, they were insular," he said with cold intensity. "They knew little and cared less about what happened outside their own microcosm. Their universe was created when they were born and would end with their death. They could not be bothered to collect data on the distant past and thus had no chance at all of learning to sense the broad sweep of history, of seeing the trends and developments that do not become visible until you view at least a few centuries at once. They could not be bothered to delve into the

religions, politics and philosophies of foreign nations; if they traveled it was as tourists, carefully insulated from any real involvement with the quaint, amusing peoples they saw, looking at strangers, at best, as one looks at animals in a zoo. Worst of all, they could not be bothered to investigate the future, but assumed without question that tomorrow would be like today, which was like yesterday, when the one thing we can be certain of about the future is that it will be different. Uns and Techs alike, they all thought the same. Can you honestly deny it?"

"No, but they can't help...."

"Hear me out! The second failing was that they were unimaginative. Their only way of expressing their individuality was in the things they bought, and then they made sure not to buy anything too different from their neighbors. Mostly they did not write, they did not paint, they did not compose, but if they did, they wrote, painted and composed according to someone else's pattern. If they built something, they bought a plan for it. If they made clothing, they made if from someone else's pattern. If they cooked a meal, they cooked it from someone else's recipe. If they sang, they sang someone else's song, and if they danced, they learned someone else's step. If they were asked about their religion, they would answer with a denomination, and if asked about their political position, they would answer with a party. Even their most fundamental thoughts were hand-me-downs! Holly! Could someone like you live among such people?"

"I managed it."

"But at what cost? Didn't you feel yourself little by little turning into them? Didn't you feel your mind gradually turning to silly putty? Didn't you fear them, try to propitiate them with at least an external conformism?"

Holly did not answer at once, but when she did her voice was serious, pensive. "I was protected from them by their worst fault."

"Protected?"

"Yes, their worst fault, which you failed to mention, was their passivity. They could not act against me on their own initiative because they could not do anything on their own initiative. If they were jealous of me, they were jealous of so many other people as well that they couldn't gather themselves for an effective attack. If they feared me, they feared so many things and so many people that they did not know which way to flee. At best they were able to organize various delaying actions and manufacture a certain amount of red tape to tie me up with, but since they couldn't act except in groups, and groups can't make decisions very fast, I could always outmaneuver them in the end.

You see, they thought of themselves always as victims...victims of their parents, of society, of history, of their own sinfulness. If they were also my victims, they could not separate that in their minds from their general overall victimization, and thus sooner or later they'd give me what I wanted, do what I wanted them to. When they couldn't do anything else with me, they generally elected me their president."

Douglas said, a little too quickly, "That won't happen here."

"Of course not," Holly said, then abruptly added, "Look down there! Isn't that the Mississippi?"

He peered down. "So it is. We're making good time."

Holly thought, *You and I are indeed the same, Brad, but I am the stronger.*

*

Two yellow-robed men made their way through a deserted passage. Neither spoke, and they walked softly, as if afraid of being heard. They stopped in front of a large air-conditioning vent. The shorter of the two, the one with the club foot, looked carefully both ways, then took out a rude, handmade key and opened the grating. He climbed into the airpipe and motioned the other to follow.

"Come on, Newton," he whispered.

When they were both inside, Victor closed the grate and locked it. Still taking care not to make any noise, they padded along the tube into steadily darkening shadows. They rounded a bend in the pipe and found themselves in darkness so deep they could not see at all. A cold draft tugged constantly at their thin garments, and from all directions came a steady murmur of distant voices and the faint, faraway whirr of a giant fan.

Victor laid a restraining hand on Newton's arm and whispered, "Not so fast, you idiot."

A tiny spot of light flared, Victor's miniature flashlight. He pointed it ahead and Newton saw a T intersection with a larger vertical passage.

"If you had stepped into that shaft in the dark," Victor remarked off-handedly, "you would have fallen fifty stories into a rather large propeller. I hope you aren't afraid of heights."

Newton shook his head, but felt more than somewhat queasy.

"Good!" said Victor in a low voice. "Because now we're going to climb up the side of that shaft with nothing to hang onto but a knotted rope."

"Victor, wait."

"What's wrong?"

"Nothing." Not in front of Victor. Not after the way Mickey had looked at him.

The upward-rushing air smelled faintly of ozone. It was negatively ionized; negatively ionized air was supposed to improve morale.

Victor groped out into the void and located the rope that hung down from somewhere above, then handed it to Newton with the instructions, "Follow me up. If you lose your grip I want you under me, not over me." He clicked off the light. Newton could tell that Victor had started up by the way the rope jerked and tugged, and by the sound of Victor's labored breathing overhead.

Taking a deep breath, Newton too began to climb. Immediately his untrained hands weakened. He tried to return but couldn't find the passageway he'd come from. With no way to go but up, Newton braced his plastic-sandaled feet against the smooth, cold, steel wall and climbed, slowly, painfully, hand over hand.

Too late it occured to Newton that Victor hadn't told him how far he'd have to go. An awful dizzyness came over him, and his palms broke out in dangerous, slippery sweat. If the rope had not been knotted, he would have fallen. Panic came to his rescue, pumping new strength into his flabby muscles and numbing his mind. Like a climbing machine he kept on somehow until suddenly he realized that Victor was no longer on the rope. For a moment he wondered if Victor had fallen, then the little flashlight snapped on and Victor called out in a hoarse whisper, "Keep coming. I'll give you a hand."

Faint with relief, Newton let Victor drag him to safety in the mouth of another horizontal airshaft. For a little guy, Victor certainly was strong.

With the flashlight again off, they lay side by side against the curving wall, panting.

After awhile Newton wheezed, "I'm glad that's over."

"What do you mean 'over'? We have two similar climbs before we reach Baboo's floor."

"I can't make it."

"Then I'll have to leave you here."

Somehow, Newton never quite knew how, he made it.

Baboo's floor looked exactly the same in every detail as Newton's, including the people, all dressed in the same yellow robes, one size fits all, all clip-clopping along in plastic sandals, all with haircuts that ranged from baldness to a shaggy crewcut; thus nobody noticed Victor and Newton as they elbowed their way through the crowd just emerging from the gym. The Techs and security police never glanced at them, nor did the armbanded trustees.

When Newton remarked on this, Victor said, "Even if someone did spot us, I don't think he'd try to stop us."

"Why not?"

"They're afraid of us, sweetheart. Sick with fear! When someone messes with the Underground, he tends to meet with what you might call an accident, a fatal accident, like maybe a filing cabinet falls on him, or he slips up with the tablesaw in shop class."

After that Newton noticed that an occasional trustee did look at them but then quickly looked away. Newton was impressed.

"Here we are," said Victor.

They stepped into a large bunkroom similar to Newton's except that the bunks were single-deckers instead of doubles. Newton had learned that single-deckers were a mark of superiority in the subtle class structure of the dorms, but the effect was marred by a maze of mattresses on the floor near the center of the room.

On these mattresses sprawled about twenty-five miscellaneous Uns of both sexes and all ages talking together with an animation and light-heartedness Newton had never before seen in the camps. In the middle of this roughly circular area of mattresses stood a single bunk which, because it was higher than the surrounding pallets, reminded Newton of a stage or perhaps a royal dais. Baboo lay on the bunk, lazily playing a rectangular, crude, probably homemade string instrument. He was a giant of a man, a very black Negro with a bald head and slightly bulging stomach that in no way detracted from an overall impression of physical strength, as if he might be a retired weight lifter or wrestler, yet in the man's face was a look of tired, wistful amusement that made Newton feel that in spite of his great strength he was gentle and understanding, the sort of person everyone turns to in times of trouble.

Baboo waved and called out, "Hello, Victor. Welcome to Etnroa." Then he continued playing. The instrument had twelve strings and Baboo tunked them gently with a little rubber-headed hammer, at the same time striking off harmonics with a battered fountain pen. The tone was sad and sweet, a little like a harp, a little like a guitar, a little like a gypsy violin or the voice of an old-time blues singer. Newton had never heard anything like it before, and it held him spellbound. He recognized, under a cascade of shimmering figurations, the tune he had heard the blind woman singing, but it had been transformed into something unearthly, hypnotic.

Newton heard himself blurting out, "I'd... I'd like to learn to play that."

Baboo smiled. "Okay. I'll teach you."

Victor led Newton toward the bunk, picking his way through the helter-skelter mattresses, trying not to step on either Baboo's disciples or their beds. Some of the disciples greeted Victor by name, others simply called him brother, but unlike their leader they seemed wary and distrustful.

"Baboo," said Victor, "this is my friend, Newton McClintok."

Baboo's smile reminded Newton of some oriental Buddha, or the Mona Lisa, or some ancient Etruscan god. "My name is Bob Osborn, but everyone calls me Baboo."

"*The* Baboo," added a young blonde sitting with her back against the foot of his bunk. She pronounced it in an awed tone, as if it were a holy title.

As they shook hands, Baboo asked, "Are you in the Underground, McClintok?"

"No such luck," said Victor. "He's like you, Baboo. Above it all. That's why I brought him here. I thought you two deserved each other. Baboo is quite a celebrity, Newton. No kidding. Nobody has ever heard of him in the big world of Techs outside, but in the camps everyone sings his songs from here to Timbucktoo."

"I haven't been off this floor, let along out of this building, for fifteen years," said Baboo, "but my spirit has been everywhere. A song is so light, so portable, nothing can contain it. It can pass the tightest customs inspection undetected, hide away in the most tightly-locked prison, never spoiling, never even growing old, as powerful, as imaginary, as eternal as the Kingdom of Etnroa itself."

"Absurd!" said Victor, but his tone gave Newton the impression that this was only the latest episode in a continuing debate between the two men, as if they had long ago given up hope of converting each other, but still carried on the argument for the sport of it.

"Develop a taste for the absurd, Victor," said the big Black. "Only then can you love humanity."

"I love humanity already. Unlike some people I might mention, I'm ready to give my life for it," said Victor.

Baboo regarded him sadly. "By violence and killing you expect to create a world of brotherhood and peace? Love thy neighbor... or else?" He began playing again, softly, disconnected unrhythmical phrases.

Victor appealed to Newton. "That's all Baboo does for mankind. He sits there and plays that poom-poom and makes up songs. It's not even a real instrument, just something he banged together out of the remains of a discarded piano."

"Just a harmless old fool," agreed Baboo. "Crazy old Un. Just sits around and sings his dumb little songs. That's me."

Some of his disciples laughed.

Victor reddened. "Go ahead and laugh. When the blowup comes you'll have to take sides, and I think you'll be with us."

"Can you give me a promotion when I join your army?" asked Baboo.

"Sure, with your following."

"I'm a king already," said Baboo reasonably. "What's higher than that?"

His disciples laughed again. Newton felt sorry for Victor, waging his war of words on Baboo's turf, surrounded by Baboo's followers.

"I have some errands," said Victor. "Newton, you can stay here and get your fill of this crap. I'll come back for you in about an hour. Okay?"

"Okay," Newton agreed, and Victor stumped away.

"Sit down, young fellow," said Baboo to Newton. "Make space for him there, Miss Hareesay." The blonde scooted over. Newton settled himself on the mat. "Any questions?" the big man asked blandly.

Ill-at-ease among these strangers, Newton said, "Nothing much, only...."

"Yes?" Baboo prompted.

"What is all this? Are you a song writer or some kind of spiritual leader?"

"My kingdom certainly isn't spiritual, just cheap."

"Cheap? I don't understand."

"What could be cheaper than a song? Money is valuable. If I give you money, you become rich while I become poor. Power is valuable. If I give you my power, you become master while I become your slave. If I give you my fame, I become a nonentity so you can be a celebrity. By each of these gifts I benefit you only by harming myself. Isn't this the world's one great unsolved problem? If one of us wins, the other must lose."

"But a song..." said Newton wonderingly.

"If I give you a song, I still have it. We both win, and nobody loses."

Newton stared up at the smiling dark face, speechless. He

could not argue with what Baboo had said, and yet common sense told him that it was impossible that this penniless, powerless unknown Un held the answer to the question nobody else in all the centuries had been able to answer, the solution to the problem that threatened to destroy civilization.

Baboo handed Newton the crude musical instrument, saying gently, "This is the poom-poom. I'll show you how to play it."

Chapter 9

Through the gray midafternoon rain, the silent man could barely see the Golden Gate Bridge across the bay through the picture window that stood ajar, letting in an occasional cold wet wind that set the curtains flapping and the papers on the desk fluttering as if trying to escape from the black, leatherbound Bible that weighted them down. When the wind hit right, the drizzle spattered on the narrow, iron-railinged balcony outside, and a few drops even reached the thick, luxurious carpet within, but the man made no move to close the window.

He was small and fat and expressionless, clad in the black coveralls and turn-around clerical collar of a chaplain. He was, in fact, Chaplain Bill himself.

But that broad, friendly smile the Uns were used to seeing had totally vanished.

He meditated, meditated on his own loneliness.

He thought about how nobody ever came to see him voluntarily, how he always had to send for them, and then they never confided in him. Sometimes even if he sent for them they didn't come, though they knew he would report this to Police Captain Clark. What Bill valued most was "being liked," yet for some unknown reason people tended to dislike him on sight. Captain Clark barely put up with him, always acting busy when Bill called. Bill called often, but the Captain always cut short the conversation unless it was about business.

Normandy Taylor, the recreation director, hated Bill and told him so. "You make me puke," she told him, but he took what consolation he could in the knowledge that she was a Lesbian and thus hated all men. The rest of the staff perched either too low or too high on the totem pole for Bill, or were unsuitable for some other reason.

The Trustees all gave him the Big Hello, but he knew their ulterior motives: they buttered him up like that solely to protect their jobs, their pitiful, unpaid jobs. He knew how they whispered about him behind his back, how they snickered and made him the hapless protagonist of their dirty jokes. They had created a second Chaplain Bill all their own and built up an entire grotesque mythology of misadventure about him...Bill the Liar, Bill the Idiot, Bill the Windbag. They'd stolen Bill's identity and passed it onto their monster, so now the monster was real and Bill himself ignored. They didn't know Bill, didn't see him as he saw himself, kindly, understanding, fair. They didn't want to know him. That would spoil the fun!

Worse, lately Bill had caught himself playing the role they'd cast him in, playing the monster with *brio* in a broad, operatic style until something awoke him from his trance and he brought himself up short, choked with shame and horror. He theorized the existence of a perverse demon within him, within us all, that drives us to do what people expect us to do, no matter how degrading.

At other times, much to his mortification, he found himself tagging after someone, bothering someone, clinging to someone, being a pest and knowing he was a pest, as the demon seemed to whisper to him, "Better insufferable than suffering."

At last he spoke, muttering indistinctly. "Where do the Uns go with their troubles?" He knew the answer. His spies had told him.

"Baboo!" he answered himself, then laughed harshly.

The Uns told Baboo everything, listened to that black bastard as if he were God in a Burning Bush.

Chaplain Bill gripped the arms of his chair with all his pudgy little might, then spoke to the empty office in a bitter, self-mocking western accent.

"Baboo, pardner, this town ain't big enough for two saviors."

The wind and the blowing curtain paid no attention.

*

"I'm not really a member of the Underground," Newton told himself. "I'm just taking advantage of free music lessons."

Newton did not like to think of himself as a member of anything. So what if the keys that let him in and out of the air-conditioning system were Victor's! So what if the shadowy presence of the Underground prevented anyone from stopping him and asking him embarrassing questions! So what if members of the Underground sometimes went along with him!

He was, of course, carrying messages for Victor, but he did not understand the messages himself. He simply went where Victor told him to go and held his hands in a certain way, with some fingers closed and some fingers open, but did not even try to learn the finger code or attempt to guess at who was receiving the messages. When he went into a toilet booth on some distant floor, in some distant part of the Berkeley Un complex, he simply remembered the way the obscene figures in the graffiti held their fingers and passed the information on to Victor, never attempting to decode anything or find out who drew the pictures. Thus he maintained his proud aloofness.

He cared not at all that he took considerable risk, that he could be arrested for, at the least, leaving his appointed area. Once you are an Un, he reasoned, what worse can happen?

He also told himself, "I'm not one of Baboo's disciples." Yet it was to see Baboo and to mingle with these disciples, the Etnroans, that he daily made the dangerous climb up the airshaft, pushing out of his mind the fear of falling that never quite left him.

At night he lay awake composing a speech to be recited to Mickey or Victor as soon as an opportunity presented itself, turning it over in his mind, taking out a word here and putting in a word there, polishing it and simplifying it.

SOMETHING FROM NOTHING
by
Newton McClintok

You think I'm amoral, that I have no values. Well, you're wrong, both of you. I believe in honesty. That is, I don't believe in trying to fool anybody, especially not myself. I don't believe in trying to cover up the plain facts of our situation with some kind of pink smokescreen of dreams. I don't live in a dream past of eternal picnics or a dream future of impossible communist utopias, and I bet if you two did have your dreams come true, you wouldn't be any happier than you are now. You'll never be happy anywhere, because you'll have to take your hateful selves along to the Promised Land, your crumby nothing selves. I know I'm nothing. I admit it openly. I shout it to the skies!

And that's where I have the jump on you both. You think you're something, so that means you're less than nothing. You're notings with delusions of somethingness!

Unfortunately the opportunity for reciting this speech never arose.

After his first few visits, Baboo assigned Newton to one of several "Teaching Circles" for novice Etnroans. Presiding over this group of twelve assorted Uns was a genial, rotund Santa Claus of a man, white beard, twinkling eyes and all, who introduced himself as Brother Judd.

Each afternoon, his chores for the Underground completed, Newton checked in with Baboo in the bunkroom for which, it seemed, Baboo never departed, and proceeded from there to a lounge where Brother Judd gaveled the meeting to order and moved to the first item on the agenda, which was always a lesson in the fundamentals of music.

Each student was given a poom-poom to practice with but was not allowed to take it out of the room, so soon the air was filled with a frightful din as twelve rank amateurs attempted to make the crude instrument produce some recognizable approximation of music. Brother Judd circulated around the room, beaming and nodding, giving each student individual attention. It was at such times that Newton asked questions that had nothing to do with harmony, melody or counterpoint.

"Brother Judd, where do these strange names come from? Judd. Baboo. Etnroa."

"From the ouija board, son."

Newton broke off his futile attempts to play the poom-poom. "The ouija board? Then they don't mean anything?"

"On the contrary, my boy, they mean whatever we want them to mean. Ouija board words are so much more docile than words that come to us loaded down with previous associations. You'll have a ouija board name yourself someday, when you become a citizen of Etnroa."

"*If* I become a citizen," Newton corrected him.

"Oh ho! What have we here? A rebel? I know your kind, spiky as a porcupine in the beginning, loyal as a spaniel at the end." He patted Newton patronizingly on the cheek.

"Don't bet on it, Brother Judd." Newton eyed the big man coldly.

"Take the word 'Etnroa.' Baboo got that from the sliding planchette, and later found out it consisted of the most-used letters in the English language, starting with the most-used of all and working down. Could that be mere coincidence?"

"Coincidence or not, Etnroa still doesn't mean anything."

"Ah, you poor ignorant lad, Etnroa happens to be the most meaningful word you're ever likely to hear. It's the name of the Kingdom of Pure Song, the realm from which comes all inspiration in the arts and sciences, the source of all beauty, the true home of us all. Tell me, boy, do you feel at home here?"

"In the Un camps? Of course not."

"How about in the world outside the camps, the world of the Techs?"

"No...." Newton admitted reluctantly.

"How can that be? If this isn't your home, you must have some sense, however dim, of another place, a place not like this. Ah lad, I see in your eyes that your mind says no but your heart says yes. You haven't altogether forgotten Etnroa after all. It haunts you still, make you dissatisfied with old Mother Earth, but you can't quite grasp it. Believe me, I know how you feel. I was the same way myself once. You should read Plato, or the First Century Gnostic philosophers. They knew a thing or two! Far Etnroa calls you, the same as it did me, but so softly you can hardly hear it. Sometimes it calls you in a certain poem, or a certain painting, or a certain story. Sometimes it calls you from the sky at dawn, from the face of a young girl, or from a storm at sea. Most of all it calls you from song, from a tune somebody whistles as they pass you in the fog, from a symphony, from the shimmering tintinnabulations of Bali's gamelongs or the cry of a bird at night. We're citizens of Etnroa, you and I, but citizens in exile, and Baboo, in a manner of speaking, is our king, visiting us here in this lost outpost. What do you say to that, rebel?"

"I say you're crazy."

"Ah, you're like some poor wistful young virgin being seduced, crying no, no, no and meaning yes, yes, yes. Look at history, the long sweep of it. Don't you see? Faith has tried and failed. Reason has tried and failed. Why not give song a try? There's a kind of instinct in us, I tell you, drawing us, drawing everybody to Etnroa. Why do you think that, time and again, the oppressed and disenfranchised have become their society's musicians? The Gypsies in Spain and Russia, the Blacks in America, the Troubadours in France, the Greeks in ancient Rome, the Jews everywhere. Whenever people have nothing, they start singing."

"That doesn't mean anything."

"You take too passive an attitude toward meaning. If something lacks a meaning, you can put a meaning on it."

"How?"

"Make one up!"

"That's not real."

"Every word we speak was made up by somebody sometime. Every word came out of the imagination, out of Etnroa! Everything this poor old human race has built came out of the imagination, out of Etnroa. What is a building? What is a train? What is a computer? They're all just frozen dreams, gifts from far Etnroa, the crumbs that fall from the tables of the feasting gods. Come now, boy, let's take the word Etnroa apart and see the meaning of its parts."

"Its parts? I though you told me the whole damn word came from a ouija board. How can its parts have meaning?"

"I'm glad you asked that question! Maybe you've noticed how Etnroans use the word et. It's a new pronoun! In English you have he, him and his. You have she, her and hers. You have it, it and its. But if you want to speak of someone who might be either male or female, you have to say something like 'his-or-her pen,' 'he-or-she might come.' Or you look at a baby and say 'it,' as if a baby wasn't alive, but just a hunk of inanimate matter like a stone. There's a hole in the English language, and you see it whenever you want to talk about people as people, regardless of age or sex, but until Baboo came along nobody tried to plug that hole. Now we say 'et.' That's close enough to 'it' to be treated in the same way, but it means 'A Creative Consciousness,' a consciousness capable of imagination, of making something new, of serving as a bridge between our world and Etnroa. Man or woman, child or adult, we're all ets."

Newton laughed. "Has Baboo really done all that? There's more in ets philosophy than there is in Heaven and Earth. Did et think of all this, or did you?"

"Jest if you will, lad, but I'm glad to see you've learned to use the word."

"That takes care of the et. What about the nroa?"

Brother Judd closed his eyes and nodded wisely. "Nro is the creative force that brings all new things into being; the energy of inspiration. When someone asks, 'How's it going?—the it they mean is the nro. Maybe you've noticed that when one of us meets another, et says 'Nro' for hello, 'Nro' for goodby, 'Nro?' as a question for 'How are you?' Nro is the all-purpose smalltalk word, but don't for that reason think there's anything petty about it. When you say 'nro' you mean, 'All's well. The creative force that brought us into being continues to flow smoothly.' You mean, 'Whether I can hear it or not, Etnroa still sings somewhere, and its songs still echo faintly here below.' "

Newton said, amused, "You certainly do have a complicated religion, Brother Judd."

"Not at all! First, it's not a religion. It's not something you believe, it's something you do. Second, it has only three parts."

"Three parts?" Newton said suspiciously.

"You've seen two out of the three already, lad. The first is song, and you've heard the songs. The second is the circles, and this class is one of the circles. The third is nrobooks."

"The nrobooks?" This pricked Newton's curiosity. "What's a nrobook?"

The bearded man studied Newton a moment before answering, "All in good time. I don't think you're ready for that yet."

He strolled on to the next student, leaving Newton staring after him, hooked good and proper. Hating it and liking it at the same time.

*

Valhalla drifted northeast in the lower stratosphere at a smooth one hundred and fifty knots, ballast ball hanging straight down like a surveyor's plumb bob in the cold, unturbulent air, triangular facets flashing in the brilliant afternoon sun. Below, hard-edged under the cloudless sky, lay the Atlantic seaboard like a lawn in which each blade of grass was a skyscraper. From this altitude Holly could not tell where one city left off and another began, nor, looking south or looking north, could she see any end to the sprawling megalopolis that stretched from horizon to horizon.

What a contrast, she thought, to the emptyness of other parts of the world, of the western United States, of the plains of Russia. No wonder the people of the East Coast had never been able to understand the people of the West Coast. Their relationship to nature had always been different. Even now, when some of the western cities had grown far beyond reasonable bounds, a spirit lingered of the deeply-felt love/fear attitude of the pioneers, of the Indians, toward the ultimately mysterious, utterly fickle Calafia, black goddess of the sunset realm. In a place like New York City, cut off from the whisperings of Calafia, one might actually come to care what some Jewish mother-in-law said.

Holly turned from the curving floor-to-ceiling window and asked her companion, "How long does the Valhalla take to circumnavigate the earth?"

Smith answered, "An average of thirteen days."

Sewall Smith was a small, androgynous elf of a man, a kind

of Peter Pan as played by an adolescent girl. Holly could not imagine him ever having been a child, or ever growing a day older. He coyly asserted his individuality by the floral borders he had embroidered on his "company blue" shift, accentuating the boyish-girlish appearance that had made it so difficult for Holly to guess his gender when they had been introduced.

She had thought him a foppish fool at first, but she should have known better. There were no fools allowed in Valhalla, and Smith's childish manner concealed an IQ equal to Holly's own, and considerable talent as an architect, watercolor painter and composer. Here on board he had distinquished himself by a mastery of navigation that would have done credit to some crusty mariner of the Age of Sail.

"I figured it was something like that," Holly mused. "You know, that's fast enough to make use of these things for regular transportion."

Smith nodded. "Brad plans to build a fleet of craft like this one, after the Blowup, to carry intercontinental freight and passengers. I've been working on the designs. He calls them 'Yaos,' after the Chinese word for 'Drifting like down on the wind.' "

"Yaos, eh? A yao won't be as fast as a magnetic train."

"True, but it won't require thousands of miles of vacuum tunnels and monorail tracks that have to be kept in repair, and it won't use any fuel at all, or create any pollution. Those magnetic trains such a lot of juice, Holly baby. We're not like the coocoos of the Twentieth Century. We think about what happens downstream, about what happens later on. They were so worried about atomic radiation, which even they they should have seen could easily be contained, while hardly giving a thought to the way their jet planes were destroying the ionosphere. Thanks to them we still can't, to this day, take a good sunbath without risking skin cancer. Actually, Brad figures that after the Blowup we may be able to built a civilization that can dispense with nuclear power altogether. You'd be surprised how a whole new menu of technologies comes into view when you step backward from the extreme speeds and power levels we've inherited from the Industrial Era."

Holly looked upward toward the high blackness. "We need high speeds and power levels to reach other planets."

Smith said seriously, "Do we really need to reach other planets?"

"I've always thought so."

"What have we gotten from outer space so far?"

"A place to fight our wars. Can you imagine what would have happened if the Russo-American War had been fought Earthside?"

"After the Blowup we won't have any more wars. If anyone tries to start one, the Prometheans will stomp him flat. If history teaches us anything, it is that peace only comes when one power has undisputed technological superiority. I don't know about you, but as for me I think it's a good trade. We get peace, and kiss the stars goodbye."

Holly reflected moodily on this. Every century, she realized, rejects the century before it, swinging the pendulum as far as possible in the opposite direction. Perhaps the people of the Twentieth Century had been a little narrow-minded with their belief in technological progress at all costs, in their gut feeling that if you can do something, you should do it; yet she could see a kind of courage in it, an adventurousness she had to admire. Her ancestors had taken risks, and now she had to live with both the benefits and the liabilites of their decisions. So be it! She couldn't sunbathe, but she could drift through the sky in a yao. Tit for tat! No reproaches and no regrets. The human race should have stuck with that plan, that attitude, should have colonized the planets instead of letting machines do it, should have somehow figured out how to bridge the gap to the nearest stars. There would be mistakes, yes. People would die, yes. So what! Maybe we'd all die, reaching for the stars. So what! At least we'd go out in style.

And she thought, *The stars are still there. We can still do it. When I take over....*

"Meahwhile," said Holly, "let's shovel the shit."

Their rest period over, Sewall and Holly got back to work, unstrapping and unplugging the spent barrel of excrement, sealing it, and hefting it onto the small freight elevator that would take it up to the indoor farm, then hauling into the empty brackets a new barrel, fresh from the public lavatory, strapping it down firmly, uncapping the pipe on the top and, trying to ignore the brief whiff of escaping stench, attaching the plastic tube that would convey methane gas either to the kitchen, where it would be used for cooking, or to the nearby lab, where genetically-engineered bacteria would convert it to Pruteen, a kind of protein used as a food by the crew. The sun, streaming in through the wide windows, provided more than enough heat to keep the process bubbling merrily, never missing a day because of a cloudy weather; this in spite of the fact that the temperature just outside the window was seventy degrees below zero Fahrenheit.

Smith, sweating and puffing with the exertion, said, "This is real work."

"I guess so," Holly agreed, still somewhat lost in her own thoughts. "But someone has to do it."

"That's more or less so. Each one of us takes a turn at it sooner or later."

"Except Brad," Holly said pointedly.

"Except Brad. But you could trade duty with someone. I've traded duty plenty of times. You and I don't really have the muscle for this sort of thing. I assure you I wouldn't be here if I could have found someone to swap with."

Holly laughed. "I swapped to get here."

"You're kidding! You mean you like wrestling with a barrel of shit?"

"No, but I like doing things nobody else wants to do."

"Even in rough weather, when the deck is tilting like a seesaw?"

"Even then. I'm getting good at it. An expert."

Smith shook his head wonderingly. "You're crazy, you know that."

"Maybe so, but I'm also getting to be indispensable."

An empty barrel came noisily down the freight elevator. Holly tackled it singlehanded and had it on the handtruck before Smith could help her.

He opened the door for her as she wheeled the handtruck through. The passageway beyond was much cooler; the chamber they had just left was always swelteringly hot, particularly during the afternoon. She strode along jauntily, Smith close behind.

"You're up to something, aren't you?" Smith demanded.

"Why do you say that?"

"I sense it. You have some kind of weird master plan. Otherwise why would you act so strangely?"

"Just because I willingly do what others are trying to escape doing?"

"Right."

"Instead of suspecting me of all sorts of evil plots," she said. "Why don't you remember, the next time you're looking for someone to swap duty with, that you always have good old Holly to fall back on."

"Thanks, Holly. And if you ever want a favor, you can count on me." Like most of them, she had found, he respected rather than resented her attitude.

"I'll hold you to that," she said lightly, thinking, *Bingo, One more chicken in the stew!*

They entered the narrow room under the public toilet and snapped on the dim light. The smell was bad, but Holly ignored it. With expert fingers she swung the empty barrel into its reserve chamber and strapped it firmly in place. It would be ready when she returned the following day to switch it with the barrel that was now in place under the toilets, loading up.

"Let's get out of here," said Smith.

"Just a minute," she said, then quickly and expertly checked all the equipment.

"What could possibly go wrong here?" Smith whined impatiently.

"Nothing, during my shift," said Holly curtly.

When they were out in the passageway again, the door dogged shut against the escape of any offending aromas, Smith said, "You're amazing, Holly. So by-the-book. So military."

"Call me corporal," she told him, smiling. "The Little Corporal."

They both laughed, but she could see from his puzzled expression he didn't know what was funny.

*

See Piggy.

Piggy is a girl. She is three feet tall. She has blue eyes and long yellow hair.

See Piggy's toothbrush. She brushes the hair of her doll with the toothbrush. Funny, funny Piggy!

Piggy has a dirty face. Bad Piggy! You should wash your face.

Piggy laughs and plays.

Play, Piggy, play!

Piggy plays with her doll and her toothbrush.

See Mickey.

Mickey is Piggy's new friend. Mickey and Piggy met today for the first time.

They are eating.

They are eating algae soup in the mess hall.

Mickey is a big girl.

She is nineteen years old.

Piggy is a little girl.

She is thirty-two years old.

Chapter 10

Some days the instructor didn't bother to show up. No substitute instructor replaced him, since officially he was there. Officially he never missed a day. If anyone asked where he was, someone in the class piped up, "He just went down the hall," or "He must have gone to the john." The Uns covered for him, not because they liked him, but because they wanted to encourage him to new heights of truancy.

In his absense, they could do as they liked.

Victor labored cheerfully on zip-guns and crude hand grenades, as did many of his friends. Newton, less ambitious, worked slowly and awkwardly on a poom-poom, a miniature version of Baboo's, and though they had different projects, Newton and Victor often shared a table.

One day Victor asked, "Well, Newton, have you met Piggy?"

"No. Who's Piggy?"

"A dwarf girl. Feeble-minded. Sooner or later you'll bump into her wandering around the halls. She never takes a bath. I hear she's not even housebroken." Victor laughed gloatingly.

"So what?"

"How do you think our friend Baboo would react to someone like that? Would he say, 'I am you' to Piggy?"

Newton realized Victor was baiting him and pressed his lips tightly together, working on in silence.

Victor continued with glee, "You. Me. Piggy. Baboo. We're all in the same boat, right? All losers! All sick, suffering idiots stumbling up the steps of the gallows! Right? Every man jack of us! That's the real meaning of 'I am you!' "

Newton said nothing.

"We're all terminal cases. We're all going to die. That's it, isn't it?" Victor punched Newton playfully in the arm.

"Have it your way," said Newton.

"All dying! Waiting for those bony knuckles to rap on the door. Won't be long now, Newton, until the skinny liberator sets you free. But some of us have figured out how to fool him. He can take me away, but the Movement remains. The Movement is my real soul, my immortality."

Newton quoted himself with a shrug. "A fool's paradise is better than none."

"Did Baboo tell you that?"

"No."

"Who made that up?"

"I did."

"Don't lie to me, sweetie. You don't have the brains to make up something like that, you dumb, stupid, idiotic Un." All this in a bantering, good-natured tone.

Newton speculated on the hypothetical situation Victor had proposed. Could one actually equate oneself to a feeble-minded dwarf? Could one say, 'I am you' to someone more like an animal than a person?

A half hour later the question became, not hypothetical, but practical.

Newton met Piggy.

Piggy and Mickey sat side by side on Mickey's bunk as Newton entered the bunkroom, and Newton knew who she was before being introduced. Who else could it be under that birdsnest of tangled cornsilk hair? Who else could it be with that toothbrush and that battered, eyeless, one-armed doll?

Newton thought, Mickey can say 'I am you' to Piggy. They're both girls. And they're both hunchbacks.

Freaks.

"Hi, Mickey," said Newton.

Mickey sprang up. "Newton, I want you to meet my new friend, Piggy."

"Hello, Piggy," Newton said doubtfully.

Piggy sat motionless, looking up at Newton with a coy smile and empty eyes. She could have been a shy, somewhat ugly child except for her skin, dry and parchment-like, the skin of an old woman. Mickey threw an arm around those twisted dwarf shoulders, crying out, "Give her a hug, Newton. She likes that."

Newton wanted to obey, to prove he really believed in the Etnroan philosophy, but he remained frozen in the same position. He couldn't do it.

Piggy stank to high heaven.

*

Captain Clark and Normandy Taylor often shared an off-duty drink in Normandy's room. They loved each other, though they would never be what is called "lovers." Normandy found only members of her own sex attractive in a sexual way, and Captain Clark, in fifteen years of a formal monogamous marriage, marred by many long separations, had never been unfaithful to his wife.

He sat back in an overstuffed chair and held his drink up to the light. "You know Victor Tarachenko?"

The restless Normandy, moving ceaselessly around her small but tastefully furnished room, answered, "That troublemaker? What about him?"

"A persuasive recruiter, that. All things to all men. How long would you say before he had the whole floor in the underground?"

"Arrest the bastard."

"For what, my dear? I can't prove anything. Before arresting someone I must have proof that will stand up in court, particularly with someone highly placed in the underground who will doubtless have wealthy and powerful friends on the outside."

"Send in some finks. You can nail him somehow, by fair means or foul," she said. "Frame him if you have to."

"I have no orders to do anything of the sort."

"Do it on your own authority."

Captain Clark sighed and shook his head. "I can't afford to do that, Norm. I'll lose my job and become an Un myself. In a few months I come up for retirement. I can't throw that away. I have a wife and kids to think of."

Normandy loomed over the sprawling policeman, one hand holding her drink, the other gesturing emphatically. "Listen, Cap, if somebody doesn't do something soon, those animals will stampede and trample us all. Every day I walk around among them as if everything was peachy, but I can feel their hatred like a poisonous fog all around me. I'm afraid to stand where one of them can get behind me."

"Try and understand, Norm. Those so-called 'animals' aren't criminals or, for the most part, even insane. They've committed no crime, let alone been convicted of any. They're not unemployable because they're evil. They're unemployable because, for some reason or other, there's nothing they can do quite well enough to compete out there." He gestured vaguely in the direction of the outside world. "Why, if we had voting booths in here, they could vote! Did you know some of them have been demanding the right to vote?"

"And I suppose you'd like to let them vote?"

"I don't know, Norm. I just don't know. If I was ordered to...."

"Those Uns would vote themselves right out of here, and who could blame them, but they'd flood a world that had no place for them, swarm like locusts through the streets of our cities. You know damn well that however law-abiding they may be now, they'd start robbing and killing if they got hungry enough. Our society can't handle that, Cap. The camps are our society's answer to the Un problem, a damned expensive answer, but the only one a humane culture is likely to come up with." She flung herself into the overstuffed chair facing Clark and ran her powerful fingers through her short red hair. "The cost-effective thing to do is line them up against a wall and shoot them, but the people on the outside won't sit still for that. The big brass doesn't understand how it is down here in the dorms. They listen to those 'happy Un' songs on the video and by God, they believe them. And they expect us to make reality match their self-deceptions, make the Uns happy and healthy, wet nurse them and change their diapers for them while all along these Un animals, far from feeling any gratitude for our efforts, only want to kill us. They want to kill us, Cap. Do you realize that?"

Captain Clark nodded sadly and drained his glass.

*

The Atlantic stretched greygreen in all directions under a transparent gauze of light stratus clouds below the Valhalla, while above it sparse white cirrus curled across the zenith like the long locks of hair of some immense albino goddess. The ballast ball swung gently, evening out the buffeting of the turbulence in the outer reaches of the jet stream, for the Valhalla had strayed from the calm center of the sky river into its slower, rougher edges. Even so, because it moved as part of that river rather than battering through it as a jet plane might have, the Valhalla remained firm and steady, rising and falling gently rather than with the giddy suddeness of so-called "air pockets."

On duty in the navigation room were Sewall Smith, Juanita Castro, Hal Waterman and Holly, seated at a horseshoe-shaped console of controls in front of a broad window that began as a continuation of the floor, then curved up to meet the ceiling at an acute angle. Overhead, tilted for maximum visibility, a series of computer display screens, television screens and digital instruments kept them supplied with rapidly changing data and a central holovision simulation portrayed their position and the nature of the surrounding air currents in three-dimensional color.

"Are we in any real danger?" asked Holly.

"Not at the moment," Juanita answered. "But like most complex machines, the Valhalla does not easily forgive mistakes. If we find ourselves in the wrong air current we must somehow get out of it."

"And if we don't?" Holly continued.

Smith answered her question. "We could drift into a region of stagnation. The equatorial doldrums, the Sahara High, the Indian Dome. And there we would stay, perhaps for weeks."

"What harm would that do? The Valhalla is a self-contained ecosystem, isn't it?" said Holly.

"Almost self-contained," said Smith. "We wouldn't be in any real trouble there. But we do need the sun. We can't afford to get stuck in an arctic or antarctic night."

"Because of the blizzards?" said Holly.

"No, we'd be above the blizzards, and surprisingly enough, the weather is milder north of the Polar Front than south of it. The North Pole itself gets less snowfall than parts of Virginia. It's the sun's energy we'd miss. Nothing to activate our banks of photovolatic cells and charge our batteries. Nothing to keep the plants growing in the indoor farm. Nothing to warm us up after the night cools us down," said Smith grimly. "If we got stuck in the Arctic Turntable, the Valhalla could move around and around in those permanent easterlies for centuries, with a cargo of corpses that defrosted every summer and refroze the following winter."

Juanita said, "But we are thinking beings. We can plan. You will never get lost if you make sure to stay found, as the old mountain men used to say. And you will learn, Holly, to know the air as a living thing, with certain habits and a certain form. You will develop an instinct for it, I promise you, so that you can look at the pattern of the waves on the sea and know if there are islands nearby, if you are near the center of a low or on its edges, if there is a wind at a higher altitude moving in the opposite direction from the surface wind. A wisp of cloud, a certain color in the sky, a certain formation of ducks.... One clue and you will see in your mind's eye the way the winds roll for a thousand kilometers in all directions. They do roll, you know. Vertically, horizontally, they roll constantly like immense donuts."

Hal spoke for the first time in many minutes. "You get a special feeling for life up here, Holly. You could never explain it to a Mundane, but you begin to understand how everything in the universe rolls and flows and changes, even human civilizations, even thoughts in your mind. Mundanes live essentially in two dimensions, in a flat cosmos, but we live in three dimensions, in the cosmos as it really is. Mundanes wonder why our galaxy has a spiral shape: we look at it and wonder how it could have any other. It's a cyclone, isn't it? In some different, thinner medium? And don't its arms roll vertically as well as horizontally, like the arms of a cyclone, only too slowly for us to see?"

Holly was always surprised to catch the cynical Hal in one of these rare philosophical moods. She could easily understand the other Hal, who joked at even the most serious matters, but this other Hal had an element in him, an element shared with the other Promethians, that she had to call religious, even mystical, as if the weather had become God. She wondered if she would feel the same way when she learned as much as they knew about the atmosphere, when she too could sense the rolling of the vast invisible donuts.

She tried to picture herself explaining the Promethean attitude to Newton and realized uneasily that she had already changed so much there were certain things she could not communicate even to that most sympathetic of all listeners.

Smith broke into her thoughts with a worried remark. "Juanita, I don't like it. The curves aren't bending right. Something's building up. I can feel it."

"I know what you mean," said Juanita in a low voice.

"Can we find the center of the jet stream again?" asked the suddenly-practical Hal.

"No problem," Smith answered, "but I'm not sure it will take us where we expect."

"Let's ask Brad," ventured Juanita.

Holly, too, had her instincts. Without pausing to think, she fired her verbal dart. "What does he know?"

The others looked at her, shocked. She waited, seeing human currents that were every bit as real to her as the rolling air currents were to the Prometheans. Juanita, the rejected lover, harboring a resentment she would not voice even to herself. Hal, the second-in-command, who had said yes to Brad many times when he meant no and hated himself for it. Smith, peacock-proud of his ability as a navigator, a small man, effeminate. How many times had classmates called him a sissy? She waited, waited to see which one would tumble first.

"Right," said Smith. "What does he know?" He laughed like a man who has found a sudden unexpected freedom. "We're the ones who do all the work around here."

Hal and Juanita glanced at each other, but said nothing.

"We'll get back in the jet stream," said Smith firmly, taking command. "I'll keep on top of this and see what develops."

A wild elation welled up in Holly, and she thought of chess, of something Newton had told her. "It's not taking the queen that wins the game; it's the passed pawn."

And now she had her passed pawn.

*

"Check."

"Hmm. I can still move my bishop."

"Check again."

"Well, Miss Taylor, there's always my knight."

"Check and mate!"

"I'll be damned." Newton fell back in his chair, stunned. In his early teens he had worked out a positional strategy which he had thought guaranteed victory, at least to the one playing whites. He had perfected it in game after game with his wife, Holly, who toward the end had come dangerously close to seeing his trap, buried though it was in a series of seemingly innocuous moves. A worthy opponent, he had thought. But Normandy Taylor had cracked his system in a single game. He glanced around the lounge to see if anyone had witnessed his defeat. Nobody else was even in the room.

"Don't forget your bet," said the redheaded recreation director.

"How much was it?"

"A whole day."

The Uns had no money, so they played games for units of time. The loser would be the winner's slave for however long the bet was for.

"A whole day," Newton echoed tonelessly.

"You couldn't resist the temptation of making a slave out of a Tech, could you, Newton?" She began putting the cheesmen into their box. "Did you really think I'd play if there was the remotest chance of you winning? But cheer up. One day isn't much. I know a guy who bet ten years in a poker game. He's still working it off."

"When do I start?"

"Right now, cookie."

"Nothing illegal," he said hopefully.

"Don't worry. Nothing illegal."

She made out a pass for him and sent him to the staff wing to wait for her in her apartment. The pass got him by the armed guard and a heavy steel door into a part of the dorm he had never entered in all his wanderings as Victor's messenger. With a little searching he found her apartment. The door, as she had said, was unlocked. As he entered the lights turned on and soft music began to play. He almost tripped over someone in a sleeping bag on the floor.

"Who're you?" the someone numbled sleepily. "What you doing here?"

"I'm Newton McClintok. I lost twenty-four hours to Miss Taylor in a chess game."

"I'm George. I lost two months. I've got one week, two days and..." He peered at a digital clock on the wall. "...seven hours, fifteen minutes, and twenty seconds yet to go. Pleased to meet you!"

He sat up. They shook hands listlessly.

"What's your hobby?" George asked abruptly.

"My hobby?"

"Sure, every Un has a hobby. You gotta do something."

"I—I'm a student."

"Everybody is a student, Newton. A student of what?"

"Music, I guess."

"Is that all?"

"Maybe philosophy."

"Everybody is a philosopher around here, Newton." George sounded disappointed.

Annoyed, Newton said, "What about you? What are you, George."

"A poet." He smiled proudly.

"Everybody is a poet around here, George."

"I'm a special kind of poet. I rhyme."

"Then we have something in common, you and I. We both live in the past."

"Want to hear some of my poems?"

"I'd just as soon not.'

"Just two little short ones?"

"No, thanks."

"One?"

"No."

"Jesus, what a sorehead," said George resentfully.

George looked more like a big, bruised teddybear than a poet, but his eyes were expressive. They seemed to be saying, "Kick me! Then at least you'll be noticing me." He had apparently made use of his time in Norm's apartment to grow a not-too-successful beard.

Newton said, "What do you think she'll have me do?"

George rolled his eyes heavenward. "Lord knows! Techs have inventive minds."

"I guess they do. Say George, do you mind if I play the television."

"I'd rather you wouldn't."

"You don't get to see a good set like this is any Un lounge. Three-D, supersonics, full-wall screen."

"I don't like TV." George lay back in his sleeping bag.

"Are you going to sleep?"

"Any objections?"

"This is the middle of the afternoon."

"You think that matters to someone who hasn't seen the sky for two years, four months, six days, five hours, fifteen minutes and—"He glanced again at the clock. "—twenty-five seconds? I got no appointments. Do you? I don't even go to the meetings of the poets' club any more. Why bother? I haven't written anything for ages, ever since a friend of mine—the bastard—won the club's big cash poetry prize. He bought his way out of here with it, and now he's out in the real world somewhere, acting like he's a Tech with a job and everything, going to Tech parties, mingling, scoring. He'll be back, though, when his money runs out."

At last Newton's interest was aroused. "Are you saying an Un can buy his way out of here?"

"Sure. Win a contest and out you go, for a while. Write a poem! Enter it. Doesn't have to be good. That damn poem that won didn't even rhyme!"

Digesting this new information, Newton collapsed into a contour chair that quickly adjusted itself to the shape of his body. Normandy Taylor's books were on a shelf, right about at eye level. They were, judging from the titles, all about abnormal psychology. He reached for one, but George cautioned him, "Miss Taylor doesn't like Uns messing with her stuff."

Newton withdrew his hand. "You don't think she'll make me do anything illegal, do you?"

"Naw. It might be indecent, but it won't be illegal."

"What do you mean?"

"You'll see."

And indeed as he spoke the door opened and Normandy Taylor came in with a group of other women, all trustees. They

117

giggled and kept exchanging meaningful glances.

"You boys are headed for stardom," she announced, showing them a compact video tape recorder. "Hollywood revisited! One of the girls has written a cute little script entitled 'The Gorilla and the Fair Maiden.' You George, put on this gorilla costume." One of the trustees delightedly opened a box she had brought, revealing crumpled black fur and a disturbingly realistic gorilla head. "And you, Newton," Normandy continued, "will slip into something more comfortable, one of my most frilly nylon tricot nightgowns, and play the fair maiden."

"Nothing illegal!" Newton objected.

"Of course not," said Norm, soothingly, taking out a tube of vaseline. "Just good clean family entertainment."

"I figured it would be another one of those," George sighed, struggling into the gorilla suit.

Chapter 11

Hal Waterman raised his glass of homebrew in a toast.
"To Holly!"
"To Holly!" chorused the Prometheans, amid a general clinking of glasses around the crowed lounge. She sat near the center of the triangular room, under the skylight, and the sun streaming in spotlighted her as if she were an actress in theatre-in-the-round, calm, self-possessed, sure of her lines, surrounded by her devoted fans who had all leaped to their feet for the toast. Everyone was here, except for the skeleton crew on duty and President Brad Douglas.

They honored her for having worked out a way to avoid unnecessary steps in the tending of the vegetable beds, a small thing really, but impressive to these exiles from a society that valued efficiency above human life. It had not been easy to find something these bright people had overlooked, but she had told herself that nothing is ever so good it can't be made better, and she had found it.

"Speech!" called out Juanita Castro.
"Speech!" echoed Sewall Smith.
They were joined by a boisterous ensemble of slightly drunken voices crying, "Speech! Speech!"

Holly waited a moment, as if hesitating, and as she had expected the shouts grew louder. She set down her glass on the table beside her, slipping it into the tight-fitting pit in the tabletop that held it upright against the constant swaying of the deck, paused again, teasing them, then at last stood up and raised her hand for silence.

Over a brief flurry of applause, she began, "Thank you, my friends, my comrades, my co-workers. You really shouldn't single me out for special attention. If I know anything, you taught it to me. If I can do anything, you showed me how. Give credit where credit is due! To wise, gentle demonic Hal Waterman. To patient, motherly Juanita Castro. To Sewall Smith, who has forgotten more about clouds than I'll ever know. To all of you. As I look around this room, I can't see a single person who hasn't taught me something. In honoring me, you indirectly honor yourselves, my mentors, my teachers, my guides." She reached for her glass. "So I say, if we drink a toast, let's make it a toast to us all." She raised her glass. "To us!"

"To us!" they answered, flattered, delighted.

Many of them drained their glasses, but Holly only sipped. She could not afford the luxury of drunkeness when one false word or action would spoil everything.

Suddenly the intercom boomed, "Holly McClintok! Come to my cabin." Brad sounded impatient.

Holly marched without hesitation to the spiral staircase at the inner point of the triangular room. As she passed Juanita, the woman impulsively caught her hand and gave it a squeeze, whispering, "He sounds angry. Good luck, baby."

Holly caught a blur of guilty expressions out of the corner of her eye. In some part of their minds, these clever, clever people knew they were doing something wrong, but they didn't know what. Mutiny? If anyone had suggested such a thing, they would have laughed uproariously.

A little too uproariously.

Holly thought, *How wonderful is the human mind. It can know something and not know it at the same time.*

With a feeling, not of fear, but of fierce exaltation, she bounded down the stairs, visualizing herself as Joan of Arc riding forth to battle so vividly she could almost hear the distant trumpets sounding the charge.

She paused a moment in front of the elegantly carved door she had come to know so well, with its familiar image of the hybris-doomed Prometheus and his fat fireball. For the first time she noticed how much it resembled something from the sports page of the news printout, a basketball player dribbling across the court or a soccer player or a volley ball player perhaps. Laughing softly, she knocked.

"Come in, Holly," came Brad's voice, more subdued than Holly had ever heard it before.

She stepped into the Round Room and gently closed the door behind her. Douglas did not advance to shake her hand, nor did he cheerfully offer her a drink. Instead he sat slumped in the conversation pit, peering moodily down through the round window in the floor. She could not say how he had changed. His disheveled white hair was no longer, his conservative grey business kilt no more rumpled, his lean face no more wrinkled.

Yet he looked old, really old, in a way he never had before.

"What's going on out there, Holly?" he asked softly.

She started toward him. "What do you mean, Brad?"

"I heard cheering. I heard people calling your name."

She sat down across from him. "The crew threw a little party for me." She said guardedly, "They made a big fuss over an idea I'd suggested for running the vegetable boxes better. You know how they blow things all out of proportion as an excuse to have some fun."

"We don't have much fun up here, do we?"

"Well, you know how it goes."

He looked up, meeting her gaze for the first time since she'd entered the room. She saw his eyes were bloodshot and ringed with dark circles. "I used to think I knew how it goes, Holly, but I'm not so sure anymore. Maybe you'd better tell me."

She shifted uneasily. "Could you rephrase that question? Be more specific?"

"I never did mix all that much with the crew, you know. Too much familiarity hurts discipline. But I always felt a certain warmth. I don't call it gratitude, though you people should be grateful to me. I call it camaraderie. I don't feel that any more. I enter a room and people stop talking, though I heard them laughing and chattering together a moment before. That didn't used to happen, Holly."

"We've been cooped up in the Valhalla a long time. Sometimes tempers get short."

"They don't treat you that way."

"Well, I'm out there with them all the time. They know me. You should get out of this room and mingle more."

"I don't push in where I'm not welcome. I don't feel a rapport with just anybody."

"But these people are hand-picked to be your peers, your friends, your equals. You tested them, looked over their records, weeded out the undesirables. If you can't get along with them, who can you get along with?" A sense of growing horror had begun to creep over her, and a gnawing pity. Some part of her wondered if she could go on with her plan.

"Out of all of them," said the old man softly, "only one really talks to me."

"Who?"

"You."

"My God, Brad, how can you say that?"

"Sometimes I think everything I've ever done has been motivated by a search for someone like you. I looked for you among my classmates when I was a child. I looked for you in the Mensa Society, I looked for you in Sigma. I was looking for you when I built Valhalla, when I set my agents to screening the graduates of all the schools in the world. I thought I wanted a group of friends, a brilliant coterie like Virginia Woolf's Bloomsbury Group, William Morris's Pre-Raphaelite Brotherhood, Tolkein's Inklings, Asimov's New York Futurians. I thought that in all this vast human race there must be at least twenty or thirty people I could talk to. I never realized until now the mathematical fact that a set is still a set if it contains only one member. You can I are alike, Holly except for gender. You and I are like each other in every other way except one."

"What's that?" said Holly guardedly.

He gestured toward the door. "You can go out there and talk to those people. You can talk to them, and you can talk to me. I don't understand that. That seems impossible to me, a miracle. I could never do it. When they laugh with you, when they chatter away with you in that meaningless babble of theirs, you somehow find it in yourself to babble back. I hear it and hate you, envy you more than you can possibly imagine. To have a mind like yours and still be able to crouch down and waddle and quack with the ducks! My God, Holly, how do you do it?"

He reached out and convulsively clutched her hand. She felt an instant wave of revolsion, but controlled herself, showing no outward sign. *Let him clutch my hand,* she thought. *It's only a hand.*

"We are alike," she answered pensively. "Yes, you're right about that. Bright children in a classroom of idiots, giants in a world of pygmies. I'm sure our childhoods were virtually identical, up to a point."

"A point?"

"Something happened to me that apparently didn't happen to you. I was in kindergarden, hiding in the bushes to avoid daily beating at the hands of my classmates. Did your classmates beat you up every day?"

Brad turned quite pale. "Yes, they did."

"Then you understand. These pygmies have sharp instincts, if little intellect. They know we're not like them. They know we're a different species, that we're dangerous to them, to their pygmy world. So they attack! I wonder how many of us they kill before the age of twelve. They tried to kill me many times, but didn't quite succeed. Children are so poorly armed, with their silly little fists and fingernails, their bricks and jackknives. Did they try to kill you?"

"Yes," he whispered.

"Of course they would. And how did you react?"

"I started my search."

"Ah, then that is where our paths diverged. You found you were different and set out to find others like yourself. I found I was different, and ..." She paused, smiling, remembering. "...And I liked it."

"Liked it?" Brad looked at her with numb incomprehension.

"Yes." She closed her eyes. "I can remember every blade of grass, every stone, the smell of dust, the waxy green leaves in the bush, the distant shouts of the children, my enemies. Most of all I remember the ants, the red ants and the black ants. They fought and I watched. Do you know that whan an ant's head is torn from its body, it goes on fighting, clinging to its enemy, gnawing at its enemy's vitals? It doesn't try to understand its enemy. It doesn't try to work out a compromise. It doesn't appeal to a higher authority. It hangs on and gnaws and gnaws and gnaws. Its jaws aren't like ours. They're sideways instead of up and down, and they're sharp and strong, like a pair of scissors. When someone asked Jesus how to live, he told them to go to the ant for lessons! Ah yes, we have so much to learn from our little hardshelled friends. I hid in the bushes and watched. The recess bell rang and my kindergarden classmates went inside. I stayed there, watching the ants, until the teacher came and dragged me away. Too late! The fraction of a second had already passed, the fraction of a second when I suddenly, wonderfully understood what I was and how I should live my life, when I knew I was a lone red ant among the white ants and should behave accordingly. I was a red ant, and I liked it!"

"Did that help you to get along with people?" said Brad, puzzled.

"Of course! A red ant doesn't have to care what a white ant says or does. A red ant can move freely among the white ants and never turn into a white ant, as long as it can defend itself. The worst thing isn't dying, but becoming like them, and I knew that wasn't going to happen. I was what I was, forever! And I didn't waste one second of my precious time searching for other red ants. I knew I was one of a kind. I gloried in being one of a kind!"

"I've never heard anything so antisocial!"

She laughed scornfully. "Me? Antisocial? I'm out there, mixing with people. I know they don't really like me, but they can make use of my talents. I didn't finish my story. That very afternoon, when school let out, I formed an alliance with the biggest bully in my class. I did his homework and he pulverized whoever I told him to. My daily beatings stopped and nobody has laid a violent hand on me since. I'm a part of the world, a part of the market economy! But you... you started with a world that included the whole human race, then you narrowed it down to those who could pass the Mensa test, then those who could pass the stricter Sigma test, then only those who were hand-picked to ride in this laterday Noah's Ark. Finally here you are, all alone in one little room. Is anyone living here with you?"

"No, but...."

"Nobody has lived here with you since I've been on board. I understand Juanita did once. Wasn't she good enough for you either?"

"There have been others."

"I'll bet! You're the boss here. You get the pick of the crop. All you have to do is snap your fingers. Right? I've had a chance to study the Valhalla, and I have to hand it to you. You are a real, honest-to-God genius. The detail in this thing! The way everything fits together. I tell you honestly, I couldn't have done it. You're a superman, the genuine article, just like in the comic books. When Siegel and Shuster first invented Superman in 1933, they began by making him a super villain out to conquer the world by making the world's armies destroy each other. Only later did they convert Superman into the hero that continues to entertain the kiddies to this day. They had it right the first time, didn't they? Superman isn't really the champion of the weak and oppressed, is he? He's sitting up here waiting for the weak and the oppressed to exterminate each other. And he's all alone, without even a secret Clark Kent identity to slip into, with no Lois Lane, not even a Jerry Olsen. All alone!"

"I thought that you...." Brad began.

"You thought that I'd move in with you?"

"Yes."

"That I'd come and share your little hell?"

"You said we were alike." Brad was pleading now.

"Up to a point. Then we diverge. You went looking for

friends. I learned to live without them, to survive without them. That's a big difference, Superman."

"I could learn to be like you, Holly, if you'd teach me. I can learn anything." He smiled suddenly, a note of hope coming into his voice.

"How long will it take, Brad? Remember, I started in kindergarten. How many years have you got left? Ten? Fifteen? You're an old man, Brad. Old brains don't pick up things the way young brains do."

He jerked back as if struck, dropping her hands at last. "You can't talk to me like this! I can order you tossed out of Valhalla without a parachute."

"Can you?" she said softly, leaning forward. "An interesting experiment! Tell your crew to murder me. See if they obey."

He stood up, swaying, and took a few uncertain steps toward the intercom, then stopped.

"Go ahead," she prompted him. "Do it. I'm curious to see what will happen."

"They're with you now, aren't they?" he said in a dull lifeless voice.

"I think so. Yes."

"Get out of here."

She stood up. "Goodbye, Brad."

She walked to the door, taking her time, not hurrying, and let herself out. In the hallway, with the door shut behind her, she heaved a sigh of relief. *That was a close one,* she thought. *If he had actually told them to dump me overboard, they might have done it.*

*

Newton never got to see the movie, but he heard about it. It had regular private showings in Normandy Taylor's apartment, and by the end of the week nearly all the staff and most of the trustees had seen it.

"First-rate filth!" commented one critic.

"Rates one hundred on the pornograph!" raved another.

They especially praised Newton's performance. "His expression of bored detachment had me in stitches," chuckled Chaplain Bill, and Bill's words carried weight. He was well-known as a connoisseur of the genre.

Unfortunately Newton's fans were a more-than-ordinarily rowdy and abusive lot. They would follow him down the halls of the dorm, shouting things at him.

"How are you, Goldilocks?"

"And how are the three bears, Goldilocks?"

Part of his costume had been a blonde wig.

They would fall into step with him, paw him, put their arms around him, squeal at him in high falsetto voices, "How about a date, honey?"

"Daddy will give you a nice lollipop to suck."

"I saw you on the tube, sweetheart. You sure were sweet. You're such a sweet thing, aren't you? Isn't she a sweet thing, fellas?"

The fellas agreed, snickering and simpering.

The biggest of the lot cried, "Hey fellas, let me walk next to her. I'm jealous of you fellas!"

A huge, hairy paw lifted the hem of Newton's tunic.

"Oo, lookie! She's a he! Who ever would have believed it?"

"How does it feel to be a star, Goldilocks?"

Newton ignored them, letting them say what they liked, do what they liked with him, while he drifted off to a distant corner of his mind, to Etnroa, where Baboo played the poom-poom and a choir of Etnroans sang and danced in a stately circle. If the shouting, pushing, grabbing real world somehow broke through, he merely turned up the volume on his mind and drowned it out in a flood of beautiful sound. It was almost as good as, maybe better than, the screen.

And he took to spending even more time on Baboo's floor, where nobody knew him as Goldilocks, where Brother Judd patiently guided him through the labyrinthine mysteries of song. Newton learned fast. He could already play many of the haunting Etnroan melodies on the poom-poom, could alreay understand much of the clean, clear mathematics of music, of scales, modes and chords, of rhythm and time signatures and the time value of notes. They made sense in a way his school studies never had. And everything was clothed in the all-encompassing philosophy of Etnroa.

Brother Judd would stop next to Newton in the dorm that doubled as a classroom and say something like:

"All knowledge is latent in song."

And Newton would say:

"What about science?" (Or some such thing.)

And Brother Judd would pontificate something like:

"Science began with song, when Pythagoras discovered the simple ratios in the major chord. Science is contained in mathematics, and mathematics is contained in music, and music is contained in song."

Or if it was literature Newton asked about, Brother Judd

127

would say:

"Literature began with songs of heroes sung by the ancient bards, and in great literature that old music echoes yet."

But if Newton asked about nrobooks, Judd would frown and reply, "You aren't ready for that. Wait a while and ask me again."

And then, like as not, Newton would ask, "When?"

And Judd would answer with a question. "Why don't you sing?"

Everyone but Newton in his class sang.

Newton couldn't bring himself to do it. To the best of his knowledge he never had sung. His voice was not good, he told himself, and the very idea of making a fool of himself in public had always paralyzed him. It still did.

And though Brother Judd never said so, Newton began to see that he was flunking again. He saw it clearly, with a growing desperation, but still he could not force himself to open his mouth and croak out a few notes. He didn't mind preparing to sing. He would have been happy to spend the rest of his life preparing.

But actually singing? That would be really doing something, that would be making a commitment, a decision. That would be admitting that singing mattered. That would be caring. Then he would be hooked.

At last the day came when Brother Judd sighed and said, "Newton, Baboo wants to see you."

With some misgivings Newton made his way to the bunkroom where Baboo held court. The disciples sprawled on mats around the bunk that served as throne of Etnroa, gossiping in low voices. Baboo stared at the ceiling through half-closed eyes, reclining on a pile of pillows like some oriental potentate.

"Nro, Baboo," Newton greeted him.

"Nro, Newton," Baboo replied, still fixing his sleepy eyes on something above him. Newton was slightly flattered that the Master knew his name.

"You won't sing," Baboo said matter-of-factly.

"I can't," said Newton.

Baboo's white teeth showed in a broad smile. "Six of one and a half dozen of the other. I'm sad to hear that, but not surprised. I expected it."

"Why?"

"Some students come here and sing right away. Are they smarter than those who take awhile to start? Not always. Maybe they do it easy because they do it light. Song doesn't mean all that much to them. Then there's the other kind. Song means so much to them they can't touch it at first. It's too holy. Sometimes that kind makes the best singers, the singers with deep nro, the klains."

"Klains?" This was a word Newton had heard but didn't quite understand yet.

"A klain is a master of nro. A klain can teach. A klain can inspire. Brother Judd is a klain. I'm the klain of klains. Someday I'm going to die, and then someone else will be klain of klains. Someone with deep nro. Maybe you?"

Somewhat taken aback, Newton said, "Me? That can't sing at all?"

"That *won't*," Baboo corrected him. "Any damn fool can sing, but some won't. On principle maybe." He cocked an eye in Newton's direction, a rather playful eye. "You got a lot of song in you, boy. I can sense it. Maybe you've been saving up the song in you for years, for all your life, behind a kind of dam. It's all in there waiting, and when the dam bursts, we all better head for the hills. Right?"

"I don't know. Does it matter?" Newton couldn't keep the edge out of his voice.

"What do you think? Does it?"

"Whether I sing or not, the world will continue to rotate. I don't care."

"If you don't care, you might as well do it."

Newton's only reply was one of his typical silences.

"You see?" chuckled Baboo. "If it didn't matter, you'd do it and get it over with, just to get me off your back. It matters all right. You're ready to throw away everything you've learned and stomp on out of Etnroa forever rather than sing a few lousy notes, and I get a feeling Etnroa is all you got at the moment. Right now you'd rather die than sing! So don't tell me you don't care. Don't tell me that lie."

"And if I don't sing, nobody will ever tell me what a nrobook is?" said Newton, with a jeering tone directed as much at himself as at Baboo. *If you don't do your homework,* Newton thought *you don't get to watch TV.* Reward and punishment. Winners and losers. That was, he reflected, the story of his life.

"Dead wrong, Newton," said Baboo. "Who told you that?"

"Nobody, but I gathered from Brother Judd...."

"You gathered wrong, dummy. I'll show you a nrobook right now, if it'll make you happy." He rolled over, reached under the bed, and dragged out a book. It was as long and wide as a sheet of typewriter paper folded once, and about three or four hundred pages thick, and had a beautiful tooled leather binding. The spine bore the word "music" and a long number, while the front cover displayed, in colored leather, a sundisk with little hands at the ends of its rays, framed in a serpentine border.

"Beautiful," said Newton in spite of himself. He could honestly have said he'd never seen a better example of the bookbinder's art.

"Look it over, Newton." He handed it to him.

Newton opened the book and leafed slowly through the pages. Instead of typeface, he found a graceful and flowing calligraphy in brown ink on cream-colored paper set off with an occasional large capital letter in red. Some pages were decorated with illustrations in black ink and delicate watercolors, each a small masterpiece obviously hand-drawn and hand-painted. Some pages contained musical notations, everything from a few bars to a whole song, words and all. Some pages showed recipes and drawings of food. Some pages showed complex mathematical formulae. Some pages showed poems. Newton recognized a limerick, suitably bawdy, and on the next page a delicate Petrarchan sonnet laced with curious Etnroan words, doubtless the product of some busy session with the ouija board. Some pages showed prose, but with such a thick coating of Etnroanese it ceased to be English and Newton couldn't read it.

After a few minutes Newton raised his eyes from the text of a particularly profound, yet funny, passage to demand in wonderment, "How was this done?"

"By hand," Baboo answered softly. "From the cutting of the pages to the binding to the writing and illustrating, all by hand."

"How much would a copy cost?"

"A copy? The word copy loses all meaning when it refers to a nrobook, which is always published in editions of one single and unique copy. And you never sell a nrobook. You keep it as long as you need it, then you give it away."

"Give it away? After putting hundreds of hours of work into it?"

"What gift could be more sincere? But it takes less time than you probably think to make one of these, if you spend a few hours on it every day."

"Could you think of something to write every day?"

"If you wrote about the progress of your thought. You're always thinking, you know. You're always learning, like it or not. You're always evolving. The typical Etnroan style is like a diary that strives, with varying success, to make sense out of each day's events. On good days, when the nro is flowing through ets fingers, a writer can sometimes glimpse rather large portions of the pattern of ets life. Then et will write things that will be helpful to all the readers the book will have before it is worn out. But you've

had time to look it over. How do you like it?"
"It's amazing." Newton spoke unguardedly, forgetting his usual tight self-control.
"It's yours."
"No, no, I couldn't accept it. It's too much. I mean, what did I do to deserve...." Newton tried to hand the nrobook back.
"To refuse the gift is a great insult to the author," said Baboo, frowning.
"Who is the author?"
"I am."
Newton stopped trying to hand back the volume, and after a moment said softly, guardedly, "Now I really do have to sing, don't I?"
Baboo laughed. "Not at all! I don't want you to sing until the pressure builds up still more. When you have to sing, when you cannot stop yourself, that will be the time to sing. In the meantime, read my nrobook, enjoy it, and pass it on. At the least I think you will chuckle at the dirty jokes."
Newton clutched the book and fled.

*

That night, lying on his bunk before curfew, Newton opened the nrobook and began to read. The frontispiece was an ink-and-watercolor self-portrait of Baboo in an ornate and perspectiveless style that suggested Aubrey Beardsley or early Japanese prints, with a hint of the self-satirical cartoon, while the writhing serpentine-floral border and bold red and black calligraphy on the title page showed a strong Celtic influence. The title was "My Heart Laid Bare" by Baboo Robert Osborn, Volume forty-eight. A blank page followed, then the text began:

The previous books in this series recounted my fall from grace with my employers, my fruitless search for a new job, my arrest as a vagrant, my incarceration in what we laughingly call "The Camps," my unsuccessful quest for a religious or philosophical rationalization for my plight, my suicide attempt, my "dark night of the soul," my reading of the works of Edgar Allen Poe, and my ecstatic vision while singing the old folksong, "The Best Things in Life are Free."

They go on to tell how the Nro revealed etself to me in song, how I founded the Nation of Etnroa with myself as the only citizen, and of the year and a half before the population doubled. They go on to relate how Etnroa grew and spread, of the internal politics, the factions, the rebellions, the schisms, the defections by my closest friends, the gradual simplification of the Etnroan Way

131

into three elements; the song, the singing circles, and the nrobooks.

Since you may never to able to find these early volumes, I will repeat portions of them from memory wherever the occasion demands. For now it suffices to recall only the passage in "The Marginalia" by Edgar Allen Poe which provided the stimulus for the writing of the first nrobook.

Poe writes, "If any ambitious man have a fancy to revolutionize, at one effort, the universal world of human thought, human opinion, and human sentiment, the opportunity is his own—the road to immortal renown lies straight, open, and unencumbered before him. All he has to do is to write and publish a very little book. Its title should be simple—a few plain words—'My Heart Laid Bare.' But—this little book must be true to its title.

"Now, is it not very singular that, with the rabid thirst for notoriety which distinguishes so many of mankind—so many, too, who care not a fig what is thought about them after death, there should be found not one man having sufficient hardihood to write this little book? To write, I say. There are ten thousand men who, if the book were once written, would laugh at the notion of being disturbed by its publication during their life, and who could not even conceive why they should object to its being published after their death. But to write it—there's the rub. No man dare write it. No man ever will dare write it. No man could write it, even if he dared. The paper would shrivel and blaze at every touch of the fiery pen."

I owe more to Poe than to any predecessor. Indeed, Etnroa itself is only a word invented by me to fill the hole in the English language which et pointed out when et wrote, "I used the word fancies at random, and merely because I must use some word; but the idea commonly attached to the term is not even remotely applicable to the shadows of shadows in question."

But most of all, I owe to et the challenge et threw down to me from over the centuries, the challenge to write one honest book about my inner life.

Indeed, in my present circumstances I could not write a diary of my external life. In telling my own secrets, I would also tell the secrets of all those whose lives interweave with mine, and such a document might prove useful to the police or to blackmailers. Only my inner life remains as subject matter. Only what Poe called "My Heart." And this subject matter seems always to step back just out of reach whenever I try to grasp it, though I flatter myself I have marched deeper into this dark continent than any previous explorer.

All too well I now understand the fragment of verse left behind on some charred bits of paper by my second-greatest predecessor, George Sterling, when et swallowed cyanide in San Francisco's Bohemian Club in 1926:
"Deeper into the darkness can I peer
Than most, yet find the darkness still beyond."
Though I have become Baboo, Pope of Etnroa, Klain of Klains, all too well I understand those words. Nevertheless....

Chapter 12

Had she bluffed him? Or had Holly really won the allegiance of the crew, really fully usurped the throne? She did not know. She guessed, however, that the loyalty of the crew teetered in delicate balance, at one moment tipping in her direction, at another tipping in his.

She had played her game well, a quiet, positional game of pawn advances and bishops waiting on the long diagonals. Newton, she thought, would have been proud of her. But now the break had come and the middle game begun. Now her opponent, a brilliant man under ordinary circumstances, had realized a game was in progress and could still beat her if he could summon the will and the wit. In fact, she was sure that if the game was played fair, he would certainly win, so she had to see to it the game was not played fair.

She knew that, like Newton, Brad was caught up in the alcohol mystique, on some subconscious level believed the old witchdoctor-bard lie that alcohol brought inspiration, the lie that had cost so many creative people their creativity, even their lives. And he, somewhere deep down, also bought the old lie that the superior player in a game should accept a handicap, proving superiority by winning even when drunk. Brad might know how to design a flying city, but Holly knew how to make a man drink.

She could make him drink with a challenge. She could make him drink with a soft word. She could make him drink to regain his balance, and drink to relax, and drink to prove he loved her.

That, she realized, was her top piece in the game, her Queen. His fatal, helpless, blundering, self-pitying, drunken love for her. Alone in her cabin just before dawn she sat in the darkness, feeling the gentle pitch and roll of the Valhalla, and chuckled.

*

Mickey and Victor discussed Newton as they stood in line in the mess hall to pick up their algae soup.

"I'm worried about him," she said. "He missed supper again. All he does is lie on his cot and read some weird handwritten book and stare at the ceiling. I speak to him and he doesn't answer."

Victor replied with his habitual bitterness, "What he needs is a good fuck."

"Don't you think I've tried that, Victor? Sometimes his body responds, though not always. But his mind? In the very middle of orgasm, he's thinking of something else, something far away. I can tell."

They took their trays and found themselves a table.

"I know his kind," said Victor grimly. "He looks peaceful and detached as a Buddha, but inside he's at war."

"With who?"

"With himself. He thinks his enemy is within. He thinks he is somehow responsible for what's happened to him so he feels guilty and full of self-loathing. You know, the old Jewish syndrome. And he hates himself and spends all his energy shadowboxing inside his soul, but you and I, out here in the real world, can't hear the thud of the punches and the moans and grunts, can't see the blood-caked lips and the black eyes. Sooner or later he'll realize his enemy isn't inside, but out here. His enemy is the Techman. Then he'll join us, and he'll be the best kind of fighter, the kind that obeys orders and doesn't give a damn what happens to him, the kind that would rather kill than ball."

"Newton wouldn't kill anybody!"

"Oh yeah? He's a born killer. Why else do you think I waste my valuable time on him?"

"No, no, not my Newton." She had become genuinely distressed.

"Newton is kind and gentle. That's why everybody walks all over him. He can't even stand up for his rights."

"There's another Newton, one you don't know."

"I don't believe you."

Victor peered up at her from under his eyebrows. "Maybe I can arrange an introduction."

"How?"

He paused before answering, sizing her up. "Have you ever really looked at Newton's nose?"

"His nose?" The question caught her off balance.

"The way the blue veins stand out?"

"What do you mean? What are you talking about?"

"Newton is an alcoholic, Mickey. I can spot one a mile away. With a few drinks under his belt he'll drop his mask and show us his real face."

Mickey asked herself silently, *Why do I have to get through to Newton?*

Mickey answered herself silently, *So I can be, in his eyes at least, a women, not...a freak.*

Still she hestitated.

"How about it?" Victor demanded smugly. "Say the word and I can have my boys steal some good whiskey from the staff quarters and plant it in his bunk. Nothing easier."

"I don't know...."

"What's the matter? Afraid of the truth?"

Mickey looked away, biting her lip, and caught sight of Piggy threading her way through the crowd toward them. "Mickey!" called out the filthy little creature, her empty face lighting up. She ran over and grabbed Mickey's hand and began kissing it frantically. "Mickey!" she cried delightedly. "Piggy love Mickey!"

"Get that freak out of here," Victor growled, pushing back his chair. "Get her out before I lose my supper."

Mickey jumped up angrily. "All right, but I'm going too!" Still holding Piggy's grubby paw Mickey took a few steps away from the table, then turned, a thoughtful expression on her face.

"Victor?" she said softly.

"You want me to get the whiskey for Newton?"

"Yes." Her voice was barely audible.

Through his one good eye Victor watched Mickey leave, dragging Piggy along behind her. He grinned and muttered approvingly, too low for anyone to hear, "Hey Mickey baby, you got a nice ass on you there, a real nice ass."

*

Holly reached under her skirt and brought forth a bottle of homebrew with the air of a stage magician. "Presto!" she exclaimed.

"Amazing!" said Brad, his haggard face breaking into a smile. She placed the bottle ceremoniously in his shaking hands. He eagerly unscrewed the cap and took a swallow. "You want some?" He offered her the bottle.

"No, thanks. Not now."

"All the more for me." He collapsed into his accustomed place in the conversation pit and peered down at the cloud-shrouded mountains and valleys. "We're off course," he said listlessly.

"No," she corrected him. "We're on a new course."

"A new course? Who plotted it? You?"

"That's right, with some help from Smith. The weather has taken an unexpected turn, so we had to adapt to it."

He fixed her with a bloodshot eye. "But you have everything under control?"

"I think so."

He laughed mirthlessly and took another swig. "You understand everything, don't you? The weather, the crew, me."

"Nobody understands everything."

"Ah, and you're so humble, too. The perfect woman! Sit down. I hate to have someone loom over me."

She seated herself opposite him. "Are you angry at me, Brad?"

"Why should I be angry? Was the Neanderthal man angry when displaced by the CroMagnon man? Who are we to question the relentless march of evolution? Who are we to complain if the rise and fall of a subspecies, which once took millennia, now takes only a few years? The others, the inferior ones, want to deny me even the solace of firewater, but you bring me what I need."

"I treat you as an adult, able to make your own decisions. If you want to drink, I have no right to stop you, nor does anyone else. When they voted to cut off your booze ration, I refused to accept their decision."

He leaned forward awkwardly to pat her on the knee. "You're an anarchist or a monarchist, one of the two," he said with genuine fondness.

"An anarchist when out of power, a monarchist when in," she said, smiling coolly.

He fell back into his seat, laughing uproariously. "Beautiful! Beautiful! I love it! Yes, you're the Queen of Valhalla now, future monarch of the world."

"If I am Queen, as you say, shouldn't you tell me where you've hidden that so-called *Encyclopedia Galactica* you told me about?"

He sat up, a cunning glitter in his eye. "I'm surprised you haven't found it by yourself, you're so clever. Have you searched the Valhalla? Have you questioned the onboard computer?"

"Yes."

"And you haven't found it?"

"No."

"Why don't we make this my little intelligence test for you?" he said, hugely amused. "If you can find it, you deserve to replace me. If you can't, you won't."

"What do you mean?" she said uneasily.

"The Encyclopedia contains, among all its other treasures, certain facts you will need to know to avoid wrecking the Valhalla." He spoke these words clearly, without a trace of alcoholic slurring, looking at her with gleaming, playful, sober eyes. "You said, a moment ago, that you thought you had everything under control. Do you still think that?"

"Yes. And I think you're bluffing. In fact, I have no proof this Encyclopedia exists."

"It exists, I assure you, and for lack of it you have already made one mistake."

"A mistake? When?"

"When you changed course," said the old man with grotesque satisfaction. "Now go away and let me enjoy my moonshine."

Holly stood up and turned to leave.

"If you give up," he called after her, "you know where to find me, but if you love life don't wait too long."

Outside in the hallway, where nobody could see her, Holly leaned against the carved door, eyes closed, and struggled to regain her composure. The chess metaphors in which she had been thinking so much lately come thronging once again into her mind, but with a new, ugly emotional charge, and she remembered those times without number when she had been certain she was winning just before hearing Newton's cheery "Check," then "Mate." Was this game, played for the highest possible stakes, going to end the same way?

*

What's this?

There's something under my pillow, thought Newton.

He reached under and drew it out. A bottle of whiskey! In the dim light of the murmuring bunkroom, Newton sat on the edge of his bed and stared, dumbfounded.

A mystery! Where did you come from, little bottle?

The bottle said nothing.

Bottles have nothing to say to people, no matter how long and loud you harangue them. This particular bottle, mute, inscrutable, had printing on the label at least. "Old John Kennedy, 100 proof" in large, old-fashioned letters with fat serifs, then a lot of other useless information in smaller letters and more modern type. From the center of all this sternly stared the face of one-time

American President John F. Kennedy, an imitation line engraving, like money.

The glass in the bottle glinted faintly green. Inside he could see an amber liquid. He could tell by the broken seal someone had already sampled it, but the bottle still was three-quarters full. He ran his forefinger slowly over the smooth, cool body of the thing and discovered a small bas-relief rose on the neck.

Newton thought, *Strange how I have this impulse to speak to bottles. People often speak to things, but the things never answer. People often treat things like people, speaking of the "neck" of a bottle for example. This bottle is dead. The liquid inside is dead. I look at the liquid and it doesn't look back. Once it was alive. Strands of grain waving in the sun have a kind of life, but the reapers cut down the grain and someone mashes it and ferments it and distills it until nothing remains but the "spirits."*

Are spirits really dead? All the way dead?

They certainly look dead, sitting there in the bottle saying nothing.

But if you drink them a miracle takes place!

Like God, you give life to dead, inert matter.

The spirits live and move and have their being within you, as part of your living body. They enter your mind, sway the balance of your thought more forcefully than any logic or oratory. Do the spirits think then? Do they feel and will?

"I think, therefore I am" someone once said.

But what if you stop thinking? Do you cease to be? And if you cease to be, who does all those things you can't remember doing but people tell you you did? Is it the spirits? That's what you tell people. "It was the booze," *you say.*

Newton opened the bottle, sniffed the familiar, good, stinging smell, listened to the familiar good splash and slosh, then he drank, tasting the good old taste, the cool flow, the burn on the way down, and he felt the spreading warmth deep in his guts, the familiar good warmth.

The other Newton blinked, coughed, and wiped his mouth with the back of his hand.

"Boy, that was good, after all this time!"

And he drank and drank again.

Finally...

Bottle empty. Damn. I drank it all. Shouldn't drink on empty stomach. Feel sick. Dizzy. Mickey, Mickey, where are you? "Right here, Newton. What's wrong?" *Everything's tipping, Mickey. I'm going to fall out of my bunk.* "No, you're not." *Yes I am!* "Let me help you down, Newton. If you lie in my bunk you won't have so far to fall." Thank you, thank you. You're a wonderful person Mickey. So sweet and kind. Don't blush. It's true. Any whiskey left? No? That's too bad. I want to offer you a drink. I want to drink a toast! To you! God, you're pretty. Lie down beside me, Mickey. How come you wear this yellow thing? You should wear orange. You always used to wear orange. "No, Newton, I never wore orange." Sure you did, but never mind. Take it off. That's the spirit. That's much better. You look best bare naked. I love you that way. Did you know I loved you, Mickey? "I thought you hated me, Newton." Hated you? Impossible! Why should I hate you? "Because of my hunchback." Who cares about that? I like freaks. We're all freaks here. I hate normal people. Do you love me, Mickey? "Oh yes, Newton, I do, I do!" Are you my wife? "If you want me, Newton." I want you, always did, always will. "Why didn't you say so before?" I didn't want to take a chance. Women leave me. Sooner or later they go. "Not me, Newton." Yes, even you. You'll leave me, and it'll damn near kill me. "No, Newton. Never!" Faithful and true, that's me, Mickey, but... sooner or later I get left.

    Angrily, fiercely, she kissed his lips to silence him, then they made pledges and vows; mad, impossible pledges and vows that mere humans should never make because they can never keep them, and then they made love as if for the first time, and it was good, and he didn't care if the people in the other bunks watched.

    Next morning Newton awoke with a murderous hangover. The old man in the next bunk, grinning, told Newton what he'd done, what he'd said. Newton remembered nothing at all beyond that first drink.

    He searched for the bottle and found it tangled in the blankets, empty.

    "Mickey?" he called out weakly.

    "She went to the gym," said the old man. "You should go to gym yourself. You already missed breakfast."

    "Oh no," Newton moaned, head in hands.

    "She really got to you, son," the man said gleefully.

    All Newton could remember was a dream he'd had just before waking, a dream of Holly, the little room in his parent's apartment, the computer school, everything like it used to be so long ago.

    "Oh no," Newton repeated, the pain in his head so intense he could hardly think. "What have I done?"

Chapter 13

Brad had emerged from his self-made prison while Holly slept. She only heard about it second hand, when she came on duty. Little Sewall Smith, on the overlap shift in the insurance computer department, told her what had happened.

Sitting at his desk before a blank computer display screen, Smith spoke with awe, his voice low and shaking slightly. Holly sat at the next desk, leaning toward him as if he were telling her some kind of secret, though of course everyone on board would soon know all the embarrassing details.

"I was surprised to see him come into the general office area," said Smith. "He used to do that occasionally, but lately, since he's been sick...." Smith, like the rest of the crew, had begun using the word sick to mean drunk. "Lately he's kept pretty much to himself."

"Was he, as you say, *sick* today?" she asked.

"No, not when we first saw him. He went from desk to desk, greeting us like old times, like nothing had ever happened, smiling, joking. But it wasn't really like old times. He was trying too hard, if you know what I mean. He was putting on an act, trying to be 'One of the boys.' That never was his style. We couldn't accept it, and of course he saw that. He's no fool. That was at the beginning of the shift. Later he came back, only this time sick."

"You mean drunk."

"Might as well say it. Everybody knows that's what I mean. Yes, he was drunk. He passed out right over there, by the staircase." He pointed.

Hall Waterman, who had been passing, stopped and added to the story. "We had to carry him back to his room." He too had a note of awe in his voice. "I've never seen him like this before. I can't understand what's come over him."

Holly said quickly, "We'll have to carry on without him until he straightens out. You're in command now, Hal."

The big man paused, confused. "I suppose that's right, isn't it?" He tried the idea on for size and, after a moment, liked it. He began to smile.

Holly understood his confusion. For some time now, though she had been given no official position, Holly had been in de facto command. Now it was necessary for Hal to feel he was in control, to like the feeling, thought Holly. *Hal must have a stake in keeping Brad sick.*

But Hal was saying, "Poor guy. We should do something for him."

Holly didn't like the sound of that. "He doesn't like people overprotecting him," she said smoothly. "But I'll see what I can do."

Hal said, "I don't know. While he was drunk he said you were trying to take over the Valhalla. I don't think he trusts you. Maybe someone else should try to talk to him. You've been doing it all."

"I don't mind," said Holly.

"Maybe Juanita Castro," said Hal. "She used to be very close to him."

Holly did a quick calculation of the human factors in the situation. Yes, Juanita would be a fairly good choice. Juanita, who Brad had rejected. Juanita, who might never admit it but who thirsted for revenge. "Good idea," said Holly, yet she had a sense of something going wrong, of power crumbling ever-so-little, of the presence of Brad's passed pawn. She would, she realized, have to do something to firm up her position or sheer force of habit would gradually erode her hard-won advantage.

The crew was drifting back to Brad's side. She could feel it. In that instant she thought of her countermove.

*

Mickey had lunch with Victor again, as she had done so many times before.

"What did I tell you?" gloated Victor, talking with his mouth full. "He's an alcoholic, like I said."

Mickey answered wistfully, "Maybe, but when he was drunk he loved me."

"Ha! A drunk loves everybody and anybody. And nobody. A drunk doesn't know the meaning of the word."

"Do you know the meaning of the word?" she challenged.

"I know, baby. Believe me, I know."

"Explain it to me then."

"Love is spending time with someone, the way I spend time with you." He had dropped his usual bantering tone.

"Don't say things like that."

"I mean it." He reached out and laid his hand gently over hers.

"I know you're lying, Victor," she added listlessly, but did not draw back her hand.

"That's your feelings of rejection and inferiority talking, Mickey. You think if Newton doesn't love you, nobody can."

She closed her eyes. "It's true. He has hardly spoken to me for three days, ever since the night he got drunk. We were wrong, Victor. It was wrong to get him drunk and trick him. I should have simply accepted the obvious, that he didn't want me and never would. Why should he? I'm not smart or pretty. I'm an Un. I'm a hunchback. He at least never lied to me, not while he was sober."

"You little fool." Victor's voice held an odd mixture of tenderness and contempt. "You know why you like him so much? Because he's a baby, groping for a tit, not a real man."

"And you're a real man?"

"I can love you like a man."

"Lies. Lies. Lies," she said wearily, slowly shaking her head like a woman who hasn't slept for days. "You'd say anything to seduce me, to cut one more notch in your dick. I wish you'd stop it though, because I want so much to believe someone could love me, I might start pretending...."

"Pretend then," Victor commanded softly, his hand tightening on hers, strong but not painfully strong, inescapable and even a little frightening.

When Victor left the mess hall, Mickey went with him.

He took her to the one place he knew where they could find privacy, the air conditioning shaft, and there he spread their yellow robes to make a rough bed, a little protection against the hardness and coldness of the metal floor.

He took his time, always in control, yet always gentle and considerate. She could not help but compare him with the clumsy, drunken Newton. She never had to tell Victor what to do. He always knew, as if he could read her mind. Actually it was not her mind but her body he read. Each tensing of the muscles, each little gasp and moan had meaning for him. Her lips on his imparted as much information to his everwatching mind as if they had spoken, or more, since words can lie so much more easily than the involuntary reactions of the body and the nervous system. Victor took pride in pleasing a woman, and he had pleased many. Each in turn taught him how better to please the next.

When it was over they lay side by side, fingers interlaced, breathing deeply. In the dim light they could barely make out each others faces. The breeze was cold on their sweating bodies and the metal cold under their backs, but they lay motionless a long time, as if too tired to move.

"Victor," said Mickey at last. "Tell the truth. You don't really love me, do you?"

After a long pause, Victor answered in a whisper, "No."

"That's all right," she sighed. "You loved me the best you knew how."

"Any complaints?"

She rolled over and planted a chaste, sisterly kiss on his cheek, then giggled.

"Not so loud, Mickey. Someone might hear us."

"Nobody's here but us."

At that instant they both heard the unmistakable sound of a stealthy footstep.

Victor sprang to his feet, crouching, clutching the knife he had grabbed from the pile of clothing. "Mickey," he snapped. "Get back. Someone's standing in the tunnel down there, watching us."

"Oh my God," she murmured, scuttling a little way on her hands and knees.

"Listen, Mickey. If anything happens to me, run like hell. The grating is just around the bend in the shaft." He knelt an instant, fishing a ring of keys from his clothes and throwing it in her direction. "The biggest key on the ring will let you out. Run like hell and don't look back and keep your mouth shut. As far as anybody is concerned, you weren't here. Understand?"

"I understand."

"I have enemies, inside the movement and out. If you shut up they may leave you alone."

"I won't say anything." She clutched the keys.

"Who's there?" Victor called out.

No one answered, but something small and metallic hit the floor with a clink.

"Who's there I say!" Victor advanced toward his unseen foe, knife at the ready.

From the darkness came a flat, emotionless voice. "Go ahead

and kill me. I don't care."

Victor raised his knife.

Mickey screamed, "No, Victor! It's Newton!"

And indeed Newton came forward out of the gloom, ghostly in his monkish robes, his face expressionless. He passed Victor at a slow, shuffling pace, stepped over Mickey's legs, and continued on his way. From beyond the bend in the shaft they heard Newton's key in the lock, the grate opening and closing, then nothing but their own breathing and the distant whirr of the fans.

"Let me help you up," said Victor, extending his hand.

"No! Let me go!" Crablike she scuttled past him and deeper into the tube. "You planned this, didn't you? You sent him on some errand that would bring him here at exactly this moment. Didn't you?"

He did not answer.

"You monster!" she screamed.

Abruptly her hand came in contact with something on the floor of the tube. She picked it up and, more by touch than by sight, identified it as a cheap, handmade tin ring, the kind Uns made for each other in handicrafts, the kind they used as wedding rings.

"Come on, Mickey. Let's go."

She held up the ring and shouted, "He was going to give me a ring, damn you!"

"I know."

"You know?"

"He told me."

"He was going to finally really love me."

"I didn't want him getting too domestic. He's good for better things."

"For killing?"

Victor shrugged and began getting dressed. He tossed her her robe and took the keys from her. "Let's go," he said a second time.

"I'm not going with you."

"Then I'll have to leave you here. I'll have to lock you in."

Reluctantly she followed him.

She thought, *Victor is so clever, so ruthless, so evil. If he wants me again, will I dare refuse him?*

*

Newton never spoke to Mickey again.

She spoke to him, though, or rather *at* him.

As he lay in his upper bunk in the darkness trying to sleep, she would sit up in her lower bunk addressing an endless monolog to him in an instense low voice until someone in a nearby bed would tell her to shut up.

In the morning, before the reveille buzzer, she would begin again, first murmuring a tentative hello, then, receiving no reply, proceeding to disconnected small talk, then to apologies, then to pleas for forgiveness. When the buzzer sounded she had often reached the stage of weeping, but Newton only jumped from his perch and strode away, not looking at her.

Nine days later a morning came when she went beyond weeping.

She began with her usual timid greeting, her halting and painful little hello. As usual Newton did not reply. As usual she went on to say how sorry she was and how miserable and lonely. "I don't ask much of you. Just say something to me. Anything. Call me names. Call me a traitor, a liar, a whore, a freak, a monster! Anything! Only just speak to me."

Silence.

"Is it because I'm ugly? Because I'm a hunchback? I can't help that. That's God's fault, not mine. I know I'm a fool. I know I was wrong about you. Can't you give me one little word? One tiny little word?"

Silence.

"Newton, act like a human being! I can't stand it any longer. It tears me in two to have you hate me. It drags my guts out by the roots. If you don't love me, at least have pity on me. At least stop hurting me with your silent hate. You crush me. You grind me. What happened to the other Newton I knew? Always so gentle and kind. How can you change so? How can you suddenly start killing me, slowly and horribly? Is that what you want? To kill me? Tell me that's what you want and I'll kill myself for you gladly."

Silence.

"I'm crying again. I always used to be so happy. No matter what happened, I could always make a joke out of it, but now...." She began to sob in earnest. "Newton, stop it! I can't stand it any more. Stop it! *Stop it!*"

Silence.

Then the reveille buzzer squawked.

Cots creaked as drowsy figures sat up, yawned and stretched. The lights snapped on. Newton's feet and legs appeared before Mickey's tear-distorted gaze, dangling down from the upper bunk.

He jumped to the floor, carefully keeping his back to her, and began to walk away.

This time she sprang after him.

"I'll *make* you speak to me, you bastard!" She seized his arm. "Say something, damn you!"

He only stood there, his face turned away.

She kicked him in the shins, but her feet were bare and couldn't really hurt him.

"Speak, Newton!"

She clawed his cheeks with her fingernails. He raised his hand in a half-hearted gesture of self-defense. Screaming like an enraged bird of prey, she attacked him again with her fingernails, then with pounding little fists, then again with feet. He protected his face with his arms, but otherwise remained passive. At last she threw her full weight against him, knocking him off balance. He fell to one knee and with an unhuman howl she kicked him in the face, then kicked him again in the side, knocking him over onto his back. She sprang into the air as he lay there and landed on his stomach with both feet. "I'll kill you! I'll kill you! I'll kill you!" she shrieked over and over again as she lost her balance and fell on top of him, raking his flesh with her nails, adding more bleeding red lines to those already there.

Dimly she sensed strong arms pulling her off him. She struggled against them with the strength of a mad animal. In the dizzy whirling panorama of flowing cots and twisted faces and bodies, she saw Newton dazedly get to his feet, looking at the blood on his hands. She saw him turn his opaque expressionless eyes toward her a moment, then slowly walk away.

Her screaming and struggling went on and on until a worried-looking Security Policeman gave her an injection to put her to sleep.

Chapter 14

As Summer came on the jetstream edged further and further south, and the Valhalla followed, exploring regions of the atmosphere that, according to Sewall Smith, they had never visited before. Smith, Hal Waterman, Juanita Castro and Holly sat in the navigation room, gazing down through the broad curving windows at the gleaming waters of the Mediterranean. Below, almost out of sight in the blind spot, rocky Corsica thrust itself up through the translucent sea. Here and there they could make out the white wakes of sailing ships, but the ships themselves could not be seen from this altitude.

Smith said pensively, "You're right, Holly. The southwest monsoons are bound to carry us back from the heat equator. It's only that Brad never liked to come that far south for fear of getting becalmed in the doldrums."

"We'll see India for the first time from the Valhalla," said Holly. "And you know I'm right. There's no danger. Brad tended to be too conservative about a lot of things." Even though President Bradbury Douglas was very much alive, they had fallen into the habit of talking about him in the past tense.

Hall said, "We'll come awfully close to the Himalayas. They're the highest mountains on this planet."

Holly said, "But we'll clear them, of course, with plenty of altitude to spare."

"I guess so," said Hal. "But for some reason Brad always

steered clear of them."

Juanita Castro laughed scornfully and said, "He's crazy, that man. Paranoid. All he talks about is how Holly is taking over the Valhalla."

Hal shook his head sadly, "It might make sense if he thought it was me taking over. After all, I'm the one in charge until he recovers his wits."

"If he ever does," Juanita added. Holly smiled gently, thinking about how they had taken to locking Brad in his room...for his own good. Still, there remained in the voices of the crew a lingering awe for his genius, a feeble remnant of respect, of belief in his infallibility. To destroy that, she would have to get them to do something Brad had forbidden, and get away with it. *Pawn takes pawn,* she thought. On the other side of the Himalayas her little chess match with Brad would enter the endgame.

Smith frowned. "The wind is stange in Tibet, more like the winds of Mars than of any place on Earth. Most of the time it howls through the mountain passes and across the plateau like the demonic minions of Siva. If you have anything to say, you have to say it before midmorning. After that the wind drowns out everything. The Tsang Po they call it as they pray for it to stop, but if, as sometimes happens, it does stop, men and animals soon become stricken with ghastly, undiagnosable disease, often fatal. Some say the atmosphere there has certain properties science has never succeeded in explaining."

Holly laughed. "Stop it, Smith. You're going to spook yourself."

Smith joined in the laughter, somewhat nervously, "Those are just rumors, of course," he admitted.

Holly understand full well what was going on. They weren't really afraid of the Himalayas, but of Brad's taboo. In a sense they still regarded him as Valhalla's god, for he had indeed created it. Everything they could touch up here had originated in Brad's imagination. How could they defy him, break his commandments? Even now, when they held him under virtual house arrest? When they had cut off all his communication with the outside world, when they had usurped control of his international financial empire? How could they defy him?

Holly had long ago worked out a plan for just such a moment as this, but had hoped she would not have to use it. She did not like outright fraud. She did not like to risk discovery. Far better to take the truth and bend it a little, then a little more, then a little more. But sometimes only a fraud will do, and this, it seemed to her, was one of those times.

She said, "I have an uncomfortable feeling, all the same."

Her timing was perfect. Three pairs of fearful eyes turned to stare at her.

"Let's check over the Valhalla, just in case," Holly added. Her voice projected still more fear, but inside she felt only calm determination tinged with triumph, the triumph of an actress turning in a bravura performance.

"Don't get excited," she finished. "It's only a hunch."

Looking at their faces, she could hardly restrain herself from laughing.

*

Newton sat on the floor among Baboo's inner circle of disciples at the foot of the black giant's bunk, half-turned to look up into his glittering dark eyes.

"Did you read my book, Newton?" Baboo asked.

"Yes. Do you want it back?"

"No. Keep it until you meet someone you think might find it useful. I'm writing a new nrobook now. I can't be bothered watching out for an old one. Let it go out into the world and wander from hand to hand, making its own way if it can. But I must return your nrobook to you. Most of the pages are still blank."

He leaned forward to hand Newton a crudely-made cloth-bound book without ornament. Accepting it, Newton asked, "What do you think of it?"

Baboo reclined on one elbow and regarded Newton seriously. "I think you are a klain, Newton."

Newton paled. "I? A klain? Don't try to pump up my ego with a lot of crap. I know what I am. I don't even sing."

Baboo nodded slowly. "No, you don't, but from what you write I can tell there is song within you. When at last you open your mouth a song will come forth that will change the world. You know I feel no false modesty, that I know my own greatness with a certainty neither praise nor criticism can touch, but I tell you I hear as I read your words a voice that will be far greater than mine, so that history will remember me only because I was associated with you."

"Come on now," Newton shifted uncomfortably.

Baboo chuckled. "Ah, modesty! You may regard modesty as a virtue, but I call it a vice, the worst vice of all, that cripples us, makes pygmies of us when we could be giants. Who knows what humanity could have done without it? Certainly we would have at least reached the stars, at least learned to live forever. Don't let modesty cripple you, my boy."

"I'm not modest," said Newton bitterly.

"Then what is your problem?"

"I'm empty." His voice was grey. "To sing, you must feel, and I feel nothing."

After a long pause, Baboo said gently, "In the landscape of the soul there is a desert, a wilderness, an emptyness, and each great singer must cross this desert to reach the beginning of ets road. Jesus. Buddha. Moses. Mohammed. Each wandered through the wasteland, speaking to demons, speaking to empty air, listening to the wind, before finding ets dove, ets bo tree, ets stone tablets, before finding ets true voice. I have hope for you exactly because I see you have entered this desert, following in the footsteps of those few who have been true klains, greater klains that I. Of all those I have met since I founded Etnroa, only you have been empty enough to give me hope."

Newton stood up. "I have to go now.' He turned to leave.

"Wait," Baboo called after him. "What do you think of what I just told you?"

Newton turned back to face him, saying in a flat tone, "Do you really want to know?"

"Of course."

"I think you're full of shit," said Newton McClintok.

Some of Baboo's disciples jumped up, furious, but Baboo only threw back his head and roared with laughter. Newton could still hear that laughter behind him as he left the room and shuffled down the hall toward the airshaft.

*

Since Mickey had been drapped away that day she'd attacked Newton, the dwarf Piggy, with doll, had moved into Mickey's old bunk under Newton. Night after night Newton had listened to the ugly little woman weeping and calling out, "Mickey! Mickey! Mickey!" At first it had ruined his sleep, but after a while he got used to it, as he had gotten used to all the other strange noises made by his miscellaneous neighbors in the other bunks.

Against his better judgment, Newton had begun to talk to Piggy, even help her, from time to time, to comb the doll's hair with a toothbrush. It seemed to him a safe relationship. Piggy was, after all, more like an animal than a human being, and animals had never treated Newton badly.

He talked to her, though he talked to nobody else in his bunkroom. She never demanded that he make sense, that he pay serious attention to her aimless childlike babbling. A meaningless grunt or nod from him every three or four minutes satisfied her competely, and he, in turn, found her maundering a soothing kind of background music for his thoughts.

But now, as he returned to his bunk from his visit to Baboo, Piggy came running to meet him, screaming hysterically, "Doll gone! Doll gone!"

Much to his distaste, she flung her grubby arms around his legs so he could hardly walk and began dragging him toward her bunk, shouting, "Baby! Baby! Baby! Where baby?"

"How should I know?" Newton muttered.

When they reached the bed, Newton saw the sparse bedding had been torn off onto the floor in Piggy's frantic search. "Where? Where? Where?" she howled.

He looked at the bed, trying to concentrate, trying to get his mind off the strange things Baboo had been telling him. Had Piggy lost the doll? Mislaid it somewhere? That seemed impossible. The two were almost as inseparable as Siamese twins. Had someone stolen it? That too seemed impossible. Who would be mean enough to steal a doll from a retard?

Newton glanced around.

A small crowd had gathered, and among the others Newton saw Victor. Around Victor's lips twitched the faintest trace of a smile. "Hello, Newton. Got any messages for me?"

Newton did have messages. He had continued to carry messages for the underground in spite of what Victor had done to Mickey. "Messages? Only one, Victor, you bastard. Did you steal Piggy's doll?"

Victor raised his eyebrows, "Who, me? Don't be silly. What would I do with...."

"When she was asleep, did you...."

"You're crazy!" Victor exclaimed, but in his voice Newton caught the merest hint of falseness.

Newton turned on his heel and marched away, Piggy scampering along beside him and Victor trailing along behind, amused. He knew where Victor's bunk was, having delivered messages to him several times there, and now he strode swiftly down the hall and into Victor's bunkroom straight up to Victor's bunk.

Newton lifted the pillow.

There lay the poor, battered, filthy "baby."

With a whoop of joy Piggy rushed forward to snatch it up in her arms, covering its face with kisses, hugging it, cooing to it, drooling over it, murmuring fragmentary phrases to it.

Newton turned slowly to face Victor. It was one, thing to fuck around with Mickey or himself, but something, as pathetic as Piggy....

Newton heard a roaring in his ears that grew louder and louder. All the evil he'd ever seen on the newscasts spun in his brain. Distorted faces began to whirl around him, faster and faster. People were looking at him strangely from the surrounding bunks, seeming to hold their breath, seeming to wait for something; he didn't know what. Bright lights flashed that he somehow knew were not real, that he knew were just in his head. The roaring grew, as if he were in a subway train, rushing down a tunnel at a thousand kilometers an hour. He felt the whole weight of his life pressing him forward from behind.

"A little joke...." Victor began. Then he took a close look at Newton.

His voice trailed off.

Newton took a step forward.

Victor retreated warily, still smiling.

There was a brief rustle as Victor's bunkmates scrambled out of the way, then a strained silence fell over the crowd. Victor continued to retreat until he backed into the rear wall of the room, then he stopped, crouching slightly, waiting. Newton kept coming, one slow step at a time.

Victor lowered his guard and opened his mouth to speak, but before he could utter more than a tentative "Uh....," Newton lunged, his long fingers stretching out to grasp Victor's throat. The defense was even more sudden than the attack. A knee in the groin, a quick swipe to deflect Newton's hands, and a judo chop to Newton's neck.

Newton, bent over and dizzy with pain, fell back as Victor pressed his advantage, ducking, weaving, hacking at Newton with the bladelike edges of his hands. Newton halted, straightening, then shuffled forward, wildly throwing punches. Out of the corner of his eye he glimpsed Piggy some distance away, sitting on the floor and playing with her doll, paying no attention to the fight, then Victor caught his arm, bent over, and threw Newton over his shoulder. Newton landed on a bunk, which promptly collapsed under him.

Victor's friends sent up a whimsical cheer.

Newton rolled off the wreckage and dragged himself to his feet, swaying.

Grinning, Victor ducked another wild punch, then rammed the heel of his hand into Newton's face, right under the nose and above the mouth. Newton sagged, shook his head, and kept on coming. Victor danced backward, faked a punch, and as Newton dodged, Victor bounded into the air, his foot shooting out to strike Newton on the cheek. If it had landed on Newton's jaw it could easily have broken some bones, at least dislodged a few teeth.

Newton fell sprawling melodramatically, destroying yet another bunk. Victor's friends cheered again and shouted encouragement to their champion.

On his hands and knees, Newton looked at the floor, saw drops of his own blood landing, drip, drip, drip. Coughing and spitting, newton managed to blurt out, "I'm going to kill you, Victor."

Victor laughed.

Victor's friends jeered.

Newton crawled forward, lashed out and grabbed Victor's left ankle. Victor tried to tug free but failed, then leaned over to chop at Newton's head and shoulders with the blades of his hands. Still Newton hung on. Victor retreated, dragging Newton along the floor. Newton gave a jerk and brought Victor to the floor, struggling and flailing, his smile fading. Hand over hand Newton dragged himself up Victor's writhing body, only to find Victor's fingers groping for his eyes. Newton screamed with pain and had to let go to keep from being blinded. In an instant Victor was free and on his feet. "So, Newton," he cried, "You want to play rough? Okay, we play rough."

Newton felt fists, feet and knees thumping into him, heard Victor panting at his work, felt blood in his mouth, in his throat, choking him. Yet Newton was strangely detached, as if all this were happening to someone else. Somehow he got to his feet again and tottered toward the enemy he could now hardly see. Somehow he managed to catch hold of Victor's hand with his mouth. He bit, and every ounce of strength left in his body went into the bite. Bone crunched in the hand, breaking, the most soul-satisfying sound Newton had ever heard. Victor screamed with agonized surprise, lashed out at Newton with his other hand, and broke free.

With his good hand Victor hit Newton again and again, circling, striking whenever there was an opening. But Newton went on groping, his arms flopping helplessly in a parody of boxing and wrestling. He was drunk with his own blood now, deaf and almost blind.

"Fall, damn you!" shouted Victor, butting him in the face with his head. Newton tottered, a lost scarecrow in a high wind.

"Fall, damn you!" Victor shouted again, throwing his full weight against him. This time he fell at last, slowly, hanging onto a bunk, sliding down, still trying to right himself, until he lay spread-eagle on the floor.

Victor waited for Newton to rise.

Newton didn't move.

Victor leaned over him and said softly, triumphantly, "Wonderful. I knew you had it in you, Newton. I knew it."

When Newton regained consciousness he found himself looking up into the faces of two security policemen. His hearing had returned, though he could still hear a terrible ringing in his ears.

"Newton McClintok?" asked one of the officers.

Newton nodded.

"You don't seem to have any broken bones," said the officer. "I looked you over while you were knocked out. Do you think you can stand up?"

"I don't know." Newton whispered, but he gave it a try and found he could.

Victor and his friends were nowhere to be seen, but over in the corner Piggy continued to play with her doll and sing to it tunelessly, her back to him.

"Can you walk, sir?" the officer said with concern.

Newton found he could do that, too.

"Who beat you up?" asked the second officer in a businesslike voice.

Newton thought a moment, then lied, "I don't know."

The policemen exchanged meaningful glances, as if to say they didn't believe him.

"Let's go get your things," said the first policeman. "You're moving out."

Newton, as he began to shuffle toward the door, could only think of one thing, and he voiced his thoughts through a bleeding, swollen mouth. "Are you taking me to the Hall of Heads?"

"Good Lord no!"

Newton persisted, "Are you transferring me to a different dorm?"

"No."

"Are you arresting me?"

"No."

Newton halted and turned to face them, demanding, "Then what are you doing?"

Both officers smiled, and the first one said, "We're setting you free."

The other added, "You can go home."

"Home?" Newton tried to understand, but failed.

The policeman touched Newton on the arm with a respect Newton had forgotten policemen were capable of. "Mister McClintok, you're not an Un anymore. You don't belong here. You belong outside, in the big world."

"But...but how can that be?"

"Someone bought your freedom. Someone put up the money so you can 'show means'."

After a long pause, Newton asked hoarsely, "Who?"

They looked at each other, then the first one said, "We don't know. We thought you would. Surely you can think of someone...."

Only one name came to mind. He did not say it aloud, but a voice within shouted out the name ecstatically.

Holly!

Chapter 15

During a normal summer that river of rolling clouds that circles the Earth, that river called the North Polar Front, creeps slowly northward toward the Artic Circle, carrying the jet stream with it, a jet stream that normally circumnavigates the planet in about three days in January and ten days in July. The jet stream is never straight or smooth, but wriggles and writhes like a cobra. Even these wriggles have a kind of normality, repeating themselves at regular intervals of five and a half years, eleven years, twenty-three years and forty-six years.

Normal weather, in fact, is a sound, a very low-pitched sound, but a sound nonetheless, with its stately procession of low-pressure areas and high-pressure areas. Such a sound might be produced by an organ pipe taller than the tallest mountain, by an immense gong with a radius of thousands of kilometers, by a multitude of gargantuan monks chanting an eternal subsonic 'Om.' By linking a barometer to a very slow tape recorder, then playing back the tape at normal speed, you can hear the drone of the weather, or see it on a cathode ray tube. It has a sweet rich tone, with a timbre like a fine violin.

But where there is harmony there can also be dissonance, and winds that should be creeping northward creep southward instead, seasons that should be cold become warm, places that should be dry are suddenly bathed in inexplicable downpours.

If we had the ears to hear it, we might hear that mad subsonic dissonance, and above it perhaps the distant laughter of the gods.

Off the coast of Israel the glittering geodesic sphere Valhalla sped through the glare of noon, swinging toward the southeast, gaining speed, losing altitude. All around it banks of black clouds billowed heavenward, illuminated by occasional flickers of internal lightning.

In the main control room near the bottom of the sphere, Holly and Sewall Smith watched their computer screens and instrument readouts with growing apprehension.

"Why are we losing altitude?" Holly asked.

"The barometric pressure outside is dropping."

"At this altitude? I thought we were above the weather."

Sewall looked at her with worried eyes. "Holly! We're never really above the weather as long as we're in the atmosphere. I think we're feeling a kind of wind-tunnel effect; the faster the wind flows, the thinner it gets."

"Can't we hitch a ride on a wind going some other direction?"

"Not this time. For once the whole airmass is moving in a block. I've never seen anything like this before. Look there." He gestured toward some clouds that looked remarkably like flying saucers. In fact, Holly had seen photographs of just such clouds in collections of UFO pictures.

"I think we've sprung a leak," said Holly.

"How can you say that? None of the instruments...."

"I'm going upstairs and take a look." She left Smith sputtering and waving his arms and made her way quickly to the lockers where the pressure suits were stored. Nobody tried to stop her or even question her. The crew had come to accept her authority more unquestioningly than they had ever accepted Brad's more unquestioningly than they at present accepted Hal Waterman's though Hal was officially in command. She thought, *One more stroke, and I'll be secure.*

She zipped herself into a pressure suit with practiced ease, lifted on the fishbowl helmet and dogged it down, checked her oxygen supply and started it flowing with a reassuring hiss, then checked her torch, her sealing compound, her tool kit, the worklight on her chest. Everything was in order.

The time had come to put into motion the plan that had been forming in her mind for months, that she had gone over in her imagination time and time again so that now her actions were like that of a well-programmed robot.

Monkeylike, with a feeling of ecstatic exhilaration, she clambered up a steel-runged ladder, opened a bulkhead, and let herself into the crawlspace under the deck of the farming area.

There she closed the bulkhead behind her, clicked on her chest worklight, and crept on her hands and knees between the taut guywires and narrow plastic struts that filled this section with a forest of interlocking pyramids.

Near the outer wall she found another bulkhead above her, opened it, and lifted herself up into the narrow space between the inner and outer skin of the Valhalla. Some of the workers in the indoor garden saw her and turned to stare at her with surprise.

She closed the bulkhead behind her and continued her spiderlike progress upward. Her shipmates on the farming deck craned their necks to follow her ascent. She looked down and froze. Up here above the deck, surrounded only by triangular transparent panels, seeming to hang suspended so far above the world, she had the horrible feeling of being about to fall, to fall all the way to the distant rocky face of Israel.

She closed her eyes and breathed deeply.

Somehow she had not included her own acrophobia in her calculations, and now as dizzyness and nausea flooded over her, she felt her whole plan, not just this little attempted fraud, crumbling in her fingers. If she showed fear here, in plain sight of a major percentage of the crew, her power, which rested on nothing but a painstakingly constructed illusion of superiority, would vanish.

She thought, *I must not be afraid.*

But her whole body was shaking, and her fingers gripped a crossmember as if welded to it.

Hal Waterman's voice came crackling through her earphones. "Holly! What are you doing up there?"

When she could trust herself to speak, she answered, "Just checking something."

"What's wrong?" he demanded.

"Maybe nothing." She listened to her own voice, heard fear in it.

Damn, she thought. *Damn, damn, damn.*

Anger welled up within her, and she decided to use it, pushing the fear roughly aside with self-contempt. *I'm not like that,* she told herself firmly, *I'm not a coward.*

The shaking stopped, but a terrible weakness remained.

Careful not to look down again, she continued her climb. The pitch and roll of the Valhalla, which she had learned to ignore, now seemed more extreme than ever before, as if the Valhalla was some huge wild animal trying to buck her off. She told herself this was an illusion, but when she happened to glance at a nearby thundercloud, she realized her senses had not lied; the Valhalla was rolling to and fro with a violence that was genuinely dangerous. In this kind of weather the crew kept strapped down as much as possible, and if they had to move, they hung on to railings and hangstraps. Holly, without safety belts, handrails or hangstraps, kept on climbing.

She reached a point she thought might be the place she had planned to stop and ventured a look around.

No, not quite yet.

Hal Waterman's voice sounded again in her headphones. "Holly, I'm going to suit up and come up too." From his tone she knew he was worried about her. That was all very well, but it meant she would have to do what she had come to do before he arrived. She climbed some more.

She checked her position again. Yes, this was it.

She took out her torch and carefully and deliberately burned a hole through the outer skin of the Valhalla. Before much of the heavier outer air could enter, she plugged the hole with sealing compound and, readjusting the heat of the torch, welded it firmly shut.

Working with feverish speed, she burned another hole through the inner skin some distance away, then sealed that too.

"Here I come," said Hal in her earphones.

Ignoring the altitude and rocking of the Valhalla, ignoring her own compulsion to throw up inside her helmet, ignoring her sweat, and her fear, and her shortness of breath, she bounded along from strut to strut like some clownish highwire acrobat until she came to the other place she had so carefully selected. There she again burned holes in the inner and outer skin of the Valhalla, then sealed them.

She glanced down, fought off another surge of vertigo, and saw a pressure-suited figure climbing toward her too large to be anyone but Hal.

She hung on, waiting for him.

A moment later he scrambled up beside her. Through his bubble helmet she could see him gazing at her with puzzlement. "What's going on here?" he asked.

With a gloved hand she indicated the nearest patched holes. "We were losing altitude. I thought we might have a leak. Sure enough, some meteor had passed right through, punching one pair of holes coming in and another pair going out. Don't worry, though. I fixed it."

She saw his gaze measure the angle of the holes, make sure they lined up. He *was* a little suspicious of her, she could see that. Then he turned to her and said, "You may have saved our lives."

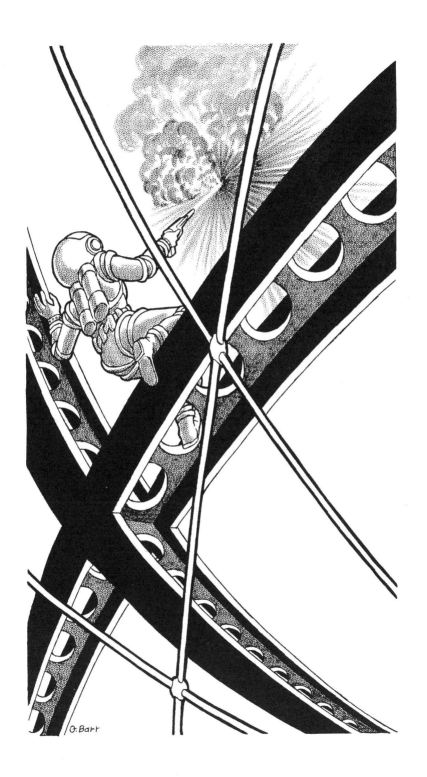

Nature or the gods coincidently joined her in conspiracy. The Valhalla stopped losing altitude.

When she got back to the locker room and began to take off her pressure suit, many of the crew, who had heard the radio exchange between Holly and Hal, crowded around her to express their gratitude and admiration. Hal stood to one side, watching.

"How did you know about the holes?" someone asked her eagerly.

"Just a lucky guess," she answered modestly.

*

Police Captain Clark sat behind his desk, templing his fingers, leaning back to look up at Newton, who stood before him, all his worldly belongings packed into a single duffel bag. Newton noticed dark circles under the officer's eyes, and a look of almost envy in them. Newton understood that envy. He was leaving. Captain Clark was staying.

"Twenty-five thousand dollars of thumbprint credit have been deposited to your account. I'd advise you to spend it slowly and carefully looking for a job, any kind of job. I mean, I wouldn't be too picky if I were you, because when that money is gone you could easily find yourself back here."

In Clark's words Newton heard a frank admission that the dorms were not a wonderful place to be, a paradise, a permanent vacation. Now, when Newton was leaving, there remained no reason to lie.

Clark went on, "And you should get rid of that yellow robe. Some people out there are prejudiced against Uns. Grey robes with a floral border are popular at the moment, and cheap. Buy some, don't rent. Renting seems cheap, but it piles up."

"Thank you, sir," said Newton.

"Will someone be meeting you to see you home?"

"Oh yes. My wife Holly."

"Good. Well, goodbye Newton. You've been a good un, but I'd just as soon not see you again."

Clark stood up, wiped his sweating hand on his tunic, and shook hands with Newton, who smiled as best he could with his cracked lip and bandaged eye.

A guard showed him out of the office and left him at the elevator. Newton rode to the ground floor and limped slowly through the lobby, looking for Holly.

The lobby was deserted.

He went through the revolving door and found himself outdoors for the first time in months. It was night. A cold rain was falling. Not a soul was in sight. He turned around and pushed back through the revolving door, looking for a public communications terminal.

Finding a whole cluster of them, he placed his thumb on the reader and watched the video screen light up with a kind of wonder. He really did have thumbprint credit, just as Clark had said!

He punched up his parents' apartment.

After six chimes Jim Moran's face faded into view, sleepy-eyed and sullen. "Who is it?" he asked.

"Don't you recognize me"

"My God, is that you, Newton?"

"That's right."

"What happened to you? You look like you lost an argument with a cement mixer."

"Don't worry about that. Is Holly there?"

"Holly? We haven't seen her for months."

"Can you give me her address?"

"We don't know where she is. Listen Newton, it's late and I need my sleep. You want to talk to someone here? One of your mothers? The old man?"

"No."

"Well, you know how it is. I gotta work tomorrow."

"I understand. Good night, Jim."

"Good night. Nice talking to you, Newton. Keep in touch."

The image faded. Newton stared at the blank screen, baffled, then punched up Social Security, accessed their computer and punched in Holly's Social Security number.

A few seconds later the screen displayed the glowing words, "No current address."

"No current address?" Newton said aloud.

He hadn't expected that. Everyone lives somewhere. Even if she'd lived on Mars, the Moon or on some orbiter somewhere, Social Security would have her address. And if she were dead, Social Security would know that, too.

The words on the screen faded.

If she'd gotten an unlisted address. Social Security would have told him that. Ditto if she used a PO box.

He considered punching up the local police station but thought better of it. He didn't want to deal with the police, no, not yet.

He punched up his parents' apartment again.

Jim Moran's face came into view, more sullen than before.

Newton said, "Can I stay the night?"

"Here?" said Moran. He sounded shocked.

"Just this once."

"No, no, that's out of the question, kid. No place to put you."

"I see."

"You know how it is. Nice talking to you, Newton. Good night."

The screen went blank.

He wondered at last if Holly had really been the one who bought his freedom. Certainly it couldn't have been one of his indifferent family. If it was Holly, why wasn't she here? If it wasn't Holly, who could it be?

He shook his head slowly, baffled, then shouldered his duffel bag and limped toward the revolving door.

He boarded a monorail for San Francisco and found it crowded with merrymakers celebrating the victory of some sports hero Newton had never heard of. They paid no attention to him. He wondered what else he didn't know about the modern world. A lot can change in a few months, and Newton hadn't been among those Uns who gathered in the lounge to watch newscasts from "The Outside."

He walked from the station to the YMCA, only to be told by the night clerk that they were all booked up. Was that the truth? Newton suspected the real reason for the night clerk's refusal was his battered appearance and his telltale yellow un robe.

Around midnight he found himself wandering the streets of the ancient North Beach district, up one steep hill and down another in the steady, monotonous rain, unwilling either to pay the outrageous rent for a decent hotel room or risk the bedbugs of a flophouse more within his means.

North Beach was a "Historical Landmark" and thus had been preserved in more or less the same condition it had been in in the Twentieth Century, except that some of the streets had been renamed—Grant Avenue had become Ginsberg Avenue and Greenwich Street had become Kerouac Street—and the whole area had taken on the unreal atmosphere of a movie set for some historical thriller about Beatniks and Hippies. Tourists loved it, and carefully avoided raising their gaze to the mountainous, looming skyscrapers that surrounded it.

Newton halted at the corner of Ginsberg and Kerouac and stared up at a gaudy, crudely-painted, spotlighted sign identifying the "Bread and Wine Mission." He had heard of the place but had never been inside. People had told him it was a cheap dive, but at the moment something cheap was exactly what he wanted. It was, of course, not a real mission, but a nightclub, a more or less faithful reproduction of the real "Bread and Wine Mission" of long ago where poets recited and protest singers protested and a heavy fog of marijuana smoke hung over everything.

Perhaps he would have gone in anyway, just to get out of the rain, but a sign in the window caught his attention, seemed to challenge him. "Greta Berg, Queen of the Uns" the sign announced, and above it, peeling away from the cardboard backing, was a sunfaded color photograph of a grinning redheaded woman clad in an un robe and strumming a guitar.

Newton went in and collapsed at a table near the door.

He glanced around. On the walls hung various surreal, psychedelic and just plain crazy drawings, paintings and prints, including one authentic Ray Nelson, a black and white india ink drawing taller than a man filled with thousands of individually-drawn figures of fat little people, no two alike, engaged in all the activities known to humanity. This masterpiece of obsession was entitled, "Complex" and, Newton had heard, once hung in the real Bread and Wine Mission back in the Good Old Drunken Days.

Then Newton realized he was the only customer. The other tables stood vacant, abandoned. He wondered if the club might be closed, but no, a waitress in beatnik-period bluejeans, T-shirt and black beret came padding toward him barefootedly, extending a dogeared winelist. Beer was the cheapest thing there, so he ordered that, though his eye lingered longingly over some of the outrageously overpriced cocktails.

At the back of the room he saw a low platform, a stage of sorts, too small for more than four performers at most. On this platform stood one kitchen stool and one old-fashioned microphone bathed in amber light from spotlights attached to the ceiling. He wondered if the show was over for the night.

No, as soon as the waitress had brought him his mug of suds, Greta Berg, the alleged Queen of the Uns, stepped from the back room and mounted the stage. She was a good deal older than her photograph showed, and a little bit fatter, but the guitar in her hand had not suffered from the passage of time. She perched on the stool and spoke into the microphone, her overly-lipsticked lips almost touching it.

"Good evening, ladies and gentlemen," she said, as if speaking to a crowd rather than only one person. "I almost didn't come in tonight, what with the bad weather and all, but the dorm captain said to me, he said, 'Greta, you got a choice. Sing or work.' So here I am." She paused for a laugh but Newton didn't make a sound. He never had liked those jokes that made the point that Uns were lazy. Now, after the months in the dorms, he hated

165

them. He knew, however, that no supposedly humorous performance was complete without some kind of dig at the Uns. He knew he would have to try to learn to laugh when everyone else laughed, to fit in here on the outside.

With a brittle smile, Greta Berg continued, "For my first number, I'd like to take you for a stroll, a leisurely stroll among the ladies and gentlemen of leisure. I'd like to sing you the Monk Wolf hit, 'My Little Un Baby and Me.' "

Newton listened to the familiar, stupid words, sipping his beer moodily. Great Berg, he noted, had a good voice, but....

She finished and bowed slightly.

Newton did not applaud.

Greta turned to the waitress, who had just come in from the back room, and said, "Some strong coffee for the gentlemen in the rear. If that doesn't work, tie a tag to his toe and call the undertaker."

Newton sat up and demanded in a level, emotionless voice, "Have you ever been in the dorms?"

"Certainly not!" She drew herself up indignantly.

"I have."

"I could tell."

"It's not like you think. It's not all peaches and cream. And plenty of Uns would work if they could, but nobody wants them."

She laughed easily, lightly. She obviously had handled his type before. "God protect us from the performer who tells the truth. Santa Claus isn't real. Does that mean I can't sing about Santa Claus."

"Maybe, if your songs say Santa likes poor kids the same as he likes rich ones."

She turned toward the empty room, appealing to some audience Newton couldn't see. "He thinks it's easy to get up here and sing." She faced Newton again to demand, "Can you get up here and sing?"

"I can't sing," said Newton.

"But you can tell other people how, can't you?"

The waitress broke in to say, "Take it easy, Greta." Newton realized she was more than a waitress. Maybe she owned the place, or managed it. Somehow there was command in her voice.

Newton said, "I can tell someone how to sing Un songs." He pulled open his duffel bag and began fumbling around in it, at last dragging out his small, homemade poom-poom.

"Is that a musical instrument?" asked the waitress.

"Yeah," said Newton, testing the strings, plucking them lightly with his fingertips to see if they were in tune. They were.

From the stage Greta challenged, "Okay, sonny. Why don't you bring that thing up here and play a few bars. I don't think the crowd will mind." She gestured toward the empty tables.

Newton stood up and limped toward the platform, poom-poom tucked under his arm. The waitress helped him up, lifting his elbow. Greta vacated the bench with a mocking bow. Newton half-leaned, half-sat on the tall kitchen stool and began to thump the strings with his little rubberheaded hammer. He was playing Baboo's "If We Could Learn."

It sounded good. The waitress smiled. Greta watched thoughtfully.

"Hey kid," said the waitress when he'd finished, "That's not bad. Play it again."

Newton obeyed. This time Greta hummed along, having picked up the tune, and began to improvise the chords on her guitar.

"That's a real Un tune," said Newton.

The waitress said, "Guaranteed authentic?"

Newton smiled for the first time since he'd come into the nightclub. "Guaranteed."

The waitress said, "Greta, you should learn some of these songs. You could use some new material." Again the note of command.

Greta hesitated, then said, "Maybe so. How about it, kid? Will you teach me?"

"Sure," said Newton. "When?"

"Why not now?" said the waitress.

Newton and Greta sat down at one of the front tables and he played and she listened and hummed and tried things out on her guitar, frowning with concentration. The waitress went out to the kitchen. No more customers came in.

The rain outside got louder.

The waitress started upending chairs and putting them on the tables.

Greta said, "It's closing time, kid. Where do you live?"

"Nowhere." Newton started packing up his poom-poom.

She touched his arm. "Why don't you come home with me." There was an odd catch in her voice.

Newton thought a moment, then said, "Okay."

The waitress winked knowingly at him as he left with Greta on his arm and his duffel over his shoulder.

Chapter 16

Brad, more sober than Holly had seen him for a long time, looked up as she entered the Round Room, his eyes dull and opaque, like Newton's.

"Juanita tells me the crew has elected you President," he said tonelessly.

"Yes, they seem to think I'm the only one competent to deal with the present situation."

He smiled with humor. "The situation you got them into."

"You might say that." She paused at the entrance to the conversation pit.

"Well, what are you here for, Holly? To evict me? You think that now you're the captain, you ought to move into the captain's cabin?"

"No, no. Not me. I belong out there with the crew. In fact, if you'd been out there more, mixing with people, you might still be captain." Without waiting for an invitation, she sat down opposite him.

"What do you want then? I can tell you want something."

"I want advice."

"From me? I don't believe it."

She leaned forward tensely. "Brad, do you know what's happening...with the weather?"

"Yes."

"Tell me."

"No."

"Is that information in the memory banks of that *Ency-*

lopedia Gallactica you were telling me about?"

"Yes, my dear, it is."

"As you probably expected, I've searched the Valhalla from top to bottom looking for that crystal the size of a baseball.'

"Maybe a little smaller."

"Where is it, Brad?"

"Why should I tell you? You of all people?"

She touched his arm urgently. "For the good of the crew."

"Your crew, not mine."

"For the good of your dream."

He placed his hand on hers and said softly, with ironic affection, "Ah, Holly, Holly, Holly, I think my dream began to die the moment I laid eyes on you. I thought if I could gather all the supermen and superwomen together, they would be peers, friends, a kind of super family. I thought Valhalla would be some kind of utopia. You see how stupid a clever man can be? How even a clever man can believe something crazy because he wants to believe it? Of course there's no such thing as peers. Even among superpeople, some are more super than others. In Valhalla things are no different than they are down on Earth. We have our winners and our losers, too. The basic problem Valhalla was built to solve remains unsolved."

"We at least have no Unemployables up here."

"Except me."

"Not even you. I have a job for you, if you'll take it. I need you. I need you to command the technical section..."

"There is no technical section. On the Valhalla everyone does everything."

"Everyone used to do everything," she corrected him. "I'm reorganizing things, setting up departments, establishing a division of labor, a chain of command."

His voice was hardly audible. "Of course you are. I said it myself. There are no peers. Why pretend that there are?"

"Then you agree?"

"Ah Holly, you clever woman, have you never wondered why I set one hundred and sixty as the minimum IQ for my little band of demigods? Why not one hundred and fifty? Why not one hundred and seventy? Why exactly that number and no other?"

She really had never thought about it, yet now the answer to his question flashed instantly into her mind. "That's your own IQ rating, isn't it, Brad."

He nodded slowly. "I have the lowest IQ in Valhalla."

She hesitated, then said, "You know I don't put much faith in IQ tests...."

"At one hundred and eighty you don't need to. A billionaire never needs to worry about money either. I know what you're going to say. The Valhalla is a work of a genius! The Valhalla proves my right to be here! Actually it proves the genius of the people I hired to do the engineering on it."

"But the basic idea...."

"That proves the genius of the one who actually thought of it, a crazy twentieth century architect named Bucky Fuller." He laughed raggedly. "You have no use for my brain here. Perhaps my body would make a good meal for the crew, but my brain just doesn't measure up."

"And that's why you couldn't mix with the crew?"

"At the lower end of the scale, IQ doesn't make much difference. You see one idiot and you've seen them all. But at the upper end of the scale two or three points can make the difference between solving a problem and not solving it, following an argument and not following it, getting a joke and not getting it. I couldn't let them see I was a wee bit slow on the uptake, that there were things a wee bit over my head. I had to keep my distance to keep my secret. I didn't set it up that way, but that's how it worked out, particularly after you came on board. With you I had to stay drunk to cover up."

Holly said, "My offer still stands. I don't give a damn about IQ. It doesn't measure anything but your ability to take IQ tests. Nobody in Valhalla cares about it."

"Except me," said Brad. "I care."

"You want to be President again? I could let you, if I could be second-in-command."

He drew himself up proudly. "You'd let me? You'd *allow* me to do that? How very kind of you. Thanks but no thanks. I wouldn't make a good puppet emperor. For that you need to be brittle and witty like Oscar Wilde, so you can make a joke of your humiliation. Go away, Holly. Go away and let an old dog lick his wounds."

Holly got to her feet. "If you change your mind, Brad, buzz me on the intercom."

Wearily he repeated, "Go away, go away, go away."

Holly went away.

It was Juanita who, some time later, buzzed Holly on the intercom.

"Holly! Come quick! Brad has killed himself!"

*

Newton sat behind Greta Berg on the creaking antique iron

bed and cut her hair.

"The hairdresser is in such a hurry he never gets it right," she had told him, and without a word he had picked up her clippers and started cutting.

"You know, kid, you're actually very good at that," she said, admiring herself in a handmirror.

"Thank you." He went on working, taking his time.

She wore a filmy, translucent white nightgown. He was naked. She asked, "Where did you learn to cut women's hair?"

"My wife taught me, or I should say my ex-wife."

"Make up your mind."

"She divorced me, a long time ago."

"From the way you talk about her, your divorce is turning out to be even more of a failure than your marriage."

"That's right. Failure is the only thing I seem to succeed at."

"You may be low man on the totem pole of material success, but of course you know the world contains more than one totem pole. The Techs may perch atop that material totem pole, but you and I have our place on another pole of which they, poor souls, are totally ignorant, the totem pole of the arts."

"Yeah," he grunted, inspecting his work.

They were in Greta's cramped two-room apartment in an ancient Queen Anne Victorian that had somehow survived not only the San Francisco fire in the early Twentieth Century, but the tireless march of Urban Redevelopment that had turned most of San Francisco into a maze of skyscrapers. It was a historical landmark, according to a sign out in front.

In return for room and board, Newton had become Greta's "househusband," doing the cooking, cleaning and shopping, babysitting Greta's eleven-year-old son Danny, and now cutting her hair. Newton's "room" consisted of an airmattress on the floor of the closet. He was, however, fairly contented. He had food and shelter. He wasn't in an Un camp. And he had not had to use any of his precious thumbprint credit.

"I sang seven of your songs last night," she told him. "Want to hear how they went over?"

"How did they go over?" he asked dutifully, starting in with the comb.

"I got a standing ovation! And the Bread and Wine Mission was packed. Those songs were exactly what I needed to give my act a touch of authenticity. A producer was there, and after the show he approached me with a contract. Congratulate me, lad. I'm about to record my first album!"

"Congratulations," he said absently.

"If we get a few steps ahead of that wolf at the door, we can rent a decent apartment. You can move out of the closet."

"I don't mind the closet."

"You're a saint, Newton, a positive saint. Wouldn't you like to have a real room of your own?"

"I don't care. Well, the haircut is as finished as it will ever be. How do you like it?"

"Beautiful! Yes, I think I'll keep you. Give Greta a kiss." She closed her eyes and puckered up.

Newton kissed her lightly on the lips and gave her a hug.

"Good boy. Now go play with Danny," she said.

Without a word, he went.

Danny didn't like children.

"They're stupid," he would often say with venom.

They liked stupid games like football and baseball. Danny liked chess. He was too fat to be good at any physical sport.

Danny didn't like adults any too well either, but he enjoyed annoying them. "They're stupid, too," he would often say.

But the stupidest people of all, in Danny's opinion, were his mother's lovers. When she had introduced Newton to him, he had said, "You call *that* a man?"

Now Newton, dressed in his yellow Un robe, came out of the bedroom and into the kitchen, which doubled as Danny's room. Danny went on reading his chess book, paying no attention.

"How about a game?" said Newton.

"I suppose. It's still raining out," said the boy, glancing at the tall thin windows where the downpour had been drumming without cease for days. Lying on his belly on his cot, he reached under and dragged out his chess set.

Greta, dressed in a peasant blouse and skirt, came into the room carrying her guitar in its case. "I'll leave you boys to your game now. I have to go practice."

"Goodbye, Greta," said Newton.

"Bye, Mom," said Danny.

She went out into the hall and closed the door behind her.

"Where does she practice?" asked Newton.

"The toilet," Danny replied indifferently. "It has a nice echo."

Danny opened the game with the old reliable Ruy Lopez, trying to play it safe. Newton had beat him almost every time, and when he had occasionally won, Danny had suspected Newton of throwing the game.

When they had been playing silently for a while, Danny said abruptly, "What's your theory?"

"My chess theory?"

"No, stupid. Your theory of child development. Everyone Mama gets to take care of me has a different theory of child development. What is it this time? Freud? Fabry? Hartshaw? Eisenstein? Miller? Or do you think I'm Rousseau's 'Nobel Savage?' "

"Nothing like that."

"What then?"

Newton considered a moment, then smiled his tight little smile. "I believe in the Theory of Creative Neglect."

After that Danny liked him a lot better.

*

Holly stood just inside the door of Brad's toilet, the only private toilet on the Valhalla. Brad half-knelt, half-sprawled in front of his urinal, his arms propped up so that the slashed wrists would not drip on the floor. The blood had stopped flowing by now, but the urinal bowl glittered with red, still wet against the white enamel. She had never meant it to go this far, although now she didn't see where else it could have ended.

On the floor lay fragments of the broken champagne glass he'd used to cut himself. The brownish red meat pushed out through his wounds. Holly felt slightly sick.

Juanita cowered behind Holly, as if to protect herself against the corpse. "Holly," she demanded. "Why would he do such a thing?"

Holly answered with a question. "Did he leave a suicide note?" She thought, *It would be just like the bastard to leave some message that would mess me up with the crew.*

From the other room Hal called, "No note. Nothing. I've searched the place."

Holly came into the Round Room. "What's that piece of paper on his desk?"

"Just some kind of stew recipe," said Hal.

Holly picked up the paper and studied it, then said, "This is the suicide note. Maybe you didn't notice, but Brad has included himself in the list of ingredients."

Hal said in an awed tone, "Are we going to eat him?"

Holly said, "Eventually. That's obviously what he wanted us to do. But first let's take him to sick bay and do an autopsy on him."

"But why?" cried Juanita. "We know how he died."

"Sure we do," said Holy grimly, "but I'm looking for something, and I think it must be somewhere inside his body. You can't miss it. It's a crystal as big as a baseball."

Chapter 17

Normandy Taylor paced her apartment, back and forth, back and forth. Once, long ago, she had been so calm, so self-possessed. Now she had to take pills all the time, and even with the pills....

Captain Clark slumped in a chair and stared into his drink. "I tried to get an order for the arrest of our friend Victor," he said.

"About time," said Normandy.

"They turned me down."

"What?"

Clark shrugged listlessly. "Someone got to them first. The big brass think the ringleader is this Baboo fellow. They've ordered Baboo's arrest. I'll have to bring Baboo in instead."

"Not Baboo! Baboo is God's older brother to the Uns. Baboo is probably the only Un known all over the world, thanks to those idiotic songs of his. If we look crosseyed at Baboo, we'll have that worldwide revolution for sure, the very thing we're trying to avoid."

After a moment Captain Clark said, "What do you think of that reverend man of the cloth, Chaplain Bill? Could he be a traitor? Could he have gone over to the Uns? Could he be setting this all up for them?"

"Why do you say that?"

"The grapevine has it that Chaplain Bill set the brass on Baboo, you know how he arranged things for that Un, Mickey."

Normandy stood, arms akimbo. "Bill, the Holy Hippo.

Frankly I don't think he has the guts to cross over, but he might be playing petty politics with all our lives. He might be jealous of Baboo as a competitor in the savior sweepstakes, and he might take this opportunity to get someone else to knock Baboo out of the race. That I can certainly believe. Bill is easily rotten enough for that."

Clark looked up at her gloomily. "Norm, you're talking about a Tech. Bill is a Tech. That means he's the best, the finest, the fittest, homo superior. Isn't the whole purpose of our society to keep people like Bill on top and everyone else on the bottom?"

Norm touched his cheek with her hand. "You've been drinking too much, Cap. If you don't get a grip on yourself, you'll be the one who crosses over."

"Maybe so." He slowly shook his head from side to side as if trying to clear it.

For a long time he sat with head drooping while Norm stood in front of him, looking down at him with sadness and infinite weariness.

*

One day, as Baboo sat on his cot surrounded by his disciples as a king sits on a throne, as a judge sits on the bench of justice, as a priest sits in the confessional booth, a haggard stranger came and stood before him, dirty, gaunt, unshaven, with yellow robe torn.

"I have come from far away," said the stranger, glancing around fearfully.

"How far?" asked the gentle Baboo.

"From the other end of the building, many kilometers from here. I have climbed through airshafts, slipped through checkpoints, hid in storerooms, all to speak to you."

"Why me?"

"Everyone says you are the wisest man in the dorms. Everyone sings your songs, believes in them, lives by them. If anyone can answer my question, you can."

"What is your question?"

The stranger hesitated, chosing his words with care. "Is it ever good... to kill a man?"

Baboo realized then that he was speaking to a murderer. "No, never."

"Not even when someone threatens your life?"

"Not even then."

Guilt made the man desperate. "Not even when someone threatens not only your life, but the lives of many others?"

Baboo considered a long time before answering, "You cannot avoid death. We all die, sooner or later. But you can avoid bringing death to others. You cannot save life, except temporarily, but you can avoid murder forever. That is within your power."

Unsatisfied, the murderer posed another question. "Have you ever killed anyone?"

"Never."

"But Mister Baboo, you must have murdered someone in your heart, in your imagination. If you're human you must have wished someone dead."

For the first time Baboo's calm was slightly shaken, as much by the pain in the man's eyes as by his words. "Yes... There have been times."

"And if you wanted to kill, don't you think a situation might arise where that desire became too strong for you?"

Baboo's disciples had been following this exchange with ever-increasing interest, and now Baboo realized, as he glanced around at their faces, that they wanted him to answer "no." Yet that, he decided, would not be honest. Baboo had not become Baboo by telling popular lies.

"Perhaps," Baboo admitted. A murmur of consternation arose from the crowd, but Baboo went on, "In such a situation we never know what we will do in advance. The situation arrives. We act. Only then do we learn, to our own surprise, what we really believe."

The murderer cried out, delighted, "I knew it! I knew you would understand! Nobody else would understand that, only you!" His voice rang with sudden freedom. "You really are as wise as everyone said!"

As if afraid Baboo would change his mind, would recant what seemed to the murderer to be a strange kind of absolution, the haggard stranger turned and stumbled away in haste, almost tripping over some of Baboo's disciples who scrambled out of his path.

"Wait!" Baboo called after him, but he did not wait, and no one moved to stop him or prevent his leaving the room. Baboo had more to say... or did he? He sighed, thinking, *I said the right thing for that one man, and for me, but for these others who think I cannot make a mistake or contradict myself... was it the right answer for them?*

He wished, for a moment, he'd never gotten started in this holy man game.

Others had come to Baboo that day with other questions.

They waited patiently their turns, but he shook his head slowly and muttered, almost angrily, "No more. No more questions today." He picked up his poom-poom and began to play disconnected fragments of melody, closing his eyes so he could not see the disappointment in his followers' faces.

He thought with wry, tired irony, *Every actor needs a backstage, a dressing room. When all the world's a stage, where are the dressing rooms? Were is mine?*

*

Greta and Danny had gone out shopping, leaving Newton to wash the dishes. He didn't mind washing dishes. Music came into his mind when his hands were busy, Baboo's songs and sometimes half-formed bits of new songs of his own, blending with the clink of the plates and spoons and forks and the gentle splash of the water. Greta had never been able to afford to repair the apartments automatic dishwasher, though now, with a recording contract to her credit, she had begun to talk about buying a new one, about buying a lot of things.

The rain had ceased, but a grey overcast still hung low above, hiding the tops of the skyscrapers he could see from the kitchen window. The weather had been strange this year. According to the radio, the weather had been strange all over the world. He wondered if Holly were actually up in a balloon somewhere in this strange weather, as she had said, some kind of balloon that never came to earth, an aerial Flying Dutchman. That could explain a lot.

A knock at the door startled him out of his reverie.

"Who's there?" he called.

"Guess," came the answer. The voice was unmistakable.

"Victor!" Newton hastily dried his hands and ran to open the door.

Victor stood in the doorway a moment, enjoying Newton's astonishment. He was dressed in the white coveralls of a high-ranking Techman.

"Come in, come in," said Newton. "Er...how's your hand?"

Victor shut the door, then held up a hand hidden in flesh-colored bandages. "Almost as good as new. These organic dressings work miracles. You didn't think you could really do permanent damage to someone like me, did you? How about you? All put back together again?"

"Sure, I'm okay."

"No hard feelings?"

"Not on my side. Won't you sit down?"

Victor threw himself down on Danny's bunk next to the refrigerator. "I brought you a present, Newton." He opened a large plastic tote bag and slowly drew forth a bottle of Scotch.

"Maybe you'd better keep it, Victor."

"You on the wagon? Okay, I admire you for it, but I think I'll leave this here anyway, in case you change your mind." He set the bottle ceremoniously on the worn, sunfaded linoleum. Newton leaned against the sink, facing him, watching him like a bird watches a cat.

"How did you find me?" Newton asked, crossing his arms on his chest and clutching his own shoulders as if to protect himself from some unexpected attack.

Victor shrugged. "My spies are everywhere."

"And how did you get out of the dorms?"

"Didn't I tell you once? I go where I please."

"And how did you get that Techman uniform?"

Victor smiled. "You might say I inherited it. The former owner has no further use for it. But you know how I hate answering questions, don't you, old pal? My business is my business. Right?"

"Sure, Victor."

"Actually I'm proud of you, the way you stood up to me. You're ready now to join us. I knew, sooner or later...."

"No, Victor."

"Still harboring a little resentment there, eh buddy? Didn't like the way I laid into you?"

"I'm not joining up with you or anybody else. Nothing personal. I'm just not a joiner."

"Too bad, Goldilocks. You could be very useful out here, with this place to stay where the police don't know you live, where Big Mama pays the rent and stuffs your face. A regular safehouse! And all you have to do is oil her springs a little every night. Out here you could do things for your friends inside."

"Forget it, Victor."

"Let's stop kidding around, Goldie," said Victor, suddenly grim. "The blowup is coming any day now, and if you're not with us, I might have to kill you. I don't want to do that. I like you. You like me, too. I can tell."

Newton said nothing.

Victor chuckled. "Can even you resist the charm of my deep, Russian soul? My sad Slavic eyes? Come on, Goldie, don't play hard to get."

"You're wasting your time, Victor." Newton knew he was afraid of Victor, and hated himself for it.

"The Big Bang," said Victor with relish. "It might come tomorrow. This might be your last chance to save your ass, baby. All we need now is a little push, a John Brown or a Boston Tea Party or something like that, something to hook the minds of the Uns, and the whole damn filthy Techman world goes over the cliff."

Newton said softly, "Ever since I first met you, you've been saying tomorrow, tomorrow, tomorrow. Nothing will happen tomorrow, any more than anything happened yesterday or the day before. It's all just talk."

"Like hell it is!"

"Yes, it's all just talk, and I know why. Because, whatever else you might have, you don't have effective communications. You have no way of reaching all your supporters, if you actually have any, and getting them all to rebel at the same time. The Techs have seen to that."

When Victor did not immediately answer, Newton knew he had hit a nerve. The reply, when it came, was surprisingly weak for Victor, "You're dumb, Newton. A goddamn dumb Un, and that's all you ever will be."

"I'm not an Un. Not any more."

Victor stood up. "Yeah? Have you ever wondered about that? Have you ever wondered how you happened to get out while the rest of us stayed in?"

"Someone bought my freedom."

"Yeah, but who?"

"I don't know."

"Want me to find out, Goldie? I can find out things like that."

"I'd be grateful if you would, but not grateful enough to join up with you."

"I'm not asking for gratitude. That won't make a man kill. I want the stronger emotions. Revenge. Hate. You know what I mean. And if it's who I think it is, and for the reason I think it is, you'll be with us, Goldie, when the shit hits the fan. You'll be with us all right." He started for the door.

"What do you mean?" Newton followed, intrigued in spite of himself.

"Hey, I got your curiosity up, didn't I? Listen, I'm not going to try to snow you with suspicions. I'm going to get you the facts. The truth, the whole truth, and nothing but the truth. But maybe you'd rather not know, eh? Maybe it won't be pretty, my sweet little Goldie. Maybe you'd like to go on thinking this is the best of all possible worlds."

"Maybe you'd like your present back," said Newton, nodding

toward the bottle which still sat on the kitchen floor trying to look innocent.

"Keep it," snapped Victor as he made his exit. "When you hear the truth, you'll need it."

Newton went back to the dishes. The water had gotten cool. Newton's hands shook, ever-so-little.

Chapter 18

According to the radar, the Valhalla had passed over the coast of India a little north of Bombay, but Holly, as she gazed moodily through the round floor window in Brad's room, could see nothing but the pinkish upper face of the cloud cover. She sat exactly where Brad had so often been sitting when she talked to him, her elbows on her knees and her chin in her hands.

The Valhalla's pitch and roll were as extreme as she had ever seen, and occasionally the cable on the ballast weight went slack, then tightened with a snap that shook the entire vessel, as if it might jerk itself loose, ripping out its moorings by the roots. The huge hollow sphere above her amplified the sounds as if it were some monstrous drum, and amplified also the creaks and groans from the shifting stress on its own surface.

Sewall Smith appeared at the entrance to the conversation pit, crawling on his hands and knees to avoid falling. "Smith reporting," he said, and in the red late afternoon sunlight reflected from the clouds below she could see his unconcealed fear. "Autoposy completed."

"Did you find the crystal?"

"No m'am." He tried to raise his voice to make himself heard over the din.

"Nothing at all?"

"Nothing, m'am."

"Damn. I was so sure...."

"But the weather pattern has become clearer. I think I understand what's going on."

"Tell me!"

He dragged himself into a sitting position on the couch beside her. "Combining my own data with what I can pick up on the radio from Earthside weather stations, I'm pretty certain this is all caused by the jet stream hitting the face of the Himalayan mountain range, where it's deflected upward to build some really tall stormclouds. Groundstations estimate the clouds will soon reach the upper stratosphere. Because the clouds are so tall, we're being sucked down toward the storm's base rather than being pushed away at its crest. Also we're losing altitude because the barometric pressure outside is dropping faster than the pressure inside our sphere." Holly had had the airpumps going for hours.

"What can we do?"

"Nothing!" There was panic in the little man's voice.

"Wrong. We can tie everything down and ride it out. You and I are going to watch the show from the central control room next door." She slipped off the couch and began creeping toward the door on the steeply tilting floor. Perhaps, she thought, Brad had had some contingency plan for just such an occasion, but if so it was locked away in his dead brain and perhaps in the mythical crystal. She had searched Brad's room frantically since his death, but had found nothing.

After a brief but bruising crawl, she managed to drag herself into a swivel chair in the control room and strap herself down. Hal and Juanita were on duty, grimly studying the glowing digital readouts and computer display screens. Outside the curving window the Valhalla's little electric aircraft fleet swung and bounded dangerously. In the last fading crimson of the setting sun she could see that some of them already showed damage to their wingtips and ailerons. Without these frail airplanes, she realized, they might be able to leave the Valhalla by parachute, but they could never come back.

As Smith scrambled awkwardly into a nearby seat, Holly asked Hal, "Where are we?"

Hal answered quietly, with a good deal more self-control than Smith seemed able to manage, "We're coming up on Allahabad. I calculate we'll cross the Ganges River at about twenty hundred hours."

"A little less than an hour from now," she said.

The big man nodded soberly. "I don't think we'll hit anything we can't handle before then." He laid an odd emphasis on the word "hit," so that Holly glimpsed in her mind's eye the Valhalla flung against the side of a mountain by the wind.

Juanita, too, maintained a facade of outward calm. "Pretty flat country down below now. I won't worry until after we cross the Ganges."

Holly clicked on the intercom and said crisply, "All hands stay strapped down for the next few hours. We're getting into some pretty rough weather. Stand by for further instructions." She clicked it off again.

Smith said hopefully, "We could bail out."

"No," said Holly. She thought, *If we survive I'll have it made. No bailing out, baby.* The bets were made. The roulette wheel was spinning. Now it was all or nothing!

The sunlight had gone. The only illumination came from the glowing instruments and display screens. The broad curved windows had become funhouse mirrors, casting back macabre, distorted images of their dimly-lit faces. Suddenly a gust of rain struck. Smith jerked bolt upright, letting out a little gasp. Holly smiled. Instead of fear she felt an inexplicable joy, an almost painful exhilaration. *This,* she decided with a flash of unholy glee, *wouldn't be a half-bad way to die.*

"Just passed Allahabad," announced Hal.

"I read you," answered Holly, and a glance passed between them, a glance of camaraderie, even conspiracy, a glance that said that if he must die, he was content to die with her.

Behind her she heard, above the thumping, creaking cacophony, Smith sobbing. Her lip tightened with contempt.

Juanita pointed to one of the screens where a color computer simulation of the cloud formations ahead shimmered silently. "Have you ever before seen such a cloud?"

In the center of the screen a monsterous anvilheaded cumulonimbus towered high above the skyline of the mountains, writhing and boiling like the mushroom cloud of a nuclear explosion. According to the scale at the side, the thing stood a full twenty kilometers tall, invading altitudes normally reserved for the thinnest and most diaphanous ice clouds. Around its base squadrons of flying-saucer-shaped clouds faded in and out of existence, and further up the simulation indicated hailstones spinning like pebbles in a gem tumbler.

"And it's sucking us in like a vacuum sweeper." cried Hal with awe.

"We're passing over the Ganges," Juanita reported.

The tossing and bounding of the Valhalla grew steadily more violent, so that they had to shout to make themselves heard. A brilliant flash of lightning was followed almost instantly by a sharp crackle, then a deafening boom. That flash lingered as an afterimage in Holly's eyes, and with it the tattered silhouette of the Valhalla's airplanes, all twisted and torn beyond repair.

"We're entering Nepal," called out Juanita. Though she shouted at the top of her lungs, Holly could hardly hear her. Holly slipped on portable headphones and a throat microphone and gestured for the others to do likewise, even though they were close enough to reach out and touch each other.

Lightning flashed repeatedly, and the thunder was like some cyclopean drummer using the Valhalla for his drum. Holly glanced toward Smith and saw that he had not put on his earphones. She was about to nudge him when she saw by the way his mouth hung open that he was screaming. It would be better if he didn't have a mike.

The Valhalla was rising now at last, and gaining still more speed. According to the radar altimeter, it would have to rise a lot more to avoid the wall of the mountains that loomed ahead. Holly grinned. She had always liked roller coasters. Besides, if she knew her physics, there would have to be a cushion of air along the face of the cliff, pushing them away.

In a fork of lightning she caught sight of a huge boulder, black and angular and too close for safety. The top of one of the Himalayan foothills. It passed to her right and vanished in the gloom.

Then the Valhalla gave a terrible shuddering jerk and Holly remembered the ballast ball swinging below her. It had hit something. She said, "We've got to retract the ballast ball. If it catches on anything it'll pull us right up against the cliff."

Juanita turned toward her, eyes wide. "If we retract the ballast ball, the Valhalla will turn upside down. It'll roll over, out of control."

"Everything is supposed to be nailed down on board," said Holly. "Let her roll! Pull in the ballast ball."

Juanita touched a button on the console in front of her, and Holly felt rather than heard the winch motor start, a reassuring throb in the floor under her feet.

Then she felt every hair on her body begin to move and she was about to call out "lightning" when the bolt hit the control room. Sparks arced from console to console. The computer screens went dark and the sharp smell of ozone filled the air. In total darkness Holly groped for an emergency flashlight clamped under her control panel and found it. She switched it on and swung it from face to face. Smith, Hal and Juanita were alive, but Smith was frozen with terror. She tried the radio. It still worked.

Juanita's voice came to her over the headphones. "Shipboard power is out, but these portable radios run on their own batteries."

Holly nodded, then said, "What about the winch on the ballast ball?" She could no longer feel the throb in the deck.

"It stopped," said Hal.

Holly unstrapped herself. "We've got to cut that ball loose. Come on, Hal."

Without waiting to see if he would obey, she started for the door, partly crawling on all fours, partly rolling, partly sliding. In the hallway she found a handrail and began to move toward the winch room, hand over hand in the blackness, her flashlight hooked into her pocketbelt. By this time she knew her way around well enough to do without the sense of sight.

She pulled open the outer airlock door to the winch room and braced herself in the doorway, panting, before moving on to the inner door. At that moment the Valhalla turned upside down, continued rotating. A terrible thump shook the craft. It went on rolling, over and over, then stopped, leaning steeply to one side.

"Juanita, what happened?" said Holly into her mike.

"We turned over a few times," came the shaky answer.

"But why are we still heeled over?"

"The ballast ball cable wrapped around us and snagged in the rigging that holds the aircraft. The ball hit the side, I think."

Holly thought, *Hit the side? Are we leaking?*

With the onboard instruments out, she couldn't tell.

She tried to raise some of the crew on the radio, but apparently none of them had portable sets turned on.

"Hal, you okay?" Holly demanded.

"Bloody but unbowed," came his rueful reply.

Thump. The ballast ball hit again. Holly could see it in her mind's eye, swinging free at the end of a short length of cable that held it to the wreckage of the aircraft rigging. She knew she would have to get rid of that ball before it destroyed the Valhalla.

Hal came up beside her and together they undogged the inner door of the airlock and tumbled like rag dolls into the winch room. Holly found a tool cabinet, got it open somehow, and, by touch alone, dragged out a laser torch. Hal turned on a flashlight a moment later and she saw he had opened the guard cover on the massive spool that should have pulled in the cable, that would have pulled in the cable if the power hadn't failed.

She fell against him, and he held her steady as she aimed her torch at the strand of cable where it stretched taut from the spool to the opening in the floor. The cable glowed red, then white, then let go with a shower of sparks. One end vanished through the hole.

The Valhalla continued to heel steeply over on its side.

"Juanita," called Holly into her mike. "Can you see the ballast ball?"

Juanita answered, "Yes, every time the lightning flashes. It's snagged by its cable in the rigging."

Holly looked up into Hal's demon face in the dim glow from his flashlight. Blood trickled slowly down his cheek from a deep gash in his forehead.

"Hal," she said. "Will you join me for a stroll?"

He fell in with her mood. "I'd be delighted, my dear. Outside?"

"Outside."

In the airlock they braced themselves as the Valhalla turned upside down once, twice, three times, then they dogged shut the outer door and stumbled into the locker room next door, where they quickly scrambled into pressure suits and fishbowl air-helmets.

A moment later Holly found herself outside the Valhalla, creeping down a short flight of rocking steps, the same steps she had come up on her first visit to the vessel. On that first visit she had felt, in spite of herself, a serious attack of fear of heights, though there had been no real danger. Now, when there was a real danger, her fear was gone. In an abstract way she knew one second's inattention would send her tumbling into space. In an abstract way she knew it was a long way to the ground. Yet perhaps because she could not see the ground or anything more than a few yards distant, her fear remained at bay. Hal followed close behind.

Steeply slanting rain struck her at intervals each time the catwalk to which she clung turned upward, and at those moments her helmet temporarily lost its transparency and she had to pause. The light on her chest was not strong enough to pierce the gloom very far.

"Juanita, can you see us?" Holly asked, through her helmet mike.

"I can see your chestlights," came the crackling answer.

"Are we near the cable?"

"You'll have to climb out farther."

A flash of lightning confirmed Juanita's observation. They continued onward to where the twisted, smashed remains of the aircraft bounced and dangled.

Holly thought, *We need more light.*

Then she felt her hair move again with electrostatic charge and became aware of the blue glow playing about the cables, struts, guywires and dish antennae. It grew brighter, shimmered around her, clothed her and Hal in unearthly cold flame, and now she could see the cable clearly.

In some part of her mind a detached voice said, "How beautiful." Then she had out her torch and began to cut. The wire turned red, then white, then broke, snapping like a whip, a whip that cut through other cables. The catwalk sagged.

Holly lost her grip and began to tumble into the darkness. "Hal!" she cried.

Powerful fingers closed around her ankle and dragged her back. She glimpsed his saturnian features through his helmet, grinning. He set her firmly on the catwalk, then guided her as they slowly crept back to the stairs.

"You got it," Juanita cried triumphantly. The ballast ball had fallen away and the Valhalla righted itself. There were no more alarming thumps and crashes.

The St. Elmo's fire that had illuminated her work began to fade, but in the darkness, broken only by the feeble gleam of her chestlight, she could see the stairway ahead of her. She started up, Hal close behind.

Then the hailstones began.

First they were small, hardly worth noticing, then larger. As she reached the head of the stairs she heard Hal grunt with surprise.

She turned back. "Are you okay, Hal?"

"I do believe that damn hailstone broke my arm," said Hal incredulously.

She started toward him, but he warned her, "Wait. Wait until they stop." Then he grunted again.

She hestitated. A hailstone the size of a tennis ball struck her helmet, cracking it, and she could hear the faint hiss of escaping air.

Hal grunted a third time, then fell, bounced off the catwalk, and was gone.

In her earphones Holly heard his voice, ludicrously apologetic, almost guilty, as if begging her forgiveness for abandoning her. "You're on your own, my dear."

She hung on, motionless, staring into the blackness.

The hail stopped.

In a flash of lightning she saw the sheer face of a cliff rushing downward, dangerously close, but she just looked at it.

Juanita called, "Holly, are you all right?"

As if in a dream Holly answered, "I'm fine."

"Come inside!"

Holly obeyed, without a will of her own. Out of habit she dogged shut the airlock behind her. Out of habit she took off the helmet.

After a moment she heard Juanita cry triumphantly, "We made it!" The swaying of the Valhalla was decreasing.

In a strained, unreal voice, remembering her last sight of Hal, her last sight of Brad mixed in it, Holly said, "that's nice." Then she vomited into her helmet.

Chapter 19

"They're coming to arrest you, Baboo," said Victor.

Baboo, sitting on his cot with the poom-poom in his lap, looked up and studied Victor's face. Baboo had an almost supernatural ability to detect insincerity, but he detected none in Victor.

"What do they want from me?" asked Baboo.

"Your memories, my friend. Everyone confides in you, even members of the Underground. You know everyone's secrets, and the police want to share that knowledge. Some of them even think you are the leader of the Underground."

"But I'm not even a member!"

"They don't know that, and I doubt they would care if they did. They need a victim, a famous victim, and you fill the bill."

"Who put them onto me?"

"Guess."

"Chaplain Bill."

"Right." A vivid image of Chaplain Bill's fat, envious, hypocritical face appeared in Baboo's mind, a face he had always hated, a face that seemed to sum up everything Baboo had been rebelling against when he founded Etnroa, all the repression of established religions down through the ages, all the hate, ignorance and prejudice. In a fraction of a second Baboo saw the Alexandrian library burning, the witch trials, the torture of heretics, the Spanish Inquisition, the medieval pogroms....

Victor added, "You haven't much time, Baboo."

"Time to do what? There's no place to escape to, is there?"

"No." Victor looked away, unable to meet Baboo's gaze.

"Oh, I see. No place except death. You want me to kill myself so I won't reveal what I know about you and your friends."

Victor nodded slowly. "With electrohypnosis they could drain enough information out of you to arrest hundreds of people, and with the best will in the world you couldn't stop them."

A cry of protest arose from the disciples clustered around the cot, but Baboo silenced them with an angry glance. "You're right, of course. Well, if I must die I suppose I should make a will, but I have only one possession." He ran his hand over the smooth wood of his poom-poom. "Victor, will you serve as executor of my estate?"

"If you wish."

He handed Victor the poom-poom, saying softly, "Give this to Newton, and tell him Etnroa is his too, if it can be said to belong to any one person. Now give me the keys to the air shaft."

Victor handed them over. "You picked a good place, Baboo. The fan blades at the bottom will...they may never figure out where you went."

"Thanks, Victor." Baboo stood up, towering over Victor, grinning at Victor's embarrassment. Baboo felt no unhappiness, only a strange lightheadedness, and he thought, *Only the dying are really free.*

The dying can do as they please. No one can punish a corpse. Baboo realized it had come already, the situation the murderer had been talking about.

As Baboo strode from the bunkroom, he whistled a tune, a new tune that came into his mind that very instant, and it seemed to him easily the best thing he'd ever composed, the sort of breakthrough tune that might lead to a whole new style. The people in the hall smiled as he passed. Some waved and greeted him by name.

He had no trouble climbing down the knotted rope in the airshaft, and he knew which floor to get off at. So many people had told him, at one time or another.

Out of the airshaft and into another hallway, he saw a tiny figure watch him pass then come scampering after him. He knew, from Newton's descriptions, it must be Piggy, the feebleminded girl.

"You so big, so big!" she called up to him in wonder.

With a deep, rumbling laugh he reached down and picked her up, doll, toothbrush and all. She was so small he could carry her like a baby in his great arms.

"Oooooooh," she cried delightedly. "Piggy flying!"

"Do you like songs, little creature?"

"Oh, yes, yes, yes!"

"I'll teach you one," he said, and began, his deep voice rumbling in his chest:

"Join hands, there's a new world coming.
Join hands and form a ring.
Join hands, there's a new world coming.
Join hands and dance and sing."

Piggy tried to join in, but couldn't carry the tune or even remember the simple words, so she just chanted in a singsong voice, "Dance and sing, dance and sing, dance and sing."

With a bellow of laughter he set her down.

"Piggy go with you!" she cried. "Don't leave Piggy behind! Piggy love you! Let Piggy come along, big man!"

He patted her tangled hair. "You wouldn't want to come if you knew where I was going."

Piggy burst into tears and watched him go.

Something about the proud tilt of his head made the Uns in the hall pause and look at him, his yellow robe slapping at his legs, his dark eyes glinting with a strange inner light.

A security policeman saw him and recognized him. "You there! Baboo! Stand where you are!" The Uns in the hall crowded together, blocking the policeman's paths.

Without breaking his stride, Baboo swept into the outer office of Chaplain Bill and snapped at the receptionist, "Is Bill here?"

"Why yes," mumbled the startled young woman. "But he's busy right now. I could make you an appointment...."

"I'll see him now."

To the receptionist's horror, he took a running start and flung his full weight against the sliding panel leading into the inner office. In a shower of splinters he lurched into the room, head lowered and arms swinging.

Chaplain Bill sat behind his desk, mouth open, eyes round with astonishment. "Baboo!" he said in a strangled voice.

"Did you sic the police on me?" demanded Baboo, towering over him.

"Why no. No. Of course not," stammered the chaplain but Baboo could not be lied to.

"You little bastard," Baboo whispered, starting toward him.

From the doorway came the quavering voice of the receptionist. "I'll shoot!" She held a deadly needle gun in her hand. "I swear

I'll shoot if you...."

With unbelievable speed Baboo snatched Bill in his arms and spun him around so he formed a shield between Baboo and the weapon.

"You let go of the chaplain!" she shrieked without conviction. Her gun hand shook violently. For a second they stood there motionless, then, with Chaplain Bill still struggling in his arms, Baboo dashed out through the open picture window and dove over the railing of the little porch.

The receptionist ran toward the window before the echo of Bill's scream had died away. It was a long way down, so long they were still falling when she reached the railing. To her it seemed they fell in slow motion, drifting to earth like two feathers intertwined.

It was late in the morning. The sky was overcast. A cold, damp wind was blowing. The receptionist stood a long time looking down and running her fingers again and again through her hair.

Below, a crowd began to gather.

*

Greta had planned to leave Newton and Danny at home when she went to her recording session, but at the last minute she got an idea.

"Newton, can you come along and play your poom-poom in the background? It will make the songs sound more authentic."

"Okay," said Newton.

So now here they were in the studio across the bay in Berkeley, not far from the Un dorms. The producer, a longhaired fanatical-looking fellow named Glen Frendel ruled the scene like a little Hitler.

"You're going to play?" Frendel asked Newton.

"I thought it would be nice," said Greta.

"If it isn't nice, we'll edit it out," said Frendel. "No sweat."

He set Newton up on a small soundproof booth, hooked up to four different tiny microphones and with headphones, like earmuffs, over his ears. Through the headphones he could hear not only Greta, who was wired up in another booth, but the prerecorded tracks already laid down by other musicians at various times during the previous week.

This prerecorded background sounded like the work of a symphony orchestra, but Frendel told him it had been done by three guys with a synthesizer and a performing music computer. Newton frowned when he heard the music for the first time.

He came out of his booth, after unplugging all the wires Frendel had so carefully plugged in, and said, "I don't like it."

Frendel sat at a huge, complex mixing console, with Danny, bored, perched beside him. "What do you mean you don't like it?" demanded Frendel.

"Too lush," said Newton. "This style of music should be simple and straightforward, like a folksong."

"Believe me, friend, I know what I'm doing. Do you know how many recordings I've done?"

"No, how many?"

"I don't know. I've lost count. But believe me, I know what I'm doing. Can you stay in rhythm with what's already recorded?"

"Yes."

"Then just plinkity-plink your little two-cents-worth in the right places and don't give me a bad time." He led Newton back to the booth and wired him up again.

Through the earphones Greta scolded him. "Newton, if you spoil my big break, I'll dice your ass. Will you behave?"

"Yeah, sure," said Newton sullenly.

"Ready, Miss Berg?" asked Frendel.

"Ready," she answered.

"Ready, Romano?" he said. Romano was a guitar player who had been brought in when Frendel had decided Greta's playing wasn't up to his standards.

"Ready," answered Romano from another booth somewhere.

Nobody asked Newton if he was ready.

"Greta Berg album take one," said Frendel.

The canned music started. Newton played along, none too sure he was being recorded. *He's letting me play to a dead mike,* Newton thought, *to humor Greta.*

He played anyway, and listened to Greta.

Greta had a fine, well-trained voice, but somehow it never seemed to carry conviction. It had actually been a good voice for the sort of songs she had been doing before, phoney songs, lying songs. Baboo's songs didn't sound right, coming from her, or so it seemed to Newton.

One after the other, they went through the songs planned for the album, Newton adding his "two-cents-worth" instrumental and getting more and more restless.

Then Frendal said, "That was fine, Miss Berg, but lets try some of those tunes again and see if you can put more feeling into it."

They tried again.

This time Newton couldn't contain himself, but blurted out

right in the middle, "No, no, Greta, not like that."

"Will you shut up?" she snapped.

But Frendel said smoothly, "Hey buddy, don't tell us. Show us."

A sudden anger seized Newton, a feeling that the honesty and strength of Baboo's songs were being compromised by both Frendel and Greta. The canned music had stopped. Newton said, "Here's how it's supposed to sound." He knew it wouldn't be any good, but they weren't recording now, and he thought he could at least give them the idea.

He began to sing.

This was no symphony orchestra. This was no hundred-voice chorus. This was no computer-generated soundtrack. This wasn't even the trained voice of an old pro like Greta.

This was just Newton and his poom-poom, solo, in a little booth all alone; Newton singing for the first time.

He had, he discovered as he sang, a voice like a frog with a frog in its throat, but he believed in it and there was a conviction to it, a rightness, a force, that surprised even Newton himself.

"If we could share this world below,
If we could learn to love,
If we could share this world below.
We'd need no world above."

When he came to the end he heard someone applauding over the earphones, then Romano's voice saying, "That was terrific!" At first he thought Romano was making fun of him, but no, the man sounded perfectly sincere.

Frendel's voice broke in. "Hey, kid. Let's hear some of the other songs."

Newton sang the other songs, then came out of the booth. About a dozen people Newton hadn't seen before were standing around, looking at him with wonder and curiosity.

Frendel pushed his way through the crowd, grinning. "I hope you don't mind, kid, but I called in some of the musicians who were working on other projects in the building. I wanted them to hear you."

Newton recognized faces that he'd seen on the video screen many times, faces of music stars he'd never expected to meet in person. These unreal people, these citizens of that Oz on the other side of the screen, were now lining up to shake his hand. Dazed and bewildered, he muttered thanks as they praised him, laughed with them as they laughed, smiled at them when they smiled at him. At the edge of the crowd Greta stared at him, hard-eyed.

"I guess you gotta get back to work," said one. Newton had

seen that face a hundred times, but in his confusion couldn't remember the name.

"Yes, yes, that's right," said Newton.

The show people began to file out.

Greta said, "If you're through socializing, we can finish the session."

Frendel said, "The session's finished, Miss Berg."

"But I haven't sung all the songs," she protested.

"No," he said coldly. "But he has." He jerked a thumb toward Newton. "We're going to release it exactly as he cut it. No frills. No fancy multiple-tracking. Just the straight goods."

He turned his back on Greta and began talking to Newton in a low, eager voice.

*

As Newton, Greta and Danny stepped out onto the sidewalk in front of the studio, Greta slapped Newton's face so hard he stumbled into the street and was almost hit by a passing pedicab full of tourists out for a night on the town.

"You can't live with me any more, of course," she told him as he regained the sidewalk. "I want you out of my apartment tonight, and take all your crap with you."

Newton thought about his "crap;" his poom-poom, his two nrobooks, his duffel bag, a few odd items of clothing. Baboo had once said, "Never own more than you can carry on your back."

"Sure, Greta," Newton said quietly.

Danny looked pleased.

Chapter 20

The Valhalla had lost the jet stream and now drifted slowly through the crisp morning air above the fog-shrouded Hwang Ho river in the Kiangsu Province of China, gradually losing altitude in spite of the constant pumping of its airpumps. So far their distance from the ground had remained fairly constant, but that was because the height of the mountains below was steadily lessening, but the broad green farmlands of Kiangsu Province were flat, almost as flat as the sea beyond. From here on the loss of altitude would begin to hurt.

At the end of the ballast cable swung a lump of wreakage, mostly the wreakage of the Valhalla's former fleet of light airplanes, taking the place of the vessel's lost ballast ball. In the crawl space between the inner and outer skins of the huge geodesic globe the crew worked around the clock in a desperate attempt to seal all the leaks sustained in the storm.

Holly had been directing the repair operations for the first forty-eight hours without sleep before turning the command over to Juanita and collapsing on her bunk for a few hours of blessed unconsciousness.

She dreamed formless dreams of Newton and of what might have happened if she'd never left him...glorious impossible sentimental spectacles of domestic bliss. Newton seemed so close, so real, that at times, half-awake in the dim stateroom, she would feebly call his name and reach out for him, only to hear the throbbing of the air pumps and know she was thousands of kilometers away from him.

Then she would lie awake awhile, thinking first of Newton, then of the mysterious library-in-a-crystal which, Brad had led her to believe, contained answers for all her questions. Where was it? Where in heaven's name was it?

Then her mind would stumble onward into the bleak and painful realm of guilt. It was her fault Brad was dead, her fault the Valhalla was limped through the lower stratosphere like a mortally wounded beast. Her hubris had set in motion this grotesque Greek tragedy, her pride had gone before the Valhalla's fall, her conviction of her own superiority had ignored the danger until too late, her ambition had roused the jealousy of the gods.

And in the midst of this orgy of self-recrimination, she would slip again into a troubled sleep.

Finally, though still weary and aching in every bone, she got up, put on her "company blue" shift, and stumbled out of her room to rejoin the crew's struggle against disaster. Hunger drove her first to the mess hall, where she was surprised to smell the aroma of something delicious cooking. She met Juanita in the kitchen.

"What's for lunch, Juanita?"

"Meat stew." Juanita's voice had an odd catch in it, so Holly looked at her with surprise.

"Meat? Meat, Juanita?" Then she understood. "Brad's recipe?"

Juanita nodded. "I had hoped you would sleep through this. You have never attended one of these ceremonies."

"You mean funerals?"

"We prefer the term recyclings. You have been with us such a short time I feared you might find this custom distasteful."

Holly thought, *Juanita, are you trying to pass a pawn against me?* Holly said, "On the contrary, as president of the corporation I intend to preside."

"If you insist...."

"I do insist."

"But would it not be more fitting if, for a quarter of an hour, we lived as Brad dreamed we could live, foolish as those dreams have been? He thought we could all be peers, equals, with no high ranks and low ranks, no superiors or inferiors."

"Who will preside then? You?"

Juanita's answer surprised her. "Not I, Holly. Sewall Smith."

"Smith? After he lost his nerve during the storm?"

"Because he lost his nerve during the storm. Who else on board is more in need of absolution? Of the forgiveness of his friends? Let him do it, President McClintok."

Holly smiled wryly. "All right, Juanita. Have it your way. What are you doing now?"

Juanita gestured toward two men who were busily setting things out onto a kind of utilitarian smorgasbord. "Helping with the preparations. I must make certain each bowl of stew contains at least a little meat. Will you help me?"

Holly pitched in, feeling the old camaraderie return so strongly it brought tears to her eyes.

The weary crew members began to file solemnly into the mess hall. The tables and chairs had been scavenged to form part of the new ballast ball, giving the room an austere atmosphere, like a zen meditation hall, and the crew members, in their identical blue tunics, seemed to Holly remarkably like monks and nuns of some nameless religion.

They lined up at the table and Holly handed out the steaming bowls of stew as they passed. Juanita served the drinks, small brown plastic mugs of strawberry wine brewed from the crop of the Valhalla's own indoor farm. The men who had been helping Juanita dispensed bread and salad.

The crew members sat down on the floor, more or less in the same places they would have sat when there were chairs. They did not begin eating, but looked expectantly toward the table.

Holly said, "Sewall Smith, will you lead us?"

The little man stood up, his face a mixture of conflicting emotions...embarrassment, gratitude, humility, pride. He held a battered Bible in his hands, torn paper bookmarks peeping from the pages. Someone handed him a mug of strawberry wine.

"Shipmates," he piped up. "Comrades. Prometheans. Let me begin as we have so often begun before, with a toast to the company." He raised his cup. "I pledge allegiance to Promethian Underwriters, and to the great project for which it stands, one policy indivisible, with benefits and coverage for all."

Many of the crew had joined in with Smith in reciting the vow they all knew so well, and now all tilted up their cups and sipped.

Smith continued, "And now repeat after me the famous blessing of Robert Heinlein. 'May you never thrist!' "

"May you never thrist," they echoed, and drank.

Smith went on, opening his black-leather-bound dogeared Bible, "It is written, 'Jesus took bread and blessed and broke it and give it to the disciples saying "Take, eat this is my body." And he took a cup, and when he had given thanks he gave it to them, saying, "Drink of it, all of you, for this is my blood of the covenant, which is poured out for many. Truly I say to you, I shall not drink again of the fruit of the vine until that day when I drink it new in the Kingdom of God.' "

He drank.

They drank.

Smith concluded, "So drink now, and eat, so that Brad's flesh may become our flesh as his mind has become our mind, so he may become one with us, his chosen people, so that he may look out through our eyes upon the land he had promised us and in our bodies enjoy its bread and meat and wine. Amen."

"Amen," chorused the crew.

Smith sat down. Everyone began to eat in silence. Holly looked into her bowl of stew for a long time, hoping that somehow there would be no meat in it. But there was, a small pink piece, like a bit of ham. The rest was vegetables and noodles.

She took the bit of meat in her spoon and raised it slowly to her lips.

Actually, it didn't taste half bad.

When the ceremonial meal was over, Holly stayed behind to help clean up, along with Juanita and a few other volunteers. Juanita turned on the radio and tuned in some music from the satellite relay.

Holly, collecting bowls, paid no attention until—the manic, benzedriny voice of the announcer bellowed out, in pure mid-Twentieth century style, "And now a brand spanking new superhit in the tradition of 'The Happy Un' and 'My Little Un Baby and Me.' It broke big in California three days ago, went national yesterday, and today it goes international on your rocking, stomping, wild blue satellite network. If you have feedback buttons on your radio, punch up your votes and show us how you like it. I call it a winner myself! It's heading straight for the International Top Ten on the World Hit Parade or my name isn't Kingmaker Jerry Gordon. Here it is, fans! 'If We Could Share,' sung by that rising young genius, Newton McClintok!"

Juanita laughed and called over to Holly, "Hey, doesn't he have the same name as your ex?"

"Coincidence," snorted Holly, but she paused to listen.

After a few bars of intro on a soft, haunting stringed instrument Holly had never heard before, a man began to sing. His voice was crude and untrained, but powerful and ringing with the kind of sincerity that can't be faked.

"Juanita!" Holly shouted. "That's him! That's my Newton!"

Juanita laughed again, louder. "Oh boy, Holly, did you ever make a mistake divorcing that one. Hey, you could have been

Mrs. Millionaire!"

"Shut up, Juanita! I want to listen!"

All too soon the song was over.

Holly thought, *A mistake! I certainly did make a mistake, but how was I to know he....* Then she remembered that Newton's world was on the eve of destruction.

*

From Newton's new penthouse apartment, he could see the Un dorms looming only a few blocks away, like a manmade mountain range. He liked to sit under a sun umbrella and sip ice water and look up at it, though he never once felt the slightest desire to return to it. He did think, however, about buying the freedom of certain carefully selected persons in there, in particular Baboo and perhaps Brother Judd, and maybe poor little Mickey.

He did not think about springing Victor, who seemed obviously able to spring himself.

And he was not surprised one hot, muggy evening when his terminal chimed and one of his security guards said, "A man here to see you, Mr. McClintok, name of Victor."

"Send him up," said Newton.

He went across the vast, dimly-lit living room with its potted palms and transparent walls full of tropical fish and stood waiting by the elevator, icewater in hand.

The elevator doors slid open and Victor, somber-eyed, stepped out, a duffelbag over his shoulder.

The two shook hands warily, then Newton, eyeing the duffel, said, "I hope you aren't planning to move in here."

"Don't be silly, Newton. Do you think I'd be comfortable here, knowing my comrades are back there, caged like animals?" He gestured toward the dorms, dimly visible through the floor-to-ceiling picture windows.

"I'm comfortable," said Newton.

Victor limped into the room, his feet sinking into the deep pile of the rug. "Oh, yeah? What you drinking, Goldie?" He took the glass from Newton's hand and sniffed the clear liquid within. "Water!" he cried in amazement, handing back the glass. "Maybe you are comfortable, after all. Full of surprises as ever, eh Newton?" He threw himself into the dark leather upholstery of an overstuffed sofa. "I have a present for you, old buddy." He roughly pulled open the mouth of the duffel bag.

"Not another bottle of Scotch, I hope," said Newton quietly.

"Nope."

"How did you find me, Victor?"

"A tour guide named Herron who does walking tours in this neighborhood points out your place to, his celebrity-happy customers twice a day. Wait a minute. Here it is." Victor was dragging out someting wrapped in a cloth. He unwrapped it. "Recognize it, Goldie?"

"Baboo's poom-poom."

"Used to be his. Now yours." He handed it to Newton.

Newton frowned. "Did you steal...."

"Baboo is dead." Victor seemed to take pleasure in putting it as bluntly as possible. "He willed it to you. As I understand it this hunk of wood and wire is a kind of scepter, crown and throne put together. Like it or not, baby, you are now the Grand Baboo, Pope of Fools, Klain of Klains. I hope you'll excuse my not falling on my knees before you."

Newton sat down on a footstool and began idly tuning the instrument, holding his ear close to the strings. "How did it happen?"

Victor told him, sticking to the facts but coloring them with his characteristic bitter glee. He finished up with: "So you see old Baboo finally joined the underground after all, and in fact struck the first blow against the establishment. As the new Pope of Etnroa, you should carry on his fight."

Newton felt no anger, only a great sad weariness. "Why should I fight the establishment, Victor? Look around you at this apartment. I *am* the establishment!"

"Don't you see?" Victor leaned forward eagerly. "This is that little push I was wishing for. Baboo can be our John Brown, our martyr. If the Uns hear how Baboo died, they'll be outraged, screaming for revenge. Word is already leaking out along the grapevine and...."

Newton set the poom-poom on the floor and answered calmly, "Baboo preached non-violence all his life, except for that few minutes it took to kill Chaplain Bill. Which was the real Baboo, the lifelong apostle of peace or the ten-minute assassin? As so-called Pope of Etnroa, which path should I lead my followers down? The path of war or the path of song?"

Victor threw up his hands in exasperation. "Damn it, they can sing as they march!"

Newton laughed.

Victor began rummaging in the duffelbag, again, mouth set in a grim line. "Enjoy yourself while you may, sweetheart. I've got something else to show you that maybe you won't find so humorous. You remember asking me who bought your freedom. I told you I could find out, and I did."

"Who was it?"

"Mickey, your cute little bunkmate."

"Do you expect me to believe that? Mickey didn't have any money."

"But she did have something to sell." Victor pulled out a soiled envelope full of snapshots. "Look here." He handed Newton one of the photos.

The picture showed Mickey in closeup with a curiously blank expression on her face and electrodes in the sides of her head that made her look like some sort of Frankenstein monster. Newton looked at those blank expressionless eyes that had once been so lively and playful and said uncertainly, "I don't understand. What...."

Victor explained gloatingly, "We live in a humane society, Goldie. If a criminal in prison volunteers to be a guinea pig in some scientific experiment, we pay him. A wise and liberal World Supreme Court has extended that policy to all of us, in the name of equality before the law, but for some strange reason no rich people are jumping at the chance to make some easy money, only poor people, only Uns. A lot of Uns sell themselves to the labs, leaving instructions that the money is to go to their loved ones. Mickey did that, and you are her loved one."

Newton had turned quite pale. "I'm rich now. I can buy her freedom as she bought mine."

Victor shook his head. "No you can't, Goldie. It's too late. The experiment has gone too far. She's working for the Hall of Heads. Those busy little doctors have been trying to find out which is the worst punishment, an eternity of extreme pain or an eternity of extreme pleasure. A crazy Professor called Balkani claims that pleasure, if it passes a certain point of intensity, is more agonizing than pain, more destructive of the personality. If his theories prove correct, they plan to change the wires in the Hall of Heads from the pain centers to the pleasure centers. The Mickey you knew is gone forever. There's no bringing her back."

"Are you saying she's dead?"

"She's not so lucky as that."

"Have you seen her?"

"Sure, I saw her. I saw her touching an electric pencil to those electrodes in her head again and again, each time jerking with a convulsion of ecstacy, the corners of her mouth twitching up in a ghastly death's-head grin. The whole complex superstructure of her personality has been permanently reduced to a single mechanical reflex. You know what the orderly told me that let me in to see her? 'She's doing it to herself.' That's what he said. He didn't want to take any responsibility. He just works there. He doesn't give the orders."

"Victor, we've got to get her out of there."

"I told you it's too late, and it is too late. She's totally addicted to those little electric shocks. The doctors know from experience that if they stopped the shocks she'd go catatonic and stop breathing within twenty-four hours."

Newton took the other photos and looked at them slowly, one at a time. They showed Mickey going through the process Victor had described. Newton remembered her trying to apologize when he wouldn't listen. Newton whispered at last. "I am you."

Victor misunderstood. "You're with us?"

Newton looked at the first photo again, at the blank, staring, mindless eyes. "What do you want me to do?"

"Your record is number one on the World Hit Parade," said Victor.

Newton was startled. "How do you know that?"

"I heard it over the grapevine, Goldie. Well, being number one means you go on the Top Ten Show on the Satellite Network. All over the world Uns watch that show on the funky little television sets they have in their public lounges. The authorities encourage it. A nice harmless music show! Keeps 'um from getting restless. So you sing your song and then someone interviews you. It's all live, see, and unedited. We want you to tell as much as they let you about how Baboo died, but more important than that, we want you to somehow say a certain word, the secret code word the Underground has designated as the signal for the revolution to begin. Say it once when you finish your song and, just to make sure, once at the end of your interview."

Newton said tonelessly, "What's the word?"

"Alaula. It's a Hawaiian word for the first light of a new day."

"Alaula." Newton spoke the word softly, trying it on for size.

"The important thing is that word," said Victor earnestly. "If you have to skip telling Baboo's story, skip it, but get in that word."

"Alaula," Newton said again. He would not forget it. Like so many Hawaiian nature words, it sounded exactly like what it meant, and could be pronounced easily by native speakers of all the world's great languages. He suspected a few hundred words had been considered and rejected before Alaula, so perfect in sound and meaning, had been selected.

"That's the spirit, babe!" Victor lunged forward to clap Newton on the back, then headed for the elevator. Newton followed him, still holding the damning photos.

"I'll be watching you on the boob tube," said Victor gleefully. "All the Underground, all the Uns, everybody will be watching. This show will be remembered for centuries, Goldie! Alaula! The first light of a new day!"

After Victor had gone Newton went out on the roof to stand in the hot, motionless air and stare up where the dorms blocked out the view of the stars. He thought, *I promised nothing*. To his alarm he found he had begun to feel.

*

Longhaired Glen Frendel was in raptures. "In the first second your song goes around the world. In the second second your song reaches the Moon colony and the local orbiters. Two minutes it reaches the Venus orbiters. Four minutes it reaches the Mars colony. At thirty-four minutes they hear you on the moons of Jupiter. Seventy-one minutes gets you to the moons of Saturn, two hours and thirty-one minutes to Uranus, four hours and twenty-three minutes to Neptune, five hours and nineteen minutes to Pluto. About four years from now, your voice catches up with the unmanned probe near Alpha Centauri, and from there it expands on and on to infinity. The whole universe will be listening tonight, Newton!" They were in the studio building, near the dorms, riding up in an elevator, together with a mixed crew of actors, musicians and technicians.

Frendel went on ecstatically, "I knew you were superstar material the first time you opened your mouth and showed those solid gold tonsils of yours. All you needed was the right promo, to be played on the right shows, to be endorsed by the right deejays. The public was sick of those la-de-da Un songs. They wanted something different, but not too different. They punched the feedback buttons for you, Newton. The first day they punched the buttons, and they kept on punching them. But I wasn't surprised. I knew from the first time you opened your mouth you were going right to the top."

The elevator door slid open. They stepped out to be greeted by a scantily-clad young woman with the offical air of a receptionist. "You may go into the studio now, Mr. Frendel," she said with a painted-on smile.

A swarm of reporters descended upon them in the hallway.

"Mr. McClintok, is it true you learned your songs in a real Un camp?"

"No comment," said Newton. He didn't want to think now. The reporter's voice seemed to come from a long way off.

Another reporter asked, "Mr. McClintok, is it true you've been offered a contract for a regular weekly variety show in prime time on the Satellite Network?"

"No comment," said Newton.

"That's right, boys," said Frendel, beaming.

"Mr. McClintok, we hear rumors there's some kind of revolutionary Underground in the camps. Any truth in that?"

"No comment," said Newton.

In his mind a voice kept repeating endlessly, "Alaula, alaula, alaula." It had become a kind of mantra, a kind of chant, filled with terrible power.

"Mr. McClintok, now that you're number one, what other challenges can life hold for you?" This from a pretty young woman reporter.

"No comment," said Newton.

A loudspeaker announced, "Ten minutes. Ten minutes to airtime."

They entered the studio, leaving the clammering reporters in the hall. The cameras were in place, the bright lights on. Technicians worked in a quiet frenzy of concentration. Newton was surprised at the small size of the studio, then realized that the vast scenes and flashes of a studio audience he had seen when viewing this show at home were products of the special effects department and the standard clips file.

Frendel introduced Newton to the host, Howard Canard, an odd little man with a funny tie.

"You got it straight now," said Howard Canard. "You wait for me to finish your introduction, then you sing, then you come over to the sofa and sit down with the other guests to answer a few questions. Okay?"

"Okay," said Newton.

"Hey, don't let it get to you, kid. This is just another one of those little routine performances on which your whole future career depends." He gave Newton a playful punch in the arm.

"Five minutes to airtime," said the loudspeaker.

A squad of ballet dancers in yellow Un robes filed past and began to do warming-up exercises near the back of the set. Voices said, "Testing, one, two, three, four. Testing."

Howard Canard walked over to talk to his other guests, who seemed to all be his close friends from the way they laughed and joked with him.

Nobody but Newton could hear the voice that droned on, "Alaula, alaula, alaula." Sometimes it sounded like Mickey, sometimes like Baboo, sometimes like himself, sometimes like a chorus of Uns.

"Sit here, Mr. McClintok," said someone.

Newton sat down in a camp chair and submitted to a last minute touchup of his makeup.

"Three minutes to airtime," said the loudspeaker.

Frendel leaned over him to whisper, "Break a leg, kid." Newton understood this old showbiz way of wishing someone luck. He'd seen a lot of backstage dramas in his years as a faithful viewer of the screen.

"Two minutes to airtime."

Someone handed Newton Baboo's poom-poom. He tested its tuning and found it acceptable.

"One minute to airtime. Places, everyone."

Howard Canard stepped behind a curtain. A fat announcer in a floral print jumpsuit took a position to one side of the stage area. The lights dimmed except for one spotlight that sent a bright amber glow down onto the announcer's ruddy cheeks. On the monitor screen a second hand rotated swiftly toward zero. Above the entrance a red light turned on. The second hand reached zero. The chant grew louder in Newton's brain.

A blare of jazzy fanfare sounded from the loudspeakers, mingled with wild applause, both recorded. As the music faded out, the announcer cried, "And now, from historic Berkeley, California, where everything happens first, Lunar Industries brings you 'Top of the World,' your weekly parade of the most-loved, most-asked-for songs from every nation on Earth and every colony in the Solar System, as tabulated by Muzak, the electronic brain, from the feedback you've given to audience-response radio, from the sales figures from your favorite media stores, and from the request patterns of your local stations. This is the Top Ten, ladies and gentlemen, today's gold records, tomorrow's classics. And here to bring it all to you, wherever you are, is our host, the little man with the funny tie and the big heart, Howard Canard! Heeeeeee's Howard!"

As the applause reached a crescendo, Howard Canard parted the curtains and stepped forth into the blaze of a pure white spotlight, bowing and grinning and tipping his undersize silly hat, saying, "Thank you, thank you, thank you! But what am I thanking you for? I deserve it! Hey, seriously now, have I got a show for you this time! A show to end all shows!"

Newton thought, *Alaula, alaula, alaula.*

*

In what had once been Newton's room, Newton's family gathered to watch the floor-to-ceiling, wall-to-wall screen. Front and center, in the room's only chair, sat the old man, Adam McClintok, puffing on his discreetly-bubbling waterpipe. On the bed lay Newton's biological mother, Miriam, with her new husband, Jim Moran, quarreling in exasperated whispers. Adam's wives, Wilma and Barbara, sat at the old man's feet, leaning against his legs and watching the show. Newton's brothers, Einstein and Arp, sprawled on their bellies, chins on palms.

"I wonder what's going to be number one this week," Wilma speculated.

Old Adam shrugged. "Some damn Un song, I shouldn't wonder. Nothing you could call real music."

"You're just prejudiced," said Einstein.

"What the hell do you know?" Adam demanded. Ever since Moran had joined the family, the patriarch had displayed a hair-trigger temper.

From the screen came the rasping voice of Howard Canard. "You've heard the top nine songs, and wonderful as they are, this next one will cap them all! Rocketing to the number one position on its first appearance on our show, here it is, a new kind of Un song straight from the dorms, entitled 'If We Could Share.' Here to sing it for you is the man who made it famous, that overnight success, that brilliant young innovator, Newton McClintok!"

"Who did he say?" muttered the old man.

Einstein pointed. "Look! It's Newton!"

"I don't believe it," said Jim Moran.

There, perched on a stool much like the one he'd used in the old Bread and Wine Mission, was Newton, illuminated by a blue spotlight, looking off into space as if dreaming, holding in his arms an odd stringed instrument none of the McClintoks in the room had ever seen before.

"Well, I'll be damned," murmured the old man, grinning for the first time in weeks. "Newton's a real McClintok after all. A winner!"

*

Danny Berg, staring at his little portable TV set with amazement, shouted, "Mama, mama, come quick. Newton's on video!"

Greta burst in from the next room. "Turn that thing off, and I mean now!"

*

Captain Clark and Normandy Taylor watched on Norm's three-D, supersonic, full-wall screen, Clark slouched in the overstuffed chair, Taylor half-sitting on the arm.

"George," Norm called out. "Bring us some drinks. The usual."

From the kitchen came George's obedient, "Yes, m'am."

On the screen Newton, in his yellow Un robe, strummed a few introductory chords.

"I don't like it," said Clark gloomily. "McClintok is in with Victor Tarachenko and that bunch. They shouldn't let him go on television like that. He could say anything, do anything. He could spout all sorts of inflammatory propaganda."

Norm, amused, said, "Do you think one song can inflame the world? I'm beginning to think nothing can inflame the world. For years we've been jumping at shadows, thinking some kind of revolution was going to break out, but nothing ever happened and nothing ever will."

"They should have stopped him," Clark insisted.

"They should do this. They should do that. If you want something done, you have to do it yourself, Cap. You know that. If you were worried, why didn't you stop him yourself?"

"There was no time. I heard that damn song on the radio for the first time day before yesterday, and only yesterday I learned by the grapevine Newton was going on the Top of the World show. To prevent a performance you have to go through committees, get papers from judges, all that crap. Our society has tied itself up in so much red tape it can't even defend itself."

George came in with the drinks.

Norm said, "Stick around, George. This show might interest you."

"Yes, m'am," said George meekly as he stood waiting, waiting to hear a certain word.

Newton began to sing:
"If we could share this world below,
If we could learn to love."

*

Juanita Castro tugged at Holly's arm, saying, "Come on. There's work to be done."

Holly remained seated on the floor, back against the spiral staircase, staring at the television screen in the Valhalla's nowfurnitureless lounge. Only the set remained; Holly hadn't let them pack that into the new ballast ball.

"Just a few minutes," said Holly. "Wait."

Juanita glanced at the screen. "Is that your Newton?"

"That's him."

"He doesn't look like much. I like a man with a little meat on his bones."

Newton went on singing:

*"If we could share this world below,
We'd need no world above."*

"Amen," Holly whispered. "Amen, baby."

Hadn't Newton's answer's always been deep ones?

*

In the dorms Victor and a handful of grim men and women sat in an Un public lounge and watched the set.

"Say it," said Victor under his breath, fingering the zipgun he'd made in art therapy class. "Say it, Goldie."

*

In another lounge, on another floor, Brother Judd and a crowd of hushed Etnroans watched. On some cheeks, including Judd's, tears trickled slowly down.

*

Before he had sung it with his voice, Newton had sung it a million times with his mind, so now he could let the familiar tune play itself out automatically through him like a recording while his thoughts wandered elsewhere. He thought of a phrase from Shakespeare: "Rather bear those ills we have than fly to others that we know not of." He thought of the vast but fragile web of technological civilization, of its power that could take him to the planets or bring all the knowledge of the race to his little computer console, that could provide him with food, clothing and shelter that did not fail when the weather turned too dry or too wet, of the myriad taboos and mind-enslaving superstitions that had fled before the light of science.

He thought of the generations of researchers and inventors who had built that civilization over the centuries, each adding one more brick to the slowly-growing tower. He thought of that tiny minority who had lived with the terror of ignorance rather than accept the consolation of unproven answers, of those few who had become wise by risking being fools, those few to whom humankind owed everything. Could he, with one word, destroy all that they had done?

The song ended.

He played a little coda on Baboo's poom-poom while the loudspeakers blasted out deafening recorded applause.

Victor had said to speak the word when he finished his song, then again after the interview. Newton found he could not say it.

The moment passed. Howard Canard took his arm and led him over to a couch where the other celebrities sat applauding. Newton had seen these people so many times before on the video screen they seemed unreal, now that he could see them in the flesh. Wasn't this just one more show in particularly good three-D and color?

They shook his hand and drew him down among them, accepted him as one of them. Canard sat down at a desk facing them. The desk, the only one on the set, gave Canard a subtle, almost subliminal advantage, as if he were a employer and all the celebrities job applicants.

"Well, Newt," said Canard heartily, "That was great. Did you write that song?"

"No," Newton answered. "It was written by a man named Baboo, a great man." Victor had said to tell as much of Baboo's story as they would let him.

Canard grinned, "A great man? Maybe we should have had him on instead of you. Ha ha."

"You couldn't," said Newton bluntly. "He's dead."

The loudspeakers exploded with canned laughter. Newton frowned. He hadn't intended to make a joke.

A beautiful blonde singer on his right touched his arm and said soothingly, with a heavy accent, "Never mind, darling. Hees music weel live on."

A handsome male actor/singer said, "I play a detective in my latest tape drama. Maybe I can solve the murder."

"Murder?" Newton failed to follow this irrational veer in the conversation.

Canard said, "Ha ha. You detectives see murder everywhere. I'm sure this Mr. Baboo died of wine, women and song, just like the rest of us. That right, Newt?"

Newton felt hot and suspected he was blushing and hated himself for it. "No. No, it wasn't a natural death."

The male singer said, "I was right then. It was murder, murder most foul. Now we must find out who dunnit!"

Newton blurted out, "You dunnit!"

"I?" said the singer, nonplussed.

"All of you," Newton went on, with a gesture that included

not only Canard and the other guests, but the viewing audience out beyond the cameras.

"Even little me?" said the female with the accent, pouting.

The canned laughter roared again.

Canard broke in smoothly, "Well, be that as it may, what did you think of the dancers?"

"What dancers?" said Newton.

"Well, didn't you notice our little corps de ballet over on the other side of the set?" Canard demanded.

"Ballet? I didn't see any ballet," said Newton, now completely off track.

"Sure," Canard continued gleefully, "while you sang, they danced, and through the magic of video the two images were sent out as one. They were—you know—showing with mime all the fun you Uns have in the camps, how happy and carefree you are."

The male singer said, "The camps would make a fine setting for a detective story. You could lend me your yellow robe, only wait until we're off camera. Like in my latest tape...."

Canard winked at the nearest camera, "That movie is called 'Rocket to the Morgue,' isn't it?"

"That's right," said the singer who acted the part of a detective. "I'm sure all your viewers will love it."

"I know they will," said Howard Canard. "Well, it's half past Mickey's ass and quarter past his nose, so we'll have to say goodby until next week...."

"Wait," said Newton, half-rising. "I'm not finished."

"Yes, you are," said Howard Canard. "By by, Newt."

Newton could hear the theme music fading in. He had seconds to make his decision, then it would be too late. He looked into the mindless face of Howard Canard. He glanced at the mindless faces of the other celebrities. All those centuries of struggle and dedication, all those sacrifices by the selfless men of science, all those little bricks of inspiration, one upon another.

This was the final result. These empty faces. These empty lives.

Newton raised his hand, waving goodbye, waving goodbye to all of them, forever.

"*Alaula!*" said Newton McClintok.

*

As the image faded from the screen, Victor turned to his comrades and cried out triumphantly, "He said it!"

The others were already checking their crude weapons. One of them said, "Let's go."

Chapter 21

The Valhalla had found the jetstream over the Pacific Ocean then, with the California coastline almost in sight, had lost it again. Unable to maintain altitude, she had been drawn helplessly into another storm, and there many of her patches had started to leak again. Holly had learned a disconcerting fact about geodesic spheres: since they gained their great strength by distributing stress places on one part of the structure over the entire structure, they could not be easily repaired in parts: bending one member back into true placed a stress on all the surrounding members that, time and again, made something else pop open, sometimes something on the opposite side of the sphere.

Only the constant running of the airpumps kept the craft aloft, and now that they were being drawn into storms that cut off the sun's rays even during the day, the solar batteries were running low.

So ultimate helplessness, she thought, *is the result of seeking, and gaining ultimate power. Did Newton know that too? How much had he known?*

Smith had repeatedly suggested abandoning the Valhalla and parachuting to the sea where they could be picked up by a passing ship. Holly had vetoed his suggestion, arguing that, even damaged, the Valhalla provided more protection than a rubber raft. Besides, ever since Newton's broadcast, news reports had indicated the world revolution Brad had predicted was finally breaking out. Could they could on there being any ships to pick them up? And if the ship were in the hands of the revolutionaries, how would the obviously Tech promethians be treated?

The crew settled down and began treating the continuing emergency as routine. Juanita took over command of the day-to-day struggle. Holly threw herself into one final, frenzied search for the crystal, knowing that it was only a matter of time before she would have to abandon the Valhalla.

The days had passed, and the nights. The radio had chattered of unspeakable atrocities, the television had shown images of bloodbaths, of streets strewn with corpses and cities aflame, but Holly had paid no attention, not even when, one after another, the stations began to mysteriously cease broadcasting. Smith and Juanita had brought her reports of the prometheans' efforts to keep the Valhalla flying, but she had nodded and muttered and not really understood what they said. She could not quell the revolution, nor could she somehow lift the Valhalla back into the stratosphere, but if she could find the crystal she would have the tool that might preserve civilization. And with that thought Holly's conscious mind knew what her unconscious goal had always been, since the day she'd first stepped on board. For she had seen even then that Brad and Brad's methods, could never pull it off. When it comes to saving the world for your own sake, what is the world but its people. Was that what they called "enlightened self-interest? Did Newton, in his way, already know this?

So, as the Valhalla rocked in the turbulence of the storm off the coast of California, Holly belted herself down at the computer console and tried one more time to get the reluctant microcircuitry to give her some clue.

She did not pause in her feverish keyboard punching when she heard Juanita's voice behind her.

"Holly," said Juanita.

"What is it?"

"I did not ask for this, and I do not think it wise, but...."

Holly did not look up. "Out with it, Juanita."

"The crew held an election. You are no longer our president."

"Who is then?"

"I am, Holly."

"Congratulations, dear." Holly's voice held no resentment but no warmth either. It was the voice of someone preoccupied with more important things.

"I'm glad you take it so well. The position of leadership meant so much to you I thought...."

At last Holly swiveled to face the older woman. "Tell me, Juanita. Do you have a plan to save the Valhalla?"

"No. Do you?"

"No. So why should we fight over which of us commands a doomed vessel?" A flash of lightning illuminated Juanita's haggard face. Holly went on calmly, "If you are captain I ask only one favor, one kindness of a vanquished rival. Let me continue to work on the computer."

Juanita shrugged. "As you wish, but whatever you do, do it quickly. In a half hour the batteries will be too low to sustain a stable flow of current. We will have no computer, no lights, and most importantly, no air pumps. Without the pumps the Valhalla will fall into the sea. If Brad's wonderful data bank is on board, you must...."

Holly straightened. "If it's on board, you say?" Her mind, numb with lack of sleep and repeated disappointments, groped for a memory just out of reach. She had assumed the data bank would be hidden on the Valhalla somewhere, or at least that it might be somehow concealed in the computer, waiting for the right code to unlock it.

But now she remembered the first time Brad had mentioned the crystal. She had asked him then pointblank if it were on board.

And he had smiled and chuckled, *and refused to answer!*

So it wasn't on board.

Then how could he use it?

Juanita began, "I mean if it really exists...."

"It exists, Juanita," said Holly firmly, turning back to the console.

"Holly, don't...."

"Go away. Let me concentrate," Holly commanded, and though she was now Holly's superior officer, Juanita obeyed, stumbling away on the wildly pitching deck.

Holly thought, *Let us suppose the crystal is outside the ship somewhere. When would he communicate with it? Unless he could communicate with it constantly, he'd have to save up questions and then, at the right moment, tightbeam them to the crystal and get back the answers. With such a small storage bank the speed of light might not be an important factor. The questioning and computation and answering could all take place in microseconds, even if he'd been piling up questions for months.*

Laughing wildly, she set her fingers dancing over the keyboard, then looked at the screen. The computer had indeed

215

been stockpiling questions, then at widely separated intervals had drained one bank and filled up another, drained out questions and filled up with answers.
And where was the Valhalla when this happened?
Again her fingers jigged over the keys.
When she read off the answer she laughed still louder and clapped her hands with delight.
Then the console lights faded.
The sound of the airpumps died at the same time, and abruptly all she could hear was the creak and groan of the Valhalla in the storm and the not-too-distant rumble of thunder.
She did not need the now-dead instruments to tell her the Valhalla would begin losing altitude rapidly. She unsnapped her seatbelt and crept to the door, thinking, *Now that I know, I can't die. It wouldn't be fair.*
She made it down the hall by the sense of touch alone, then saw flashlights swinging in the gloom. Juanita, Smith and some of the other Prometheans were handing out lifejackets to the grim-faced crowd. Holly accepted one of the jackets with a murmured "thank you."
Shouting to make herself heard over the storm, Juanita called out, "We're still over the sea, but the California coast is only a few kilometers to the east. Your lifejackets should keep you afloat, so don't try to swim at first. Save your energy until you get into the surf, then try as best you can to stay away from the rocks. There are a lot of rocks along here, but there's beach too. Each one of you has some chance to survive. When the Valhalla hits the water it will float for a while, I think, before it starts to break up. We'll have time to get everyone out if we all keep our heads and evacuate in an orderly fashion. Any questions?"
There were none.
Juanita led the way from the locker room through the airlock and down the damaged but still fairly firm catwalk below the sphere.
In a pale yellowish light Holly could see the whitecaps of the waves in a vast, pulsating pattern beneath her, uncomfortably close. Cold wind blew salty spray into her face, almost blinding her. Driven by a relentless gale, the Valhalla dropped lower and lower until finally it almost skimmed the wave crests, its ballast ball dragging in the water.
"Hang on!" screamed Juanita. "We're going to hit!"
The impact of the first wave carried Holly overboard, but she'd had a chance to fill her lungs with air, and she managed to hold her breath through that long cold wait in the swirling

underwater darkness when she could not tell up from down. Surfacing at last, she saw the Valhalla, briefly airborne again, rushing away from her, spewing struggling bodies, heard the distant screams of her crewmates almost lost in the howl of the wind. Then the Valhalla hit again and, slowly and majestically, as if made of cloth rather than plastic and metal, it collapsed, folding in upon itself.

Holly let her lifejacket hold her up and drifted, watching, thinking, *Goodbye Valhalla. You're not completely dead as long as I'm alive.*

*

Normandy Taylor had been alarmed by Newton's appearance on television, particularly by the unfamiliar word he had used when saying goodbye. There had been something demonic about him at that moment, something Normandy would not have expected in a passive, spiritless man like Newton, and after Captain Clark had gone home, she had lain awake for a long time, her body motionless but her mind in turmoil.

Then she heard a noise in the darkness, a stealthy footstep. She sat up and snatched her needlegun from her bedtable. "Who's that?" she demanded.

"Only me," came George's meek, wistful voice.

Normandy caught an unnatural undertone in his words, a tension, a touch of fear perhaps. She rolled out of bed onto the floor on the side away from George an instant before George's laser pistol sent a whitehot beam searing into the bedclothes, then another, then another. The bed burst into flames, and in the flickering firelight she could see him standing in the middle of the room, wide-eyed, searching for her. She aimed her needlegun and squeezed the trigger. The gun made an almost inaudible snick. George swatted at his cheek, as if at a mosquito, then crumpled to the rug. Lying on his face, he breathed twice, slow and hard, then stopped, his mouth open, saliva running out.

Nude, she dashed forward and picked up the laser pistol, then searched his body for other weapons. He had a knife and a crude, handmade zip gun.

She dressed quickly in Tech coveralls as the room filled with smoke, making her cough, bringing tears to her eyes. The automatic fire extinquisher, a sprinkler system, did nothing.

"Sabotage!" she muttered. George must have done it, or perhaps one of those damn Un girls she was always having in for the night. By now the fire had spread. There was no way she could put it out.

She thought, *I've got to get out of here, got to find Cap."*

Cautiously she opened her front door and peered into the hall. The lights were out, and she had never seen them out before, night or day. Someone, it seemed, had cut the power lines, and that meant this was the real thing, the revolution at last. She slipped into the hall, closing the door behind her. Darkness was her friend. It would hide her. She knew these passages so well she could move swiftly through them with no fear of getting lost.

Noiselessly she sped along the hall, bare feet on the cold cement floor, the fingertips of her left hand brushing lightly against the wall to give her direction, her right hand gripping the needlegun. The laser pistol she kept in her coveralls pocket. Its bright flare might attract unwanted attention.

Many times she had idly allowed her fingers to skim along the wall, just like this, on her way to work. She had not been consciously aware of doing it, but now, in the blackness, her fingertips remembered each bump, each rough spot and irregularity. Somewhere below her she heard a muffled explosion.

A light appeared up ahead. She backed into a doorway and held her breath.

"This way," came the unmistakable voice of Victor Tarachenko, full of the exhilaration of battle. He ran past, so close he could have reached out and touched her, followed by a squad of robed figures. She waited until the glow of Victor's flashlight had disappeared around a corner, then continued on her way.

More explosions sounded in the distance, and some muffled screams.

She slowed when she reached the heavy door that had once separated the staff quarters from the dorms, reached out a groping hand and found it was open. Had one of the Uns employed in the staff quarters as a servant opened it? Or had they lasered the lock? No matter.

Out of the blackness came a voice. "Who's that?"

She recognized the voice. The one they called Brother Judd, a close friend of old Baboo. Judd must have joined Victor, otherwise Victor wouldn't have left him here alive. She made certain of her own location by reaching out and silently touching a familiar lighting fixture. She knew where she was, but where was Judd?

"Who's that?" Judd repeated.

She pointed her needlegun in his general direction and waited. He took a few steps toward her, slowly, carefully. She knew there was a strip of metal in the doorway. If he stepped on the metal his steps would sound different and she'd have him located. She thought, *Step on the metal, you bastard.*

There it was, the sound of a sandal on metal.
She pulled the trigger.
Judd sucked in his breath, then fell. She waited a second, in case he might be faking, then dashed through the doorway, tripping over the corpse and almost falling.

*

Captain Clark switched on the chiming terminal at last.
On the screen the image of his superior officer, Mr. Emmanuel, swam into focus. The old man was dirty, frightened and bleeding from the mouth.
"I'm dying, Clark."
"So I see."
"I'm bleeding to death, Clark. Hand missile blew up my office. Those yellow-robed swine are coming to finish me off. I can hear them. How about you?"
"They haven't attacked here yet, sir."
"Thank god! You're in charge now, Clark. Fight 'um off until reinforcements arrive." To Clark the old man seemed almost funny, as if he were some ham actor in an old silent film.
"Yes sir." Clark switched off the terminal. He didn't want to see Emmanuel die. Not really.
He didn't have time.
Quickly he plugged in his electric clippers, expecting the power to go dead at any moment, and began to shave his head, zipping away all of his sparse, greying hair.
Still working against time, he took from a drawer a typical Un camp identification bracelet containing, in magnetic code, a complete profile of an imaginary Un, a man Clark had invented. If asked, the computer web would look up the information Clark had planted during the last few days and support every detail. He snapped the bracelet on his own wrist.
An explosion not far away shook the room and the lights dimmed briefly, then came on again.
Clark took off his uniform, placed it neatly on a hanger, and went to the closet to exchange it for a yellow monkish robe and a pair of plastic sandals. As he slipped the robe on over his head his computer console chimed, startling him.
He snapped it on, standing to one side so whoever was calling him couldn't see him.
"Cap! Cap!" The voice was that of Normandy Taylor. A moment later her face faded into view, wildeyed and glistening with sweat. "Are you there? Let me in. I'm right outside your office. Show yourself."

Clark stepped in front of the screen.

Normandy looked puzzled for a moment, then brightened. "That monkey suit...you're going to fool them." She laughed brokenly.

Clark pressed a button to unlock the entrance to his office. A panel slid to one side. Normandy stumbled in and threw her arms around him as the door closed behind her. He felt uncomfortable in her embrace. Until this instant she had hardly ever touched him, let alone hugged him, but in her terror and excitement she had apparently forgotten herself.

"What's the plan?" she demanded, letting him go.

"I'm changing sides, Norm."

She stared at him, speechless.

He added, "I have prepared a false identity for you, too, if you want to use it."

"Are you crazy?" She backed away from him.

"I would be crazy to stay here and fight. Nobody knows better than I do how fragile our defenses are, how frightfully outnumbered we are, how hopeless our situation is. This war will last a matter of weeks, perhaps days, and the techs will lose. Victor and his friends captured a sperm bank in the hospital the first thing. Do you know what that means?"

"I...I don't understand." She leaned against his desk as if afraid her legs would not support her.

"I'll explain. The male Uns, as you know, have all undergone a sterilization operation. If Victor is so concerned about a sperm bank, it can only mean that he and his friends intend to exterminate everyone not dressed in the official yellow robe and ID bracelet. He doesn't intend to let any of us live, not even as...as studs. I have a robe here for you if you'll...."

"No! Cap, think of your wife...."

He sighed. "I tried to talk to her weeks ago. She wouldn't listen. She wouldn't believe this could ever happen. Now there's nothing I can do for her except stay alive and hope that the impossible will happen, that somehow she will stay alive too."

"Do you want to be alive in the kind of world that's coming?"

He shrugged. "After the smoke clears away, we may find things haven't changed so awfully much. At least for me. I imagine the Uns will give me a job not unlike the one I hold now. Every society in history has needed a certain number of good, trained experienced cops. Now be smart and...."

She spoke softly, wonderingly. "I thought I knew you. I never knew you at all."

Impatiently he demanded, "Are you coming?"

"Never. Never in a million years. There's such a thing as honor, such a thing as duty...."

He smiled. "I never thought I'd live to hear you, Normandy Taylor, the tough old bull dyke, talking such bullshit. All the same, right now it seems to me I care more about you than anyone else on God's green earth." He gently touched her arm. "Come with me, Norm. Please."

She jerked her arm away. "You, of all people, a traitor," she whispered.

"So you're staying?"

"Of course."

"Then goodbye, babe. You're in charge now. Lots of luck."

He pressed the button to open the sliding panel, then stepped into the hall. She stood a moment, biting her lip, then ran out after him.

"Cap!" she shouted at his retreating back. "Stop!"

He glanced back at her over his shoulder, a foolish grin on his face as if he were a kid caught stealing cookies, but kept on walking.

"I warn you, Cap. Stop right where you are or I'll shoot you down." She drew her needlegun.

He went on walking and grinning, looking back at her, sure she could never pull the trigger, not on him. On anyone else maybe, but not on him.

Slowly, deliberately, she raised her pistol, gripped it with both hands, and squeezed the trigger.

He felt the sting in the back of his neck, half-raised his hand, then fell, the grin beginning to fade as the poison rushed through his veins, as the life left his body. He landed on his face and lay still.

Tenderly she removed the yellow robe from his limp corpse.

Gently she dressed him in his uniform as the sounds of battle drew closer.

But her voice was firm as she activated the computer terminal and said, "Captain Clark has been killed in action. I recommend him for a distinquished service cross, to be awarded to his widow, Mrs. ...." She tried to remember the woman's name and failed. "Captain Clark died in the distinguished tradition of...." Again she could not go on. "Exceptional bravery ...." The words stuck in her throat. At last she blurted, "Clark's dead. This is Taylor taking command. Battle sations report."

The battle stations began calling in. There were not many left.

Chapter 22

The tropical fish in the glass walls died after the power failed. Without electricity the automatic heaters and air bubblers that maintained their environment would not run. Newton watched them floating, belly up, near the ceiling of his luxurious apartment, with a felling of numb helplessness. Somehow it seemed unjust these little creatures should die because of humanity's folly, these little creatures who could not vote, let alone fight.

Newton had not fought either, but had sat out the war, listening to his battery-powered radio and sometimes going out to the edge of the parapet to look down into the street far below, eating canned food cold with a plastic spoon. He held the last of these cans in his hand now as he looked at the dead fish. It had been cream of chicken soup, and he had not bothered to mix it with water.

He looked at the fish.

He could not eat them. They had been dead too long. Besides, they were pets. One does not eat one's pets.

"I'll have to go out," Newton announced to the empty room, quiet in the slanting rays of the afternoon sun. He wondered how long he'd been here since returning from the studio the night of that incredible broadcast. He'd lost track. Six days? Seven?

He had spent a lot of time at first out on the roof watching that vast river of yellowclad humanity flow by in the streets below, watching the fires rage in the immense Un barracks nearby, listening to the screams of the dying and the sounds of battle, but after two days, or perhaps three, when the rain started, he had gone indoors to take care of his fish, and when they had died he'd contented himself with eating and sleeping.

He'd had visitors.

The first group had kicked down his front door and had almost shot him, but when they saw he wore the Un yellow robe and the identification bracelet, they had apologized and gone away.

The second group had recognized him as the one who had said the word on television, and had embarrassed Newton by treating him like a hero.

The third group had been Victor and a squad of Undergrounders. Victor had gloatingly recited a list of names of the people Newton knew who had died in the battle, watching Newton's expression for some sign of an emotional reaction. Newton had listened pokerfaced, not wanting to give him the satisfaction. Even when he heard Victor mention Mickey, and Greta and Danny Berg, and Piggy, Newton betrayed no expression. At Piggy's name Newton had glanced at his fish. Piggy was like the fish, an innocent creature paying for the folly of so-called higher lifeforms.

"Come with us to San Francisco," Victor had finished. "It's all over but the mopping up."

Newton had shaken his head and Victor had gone away.

After that nobody had intruded on Newton's solitude.

And now Newton stood with an empty soup can in his hand and said to nobody in particular, "I'll have to go out."

The elevator didn't work so he went down the back stairs.

As if chosing a direction at random, he walked west, toward the Oakland-San Francisco Bay Bridge. It was worse than he thought. All the violence of a civilization gone mad had erupted. The streets were full of rotting corpses and clouds of humming flies that swirled upward as Newton approached, then settled again after he had passed. The shelves of the neighborhood supermarket were bare, already looted. Some of the shops were heaps of smoldering rubble, others retained their display windows unbroken. In one doorway a bloated rat watched Newton fearlessly, defiantly, as if ready to fight for the God-given supremacy of the rodent race.

His brain began to reel. It was like the worst nightmares on the screen. It was unreal. It couldn't be real. He rejected it.

In the ditch beside the Powell Street onramp, Newton found

an undamaged racing bike, low and streamlined, with a grey fuselage and painted eyes and teeth to make it look like a shark. He opened the plastic canopy, dumped out the dead occupant, and, resting it on its outrigger wheels, climbed in and settled back into its comfortable recumbent seat, lifting his feet to the high-mounted stirrup-pedals. Shifting into low, he started off.

The broad ten-lane bikeway seemed deserted, so Newton pedaled toward the fast lane, shifting up quickly through the gears, retracting the outrigger wheels with a snap. A racer like this, Newton knew, could go faster than the speed limit once enforced here for powered automobiles, but could, at such speeds, become a little unstable in a strong crosswind. There was no wind today, and nothing else on the road, so Newton let himself go, pumping with firm even strokes until the guardrail separating the northbound and southbound lanes melted into a blur.

If the camps had given him nothing else, they'd given him muscles. He'd never been able to work up to these speeds before those many hand-over-hand trips up and down the airshaft to visit Baboo.

He smiled, pleased with his newfound strength and sense of accomplishment.

On his left he saw an overturned three-wheeler pedicab, then a pedibus, a four-wheeler, filled with dead teenagers. Newton glanced at them, seeing them and not seeing them at the same time, as if they were on the screen and not here in life.

A five-man peditruck stood sideways, its broad square flatbed sticking into Newton's lane. Newton swerved, easily avoiding it.

Newton knew where he was going now. It was the only logical place to go. He was going to San Francisco. He was going to his room.

Home.

He smiled again.

*

San Francisco had been harder hit than the east bay. Here, along Market Street near the rail terminal in the San Francisco Hilton, major fires still blazed out of control and the street was so clogged with debris Newton had to abandon his bike and proceed on foot.

His sandals crunched on broken glass as he passed vacant store windows. Some nude dummies stood in one, bald and armless. Looters, it seemed, had stripped them bare, Uns snatching for the first time the luxury goods they had never been able to earn.

There had been a storm the day before and all through the night, and a cold, damp wind still howled down the manmade canyons between the skyscrapers. Newton shivered, keeping in the sunlight as much as possible.

Here and there bomb craters gaped to the heavens, their quiet brown pools placid as if they'd been there for eons.

He turned a corner and in the distance caught sight of his home apartment building. It seemed intact, surprisingly unharmed. He continued on, neither faster nor slower than before.

He came to stretches of fresh damage, burning apartments sending streamers of black smoke into the windy street, fresh dead people still bleeding, dying people moving feebly and moaning. If they were in his path, Newton stepped over them. Where the way was blocked with rubble, Newton climbed over carefully, taking no unnecessary chances. At one point he heard a woman weeping and did not even turn his head.

He still couldn't bring himself to believe it was real. It seemed to Newton, a kind of dream one might have after death. When one person dies, that has meaning. When a multitude die, that is empty statistics.

All around him he began to see people, yellow-robed people, poking around in the rubble, looking for something, not speaking to each other or even looking at each other. What were they looking for? Newton did not ask, but it was probably food.

On hands and knees Newton climbed a tilted slab of broken concrete, the rough surface warm against his palms, warmed by the sun. The huge building that had shielded this area was gone. Maybe now something could grow here.

In spite of the transformation made by fire and bombs, Newton recognized this as his own neighborhood, the place he'd been born and grown up, the place he's spent his entire childhood. In fact, that blackened hulk over there had once been his gradeschool.

Slipping and sliding down the other side of the slab, he caught sight of a woman ahead, crawling down the middle of the street, her legs dragging uselessly behind her. Her clothing, torn and bloodstained, was not the yellow tunic of an Un but the white coveralls of a Tech. She was the first Tech Newton had seen alive for days. From the looks of her trail of blood, she had already crawled a long way. She seemed somehow familiar, but Newton didn't immediately recognize her.

"Newton," she called out to him.

His heart froze.

"Wilma!" said Newton.

It was one of his mothers, the one who'd been kind to him. He started toward her at a run.

"Newton," she cried. "They're dead, all dead."

He knelt beside her.

"Wilma, let me help you."

"They're dead. The whole family. Your father, Jim Moran, everyone." She looked up at him, resting her weight on one elbow. "The Uns came. They smashed in the door. They were so cruel. What did we ever do to make them hate us so much? I don't understand. You can tell me. You're one of them. Why do you hate me so much?"

"I don't hate you, Wilma."

"Then, why, why, why?"

"I'll protect you. I won't let them hurt you," said Newton.

"Did Holly find you?" asked Wilma in a strained whisper.

"What? Is Holly looking for me? She's not dead?"

Wilma did not answer.

"Did you see her?" Newton asked desperately.

Wilma said nothing.

He looked toward the apartment building, measuring the distance. If only he could get her home!

Gently, gently he gathered her into his arms, then slowly stood up. For a moment she smiled at him as if she might be about to play one more game of chess with him, one more game after so many, then suddenly she gave a little cry. "Newton. I'm hurt. Inside. You're hurting me." She coughed blood.

"No," said Newton. "Not you. Not you, too."

"Put me down." He could barely make out the words.

He laid her gently on the sidewalk. She coughed again. Her eyes glazed over and her skin took on a dull bluegray color. He tried mouth-to-mouth resuscitation. She went on looking at nothing with unseeing eyes, motionless eyes. After a while he gave up.

He left her there and continued on his way, not looking back, tears at last in his eyes.

As he cried, feeling began to return to him, things began to seem real to him again, as real as they'd ever been, in fact more real than they'd ever been. This, he finally accepted, was not on the screen. You could turn off the screen. Now the screen too was dead. A cloud of smoke from a burning storefront engulfed him for a moment, leaving him coughing and weeping, and as it cleared he found himself in the center of an intersection. He stopped and turned slowly around. In that instant the twisted

wreckage appeared, in the drifting smoke and steep-slanting sunbeams, to be a forest of wonderful metal trees and incredible metal flowers. This was Newton's world, Newton's civilization, opening at last like a flower, blooming at last after centuries of slow growing. This was the glorious end of one thing and the quiet, almost unseen beginning of another. All the centuries of struggle, of thought, of love, of plans, of hopes....

This was where they had been leading from the very beginning. One civilization the fertilizer of the next.

He began to run, his heart beating painfully hard. When a chunk of rubble or an mangled body blocked his path, he leaped over it like a dancer, like a horse clearing a hurdle. Each one, he knew, was an et.

Ahead he saw a lone human hand on the pavement, covered with flies, dust and dried blood. He kicked it, sending it spinning skyward, the fingers twitching like the legs of a crab.

He stood and watched it go.

"You flunked!" he screamed at his civilization.

"You flunked!" answered the echoes. "Flunked. Flunked. Flunked." The echoes faded away. "I didn't flunk. You did."

Some of the Uns stopped digging in the rubble to look at Newton resentfully, disapprovingly, already worried about where their next meal was coming from; it was something they had never worried about before.

At last there was no sound but the crackle of flames and sighing of the wind and, after a while, Newton's slow footsteps.

*

Newton climbed the stairs, walked slowly down the hall and stepped through the front doorway of his old home. The fragments of the door were strewn across the carpet. He tried the lightswitch but nothing happened. He called out to the voice-activated appliances, but they did not respond. A lurid red glow illuminated the whole place, full of deep black shadows. Newton realized every door in the place was torn open, and the light of the setting sun, entering through the picture window in the living room, penetrated every corner. He went into the living room. Outside, across the park, stood the gutted skeleton of the building that had been there as long as he could remember. Beyond, throwing the naked steel girders into dark silhouette, the red oval of the sun hung blazing.

Near the window lay the mutilated body of old Adam McClintok. He had obviously been tortured.

Knowing the light would not last, Newton explored the rest

of the suite. As Wilma had said, they were all here, all dead. The McClintok clan.

He went into his room and settled into his chair, his old familiar chair, and sighed.

The light began to fade.

He heard footsteps, familiar footsteps.

"Holly?" he called out. He cared, and he knew it. More, he accepted and gloried in it. Now he understood "et."

She appeared in the doorway, carrying a heavy bag. "Hello, Newton. I knew you'd come back here."

"Then you knew more than I did." He studied her in the failing light. "I see you're wearing yellow." She had on a typical Un robe and on her wrist was an Un ID bracelet.

"It's all the rage this season," she said, amused. "I have some food here. May I invite you to supper?" She set down her bundle.

"Thanks."

"Aren't you going to kiss me? I expected a warmer greeting than this."

Newton remained seated. "Why did you leave me?"

She leaned against the doorframe, folding her arms. "You left me first, psychologically. I needed an ally, a loyal, fighting ally, against this world. You wouldn't fight."

He thought about that a moment. He couldn't deny it.

"Why did you come back?"

"To bring you a gift." She came in and stood looking down at him.

"A gift?"

"A gift of knowledge. All the knowlede of our civilization neatly packed into a single crystal you can hold in your hand, all the knowledge mankind needs to rebuild, to reconstruct our society. I know where it's hidden, only a few kilometers from here. I can take you there. It's out in the valley...."

He broke in, "I don't want to know."

"What? do you realize what you're saying?"

He gestured toward the wall filled with his old floor-to-ceiling television screen. "Do you think I want to know how to make that damn thing start up again? It has stopped flooding my brain with its idiotic pictures. Good. Maybe now I'll be able to draw a few pictures of my own. It has stopped its endless yammering in my ears. Maybe now I'll be able to say something of my own. It has stopped singing to me. Maybe now my own song will be able to be heard. A man who never watched it taught me to sing."

Holly crouched beside his chair, clutched his bony hand in her soft one. "You can't throw all of science overboard like that."

Newton said quietly, "I'm not throwing away all science, only the part where we went wrong. We tried to learn how to make wonderful machines. We should have tried to make wonderful people. Instead of learning how to build things to do things for us, to replace us, we should have learned how to develop to the full our own latent powers. Those machines should have freed us. We could have been artists, singers, dancers, poets, designers. Instead we made ourselves useless. Instead we made ourselves obsolete. I used to use the word science in the singular, the way you do. No more. Now I've come to see there is no one big science. There are many little sciences, and each society finds the science it looks for and ignores all the others. I met a man who showed me another science, another way to live. I won't go back to the old ways." He could no longer make out her face in the darkness. He wanted to see her face, wanted to see how she reacted to his words.

When she spoke she sounded angry, but he knew only too well how she could pretend. "You're not talking about science. You're talking about religion."

"Religion?" he mused. "Perhaps. I've begun to wonder if those two things are as different as we used to think. Science, religion, the arts...where do you draw the line between them? In Etnroa all are one."

"Etnroa?" she said, puzzled.

And in the darkness he began to tell her all that had happened to him, about Baboo, about the meaning of song. From her questions he knew she understood, more than understood. Her mind, that frighteningly powerful mind of hers, constantly bounded out ahead of his, seeing things he had failed to see, using his words as a springboard to leap into areas of thought he had not known existed.

What did I tell Brad, she thought. That Newton's mind ran slower but deeper? Why didn't I listen to myself? Was jealousy one reason for leaving him?

When he paused, she began, eager, excited. "You have it! The real seed of the future! Not simple a recreation of the past, of a past that has already failed to produce a liveable world. What a fool Brad was, with his damned crystal! I knew it then, though I didn't know why. Its *you* who will set the tone for the coming millennium, not the old society all over again, but a new and better one, one that strikes off in a new direction never yet explored! It's you, who we thought a failure because your talents were different than ours, you who will rule!"

Newton shifted uncomfortably. "What if I don't want to rule?"

"Do you want leadership to fall to someone else by default? Would their world be better than Etnroa?" she demanded.

He thought of Victor, of Victor's cruelty, Victor's senseless violence. "No. No, I don't think so."

"You are the Pope of Etnroa! Fight for your church!"

"My church?" The word seemed presumptuous.

"*Our* church!"

"Maybe *you'd* like to be the leader, Holly."

She laughed lightly. "No, my dear. I tried that once. You have the face and voice everyone recognizes. You have the knowledge of Baboo's way. You will be the Jesus of our new religion."

"What will you be? The Mary Magdalene?"

"No, I think I'll be the Paul, the one who organizes everything. Now come along." She tugged at his hand.

"Where?"

"To the streets! We must begin!"

Chapter 23

The afterglow of sunset had not yet altogether faded, but the full moon already dominated the eastern horizon.

Holly led Newton to a pile of debris and began to climb. He followed. Around them little clusters of Uns moved, paying no attention.

At the top Newton stood looking out at the shadowy moving shapes, Holly next to him holding his hand. "What do I do now, Holly?" he whispered.

"Sing! Sing, you idiot!" she cried with exasperation.

He began, softly at first, then louder. Holly quickly memorized the song and joined in. They sang the same verse over and over again. Newton couldn't remember the other ones.

In the street, people stopped to listen.

"*If we could share this world below,*
If we could learn to love.
If we could share this world below.
We'd need no world above."

Everyone who had ever lived in the Un dorms knew the song by heart. At the foot of the pile of debris, one voice joined in, then another. Some voices called out, "I know him! It's Newton McClintok!" They pointed at him, muttered to each other, then joined in too. The song spread down the street. Newton could hear the waves of sound from further and further away. Young people, old people, men and women, all joined in, singing under the full moon, and from the smoking ruins of San Francisco the song went up, louder and louder, stronger and stronger, until it seemed to shake the sky.

Newton threw his arm around Holly's shoulders and kept on singing as tears rolled down his cheeks. Holly was crying, too, through her song, and laughing.

And thus began the Nation of Etnroa.

And thus began the Age of Song.